Fiach Fola

The Sumaire Web, Volume 2

Anna Rose

Published by Sumaire Press, 2018.

FIACH FOLA

First edition. May 9, 2018.

ISBN: 978-1393601890

Written by Anna Rose.

Also by Anna Rose

Watch for more at www.sumaire.com.

To My Father:

A special note of thanks to my always-supportive Father, who, unfortunately, passed on before he could see my novels reach actual publication. He taught me from a very early age that I could do whatever I wanted with my life, if only I strove hard enough to reach my goals. I screwed up a lot over the years, but he (and my Mom) were (and always have been) supportive of me, in spite of whatever foolish decisions I made growing up and then later on into my nominal adulthood. I know that wherever you are right now, Dad, that you're happy that I finally took that leap of faith and published my work. I'm sorry I was so blindingly bone-headed about things. I miss you, Dad.

Lest anyone think they have been forgotten, that's just not true. So I want to also thank my wonderful Mom, the miraculous Kate, the mighty Norma, and always-blunt Tammy. You've always been there when I needed support or just a big kick in the ass. And finally, a special shout-out goes to the Moose. You know who you are.

One

"**S**iofra, are we going to hunt again tonight? I'm getting hungry again. I feel like I haven't eaten at all," He broke into my reverie, grabbing my attention. "Right now, it's hard to believe that I could ever go more than a day or two at the most without needing to feed again."

Nathaniel's voice was plaintive, but I had been hearing this off and on since shortly after he first awoke in my loft. It reminded me of the scores of toddlers I had heard whining to their parents over the centuries, complaints I ignored as I went about my business. However, in this case, this was not something I could simply ignore. I had to pay attention to the needs of my own offspring. I had seen the kind of ugly that could and did happen when newly fledged vampires were left to their own devices.

"I don't want *that* to happen again," he said in what would have been a non-sequitur to anyone but me.

Yes, *that*. I never wanted something like *that* to ever again rear its ugly head. We'd been so very lucky that time, but there was no reason on earth that we should push our luck. Luck has been established to have a very bad habit of running out at the worst of times.

Nathaniel was the first vampire I had ever knowingly created. I had never envisioned such a thing ever happening in my existence, but it had, and now I was the matriarch of a family of two. Blood relations, if you will.

Yes, I pun, and you'd better get over any distaste you may have for them early on, because they aren't a rare occurrence around me. I've made a few acquaintances over the centuries who educated me well in the art of cruel and unusual punnishment, and I'm glad they taught me about this rather creative form of wordplay. It can really keep you on your toes.

I'd seen other fledglings with their makers over the centuries, but I'd never really explored the relationship they had, as I had seen no need. A self-imposed solitary existence doesn't normally create a reason to know that kind of thing. I'd watched those relationships from afar and would sometimes go to great pains to avoid hearing about the particulars. I had friends in the vampire community who were sires, but I would avoid discussing become one myself when the subject came up

Just as with humanity, there was often talk of bringing up another generation and having someone with whom to have a familial connection, but I didn't see a need for it, myself. I was happy being on my own and even cherished my solitude.

Now, I was a sire myself, and there was a bit of a thrill as I felt the connection that existed between Nathaniel and me. It reminded me of the excitement I felt when I was on a challenging hunt. A part of me I hadn't known existed actually enjoyed my new situation. Did human parents feel this way when their offspring entered the world? I supposed I'd have to ask when that unlikely opportunity presented itself.

I took out my earbuds and looked at Nathaniel, who looked back at me with an urgent expression on his face. His skin was even paler than it had been the night I turned him. His complexion would probably go down a shade or two more before it finally settled into whatever his final skin tone would be.

I could still hear Draiman's voice screaming out the song's angry lyrics, even with the volume turned down almost to the point of silence, the buds lying across my chest. To be perfectly honest, with my enhanced hearing I really didn't need the things, but it gave me a personal bubble of sorts, and I liked the singer's work, both with his group and when he performed solo.

The song he did for that one otherwise laughable vampire movie sequel had been downright infectious. I'd bought all of his group's albums and of course, any of his solo stuff as well. Ultimately, I'd found that the entire group's music was good for losing yourself and just letting your thoughts go into a primal mode. That whole "lizard brain" thing I've heard about over the years.

Not all vampires are into strictly classical music or the blues. Nor are they all into the whole steampunk movement. Yes, there are some who actually do embrace the steampunk way of life and thrive in it, but most modern vampires who are out in the world tend to dress and deport themselves like the humans around them. As for music tastes, I know a few vampires who like to do the equivalent of head-bopping to Country and R & B. I liked a little bit of just about everything. My playlist currently runs everywhere from Draiman to Kanno to Coulton, and three more wildly diverse composers you'll never find.

Draiman's stuff was good to listen to when I wanted to lose myself in something. His lyrics were always so raw and primal that I wondered if he had known at least one of my kind in his life, but I would never presume to ask, especially as I would have a lot of explaining to do for even broaching the subject. I guess I'd never know.

I noted Nathaniel's haunted eyes and finally sensed the hunger and terror that was slowly building inside of him, wondering if I even had the strength to raise him. There was trust in those eyes. Trust I did not know if I even deserved.

Was it normal for a fledgling vampire to have so much blind faith in their maker from the start? I remember that I had wanted nothing to do with my own maker, but that had been an odd situation from the moment I was turned. I should have asked more questions when I'd had the chance a few days ago, but again, I did not want to push my luck.

Had I bitten off more than I could chew by bringing Nathaniel over to this new life? Dying and disappearing just was not what it had been even a hundred years ago. Too many people noticed such things now to make it something easy to do anymore. Just ask someone who tries to fake their death to get insurance money. There always seems to be something in the news about some twit who tries to disappear and the next thing you know, the cops are all over it and the guy is being hauled into the police station in handcuffs.

At that point, you know it's going to be bad, because then the Feds get involved.

The news had been full of stories about Nathaniel's disappearance and then the eventual discovery of a very great quantity of what forensic science would later determine to be his blood. All manner of conjecture had been offered about what had happened to his body, but the only thing upon which they seemed to agree was the fact that he was dead, even with no body to tag and bag.

My favorite rumor was that he had been kidnapped by someone who was supplying the body parts registry. Currently, that theory was eating up the internet on news sites' comment sections. Most of those who commented seemed to ignore the fact that the sheer amount of blood that Nathaniel had obviously lost would have made his organs unusable.

As far as the human world was concerned, all that remained of Nathaniel Ian Bock was the bare bucketful of clotted and filthy hemoglobin the forensic technicians had painstakingly scraped out of the gutter. By the time they had finally located any of it, rain and local vermin had made the majority of what I had not consumed disappear in one way or another. Fortunately, there was still certainly enough of it all over the ground to convince them that short of divine intervention, there was no way he was still alive. Genetic comparisons between the blood and DNA from his personal items had confirmed its origin.

Someone, either a family member or a friend, had started a social media page for him, requesting any information on his location and status. I don't know if Nathaniel visited it again after the first time it came to his attention, but it must have been a personal hell to avoid going there and knowing you couldn't tell the people you once knew that you were still around.

While his family might miss him and grieve for him, as of a few days ago, they would not want him anywhere in their immediate vicinity. Well, not unless they were monumentally stupid, anyway.

For while in some ways he was still Nathaniel Bock and always would be, the truth of the matter was that he was now one who fed off of the human herd. Certain things had changed in him to make this possible, including mental changes that kept him from trying to avoid what he had to do to survive. There would come a time that he would lose major parts of his human self, his human personality, I suppose. That was a normal stage of the transformation of human into vampire. At that point, although a family member might recognize him by his appearance, his personality would be quite different.

A vampire is driven by his or her predator self. It is an unconscious way of being. Until I saw it in other humans who had been made vampire, and I had known them both before and after, I would not have believed such a thing to be true. It made me realize that I was quite different than I had been as a human girl, though I don't remember my human self. Even when I have related stories of my human past, I do it through the veil of my predator self. It's just been too long since I was a human being, with human thoughts and feelings.

For me, I had not known Nathaniel during his time of being human, so this was something that would not be shocking to me.

I was there to watch his vampire self develop and grow. I would never know him in any other way, even when dealing with the deep emotions of the very young fledgling vampire.

Physically, he was in his late twenties, but for now emotionally anyway, Nathaniel was about eight. It made me think of girls hitting puberty, when their mothers often wish they could lock them in a closet until the hormone dance was finally ended. I did not have that option, either. This was a commitment I had made to him when I had decided to turn him without his permission. I had to live with my decision, as it were. Unless he expressed a desire to permanently end himself, this was going to be my life.

If I had chosen him for beauty, which I had not, he certainly had what it took to catch a human's attention enough to lull them into a false sense of comfort and security. It was not just some vampire trick that made him attractive. He truly was quite handsome. An ugly vampire is one who ends up generally being forced to move through the shadows and be far more of a fringe dweller to survive. It cannot be an easy existence for a vampire in those circumstances.

He was easy on the eyes, having the unearthly pale alabaster skin common to a vampire of European human descent. His haunting blue-gray eyes practically forced you to want to look into them and even get a little lost in their beauty. Nathaniel's full head of thick lightly wavy dark brown hair was cut to just below the nape of his neck, and couldn't have been better if I had arranged a haircut for him before I turned him. Occasional strands of medium auburn spread throughout his mane of hair added a bit of flash to its appearance. He was also possessed of a flawless complexion that any person, living or dead, would kill for and would remain so as long as Nathaniel existed. No acne scarring or any other kind of visible damage marred his appearance. He was perfect, as only a vampire could be. There was even an almost perpetual half-smile on his face and a twinkle in his eye that made him appear friendly and downright trustworthy. That was something good to have, if you were a vampire. Your prey wouldn't know that they should be avoiding you at all cost.

"Yes, we will be going out to hunt again in a few hours. You can hold on for a little while longer," I assured him. "It has only been a little over a day since you last fed."

"It hurts so much and it's getting harder to think clearly. Even my thoughts are preoccupied with visions of my next feeding. I don't want what happened the first time to happen again," he stressed. "Will it always be this way for me? Will I always feel this sense of urgency? I can't feel the same sense from you at all, so I'm assuming things will eventually get better for me."

"I know that it's difficult for you right now, it wasn't easy for me, either, but I also had to hunt a bit further and wider to find my prey. I think it's more difficult for you because you're having to force yourself to ignore the scent of nearby humans." I told him. "You can't just kill randomly in this part of the world. People tend to notice and it's harder to hide in a culture where surveillance cameras are just about everywhere. It's entirely too easy to be noticed."

"That doesn't sound good at all," he replied.

"I know, Nathaniel. You do learn to live with it, though. You learn where the cameras are and you do your damndest to avoid them at all cost."

"Is that even possible?"

"Yes, actually it is. It can be a pain in the ass, but you can do it. And, as you get older, you will be able to go longer and longer without feeding, Nathaniel. I promise you that." I put as much reassurance as I could into both my thoughts and my voice, since as I was able to know what his emotions were, he did mine, because of our blood bond. "It really will become easier."

"Right now, that's hard to believe," he replied. His mind was spinning with chaotic emotions that were difficult for me to filter, but I did what I could to keep myself from losing myself in his despair. I was privately glad that all I felt were his emotions. I don't know what I would have done if we had possessed true telepathy. I'd never been much of one to embrace sharing. "It's a miracle to me of how you've done it."

"If I could do it, and I was all on my own when I was turned, you can do it, too, Nathaniel. I know that you can feel the truth of what I'm telling you." Putting down my e-reader and rising from the couch, I came up behind him where he sat at the computer and wrapped my arms around him, resting my chin on the top of his head. I am not that tall anyway, so it did not require much bending over on my part. I enjoyed touching him, which I believe had to do with our psychic connection. He apparently enjoyed the tactile experience as well, as he leaned backward into me, closing his eyes.

"What were you looking at, Nathaniel?"

He opened his eyes, looked up and over his shoulder at me and gave a funny little shrug. I felt a sense of mild embarrassment and consternation emanating from his mind, which only made me more curious. What could there have been to make him embarrassed, as he'd done nothing so far that should make him feel that way.

"I am surprised they haven't found any of the bodies we've left behind, Siofra. You'd think they'd find them pretty quickly." He gestured at the monitor, which held the banner of a popular local online news site. I saw political news and the usual cache of general news stories, but nothing about anything we had done over the past three weeks. "There's one story about gang activity being quiet, which probably has something to do with what we have been doing, but that's it."

We'd disposed of the bodies in places where they would very likely be destroyed before they could be found. One of my favorite places to dump a body in Los Angeles was the La Brea Tar Pits. If you chose an area with little to no human activity, you could often force the body down enough to make it disappear into the depths of the sticky stuff and get little to none of it on yourself in the process. When that couldn't be done, I liked to leave bodies in abandoned buildings where there would be little chance of discovery before they had decomposed enough to leave little trace of what had happened to render them so very dead.

Nathaniel was too young to know how things worked in our world, and if I was right, he was too distracted by the newness of his condition to really see and understand what we were doing with the bodies we left behind. If one fed discreetly and very carefully on the fringes of the human population, unless they were was particularly blatant, disappearances were rarely noted. Vampires in the twenty-first century don't have the same freedom to feed in a relatively indiscriminate manner as they did when I was turned almost four hundred years earlier, and a vampire that isn't careful isn't going to be around very long. The vampire community itself would see to that.

"That is obviously one of the unheralded benefits of having a considerate vampire in the neighborhood." We both laughed at the very bad joke. "I should have thought of that before."

Even feeding on the fringe, however, I knew that we were pushing it and that I would have to do something to address our current situation before the local authorities caught us and we were forced to do something unfortunate to someone in the wrong place at the wrong time. So far, we had fed in Boyle Heights, North Long Beach and East L.A. over the past couple weeks, and the local gangstas were now becoming much more vigilant and had started to keep close to their home territories. Between us, we had taken out eight wastes of space, leaving the streets just a little bit safer for reasonably law-abiding humans to go about their lives. Most of those humans had become food for Nathaniel, as for now, he needed to feed much more frequently than I.

Eventually, though, even those local street thugs would overcome their natural reluctance to involve the keepers of law and order, and eventually would report those members as missing persons and the cops would not be able to ignore their absence any longer. At that time, our relative honeymoon period would be over. Hunting was already becoming more difficult for us, so we kept an eye on the news for anything that would indicate a better place to hunt.

Truly, the modern world, at least in the more developed countries, was both a boon and a curse. Two steps forward and three steps back, more often than I cared to admit. At least it sometimes seemed that way. Computers and smartphone cameras made information gathering and dissemination so much easier than in decades and centuries past. There were fewer "secret wars" and governments had a much more difficult time keeping their dirty little secrets, but that same ease of information sharing made it much more difficult to work off the grid, as it were.

I more than liked computers, hell, I owned and ran an I.T. business. It was an easy way to stay relatively out of sight while making a not insignificant amount of money. I had always been one of the tech types commonly referred to as "early adopters", and I had gone from punch-card computers to the newest personal computers.

I'd even bought one of the first personal computers, one of those Apple boxes, before moving on to the standard non-Apple personal computer. Eventually, I had even learned to build my own box, since I did not like the limitations that a premade tower presented. With those first computers, I experimented and learned coding and more. When I wasn't working, I like to use them for research, playing games and the like. I was particularly fond of massively multiuser role-playing games and first person shooters. The former gave me an opportunity to relax and pretty much be myself, but still be able to have conversations with humans and not end up wanting to eat then.

I stuck to role-playing servers on the particular MMO I played, and the other players simply thought I was buried in my character. The latter were fun, too, but I did not play them anywhere near as often as I played MMOs.

Nathaniel was not a gamer-type, which was a shame, but he did not seem to resent when I would spend a couple hours here and there playing. He seemed to understand that this was my way to unwind. I would queue up the playlist of the music I kept on my computer, shove my earphones deep into my ears and lose myself in the artificial world before me. I would not lose track of Nathaniel, as I could still feel his presence in my own head.

Nathaniel liked to spend his time writing and surfing the internet, so I knew that either a second computer or a pair of laptops were in our future. Probably the latter, as laptops would be much easier to transport in the event we had to make a sudden and unexpected exit from our current situation. I had already warned him to never set down anything in writing in regard to his changed state or continued existence. Safety was our paramount concern and identifying information would be the true death of us both.

It would be a shame to leave my tower behind, but it would be too bulky to take with us, and it was not safe to leave it behind in storage. I had sunk a lot of money into that tower, and I was not willing to let anyone else have it, especially as I also knew how difficult it really was to completely wipe a hard drive. This was going to require some particularly creative destruction, which I knew would hurt to do, but also that it was necessary.

"We will be leaving here in the next few days, Nathaniel, so it will be much better soon," I told him, giving him a quick hug. "I've had you be much more cautious about feeding since your first feeding. I didn't want you to accidentally feed from someone who had already died. That's now going to change. Starting tonight, you'll feed fully so that we may go longer without hunting. I believe that you can now tell just before the human dies, so you won't face what happens when you drink from the dead. I want you to drink deeply and to take in as much as you possibly can before the human dies. That means drinking much more slowly, so that the heart will adjust to the blood loss more easily. Think of it as another lesson in self-restraint. In fact, it is what helped to keep *you* alive for so long before I found you."

"Yes, Siofra, I will," he replied, looking up at me with his enormous blue-gray eyes. The trust in those eyes was like nothing I had experienced and it shattered all those things I had once thought I knew. With only a very few exceptions, and those were innocent and very young human children, no one else had ever looked that way at me before. It was unsettling. "I can hold on until tonight, I think."

Nathaniel was full of surprises for me, and they had started early in our relationship.

On the night of the day he had awakened as a vampire, but after he had fed from me, I had given Nathaniel the opportunity to be ended completely, to be well and truly dead. To my surprise, he had declined the chance to lie at peace, oblivious to the world around him, and had instead embraced his new existence.

"No, Siofra. You told me that I'm the first human you made into a vampire, but you don't know why you did it. There must be some reason for why you did, so who am I to gainsay that? Teach me about what I am and what I have to know to continue my existence," he said, coming to me and encircling me with his long arms, resting his chin gently atop my head. Yes, he really was that tall. If it had been anyone else doing something like that to me, there was an excellent chance I would have thrown them into the nearest wall, but not with Nathaniel. "I'd have died and been completely gone if you hadn't done what you did to save me. Like I said, I can't imagine this happened just by random chance. I believe there has to be a reason why this had to happen to me."

In wordless shock, I simply nodded and hugged him close. As we stood there, embracing one another, we both felt a surge of connectedness and contentment brought on by our emotional link. It just made everything seem *right*, and I couldn't bring myself to question Nathaniel's unwavering surety.

He was a grown man, but in so many ways Nathaniel was a child again. The world he had grown up in was now a thing of the past. Nothing was as it once had been. Family members and friendships cherished and dear were gone as swiftly as one might turn off a light switch. Too many knew that he was missing and most now believed he was dead. It had to stay that way if we were to remain safe. I cannot imagine things would end at all well if he suddenly showed up and someone decided to "run some tests" to see if he was alright after having lost so very much blood. The cool skin and lack of a heartbeat was certain to be an instant giveaway that something was different about Nathaniel.

I had come from a much different time for humanity, when life was much simpler. Most everyone I had known and who might possibly have been able to recognize me had been killed just before I rose as a vampire. At that time, I had little to no realistic fear that I would run into anyone who thought me dead. I cannot imagine having to be a freshly turned human in the twenty-first century.

There had been something about this man when I encountered him that night. Something that made him different from the thousands upon whom I had fed since the mid-1600's, when I had gone from being a simple human servant girl to the deadly predator I was today.

Indeed, one of my first fears when I turned him was that I had done so because I was smitten with romantic feelings for the lad. Thankfully, I soon discovered that I did not hold those kinds of thoughts where he was concerned, nor any hope that something like that would ever develop between us.

I had seen what passed for contemporary vampire fiction, and it would turn my stomach if that organ was not already completely inert. Of course, that kind of fiction also presupposed the absurd concepts of feeding from non-human animals as an alternative food source, completely abstaining from blood (when blood is your sole source of nourishment, that's just not going to happen, Buckwheat) or even drinking dead blood gleaned from the local blood bank. It must always be fresh warm and unadulterated human blood, taken from that human's body before he or she dies.

Some bizarre supernatural alchemy requires that we must actually drink the blood from a human body in which the heart still beats. It's not magic. Magic does not exist. Sorry about that, folks. We cannot simply drain it off into a glass and drink it that way. It would be nice to pretend it was merely a goblet or tumbler full of some human normal beverage, but that's just not the cards for a vampire.

So, perhaps it had been an instance of supreme selfishness on my part that had caused me to turn him. I had been alone for most of my existence. Perhaps something deep inside me felt it was time for that solitude to end.

This was not at all about getting laid. That had never been an issue for me. Vampires don't do it the same way humans would, anyway. I've heard about human orgasms, but they did not sound anything like what my experiences with vampire orgasms had been. I had been a virgin when I left the human world to join the undead one, so while the descriptions I'd read on the subject of human orgasm could be tantalizing, they ultimately did nothing for me.

A few short relationships with other vampires had been enjoyed for a time, but they had not lasted for one reason or another. This was probably more along the lines of missing family connections and unconsciously wanting some. I had the power to make that happen, and so I had done it.

Nathaniel's tenacity in somehow staying alive when sheer harsh human biology would normally have dictated that he die as I fed from him had grabbed my attention. His single utterance, a call for someone called "Kathy", had escaped his lips as his heart began its final beats. I could not allow that strength to pass completely from this world. It would have been wrong.

Because of his tenacity, I knew that he would be okay, as long as it remained a part of him.

I still had not asked him who "Kathy" was, and would wait for him to tell me, should he ever decide to do so. We all deserve our secrets.

It is kind of funny how most humans seem to go smoothly from being human to being a vampire. While there is regret at what must be done in order to survive, rare is the fledgling that will truly balk at what feeding requires. I have wondered about it on occasion, especially now as I was raising my own child. There must be something that actually changes in the brain of the vampire to enable us to become an instant predator more deadly than we might ever have imagined ourselves capable of being.

For example, when I was turned in 1600's Ireland, I quickly realized that while I felt some small regret for feeding upon humans, ultimately, I knew that I had no choice, and so I had kept doing so. I would feed on criminals and the fringes of society when the opportunity presented itself, but when I had no other choice, the most convenient prey would do.

The majority of turns do not immediately become mindless killing machines. If you were a mild mannered schoolteacher, you are still that mild mannered schoolteacher, albeit with a vastly altered diet and lightning reflexes. I would not recommend allowing that mild mannered schoolteacher anywhere near a child for at least forty to fifty years, while they learned about what they were and how to control our baser urges. If that vampire decided to go back to teaching at that point, more power to them, as long as they kept from eating their students.

Bad form, that.

We vampires do our best to avoid turning those who are demented or simply murderous. Giving the kinds of abilities we possess to the deranged is not the most intelligent of acts. Can you imagine turning someone who is already a dangerous mass-murderer? Not the brightest act I can think of a vampire performing. It would very likely get them ended as quickly as was practical. There have been a couple of bad decisions along those lines since I was made a vampire, but again, those turns were destroyed as quickly as possible.

Perhaps it is some innate vampiric survival mechanism: Survival at any cost. In those times when I had had to feed upon the innocent, those who perhaps did not "deserve" my particular kind of attention, I made their passing as easy as possible. I had even determined to sit with Nathaniel as he went into the Void, rather than leaving him to die alone, before I instead decided to turn him.

It's easy to tell the innocent ones, when you find them as I had found Nathaniel. There is a certain scent to them that the more tainted souls lack. It is almost as though the stink of those tainted souls stick to their very essence, screaming like a claxon to anyone with the ability to scent it. When you are deciding to bring a fledgling into the world, who would you want to embrace? An innocent who might bring more good things to the world, or some megalomaniac who would revel in his or her newfound strength and use that gift to perpetrate even more evil onto the world?

That's how I viewed it, at least. For all I knew, there could be some vampire out there who liked his turns a few blocks off Main Street, and then some. Frankly, it would not surprise me if that were the case.

The few fledglings I had seen who could not embrace their transformation had been religious fanatics. Each had ultimately been ended by their maker, as that was the law of the vampire community. One never brings over and then allows to survive, someone who cannot assimilate into the vampire culture. It brings too much danger to us all.

Imagine if you will, humans knowing the truth of our existence. They would do everything in their power to eliminate us as a perceived threat, as though we were a disease to be vaccinated against. We had managed to keep them thinking that we were merely the stuff of horror and fantasy, and fully intended to keep it that way. There were some humans who knew about us, but they were carefully monitored in case they finally found themselves unable to contain the secret they bore. Fortunately for those humans who couldn't keep their mouths shut, very few of them ended up meriting a death sentence, most that broke under the pressure ended up locked safely in an asylum, where no one would believe them, anyway. The ones who died were those who had the ability and intention of offering names, dates and information on where the bodies were buried.

Our peculiar society did what we had to in order to keep ourselves safely concealed. Our survival as a species depended upon it. So I knew that if it was in my power, I would allow nothing to harm Nathaniel and woe betide the entity, human or otherwise, who tried to damage even a single hair on his head.

I was a mother bear with both fangs and talons, and I knew how to use them.

The first days following his turning had been difficult; there is no doubt about that. Taking him out for his first feeding of human blood had been nothing short of a trial designed to test the limits of my patience.

I had intended to take him out the night he rose as a vampire, but time had gotten away from us during our emotional bonding.

Dawn was blushing on the horizon when I looked out the window, and I knew we'd have to wait till nightfall before I could take him out for his first taste of human blood. By the time we finally made it out that next night, it was well after midnight, because the police had been out dealing with protestors who hadn't discovered that civil disobedience is a much better instrument of change than outright insurrection.

We visited Boyle Heights, where the police currently were not and gang violence was common. I'd read in the online edition of the Times that drive-bys were picking up in the areas, so I reasoned that any leftover blood where we hunted could be assigned to something along those lines.

It had been easy to identify and then isolate a suitable target with those criteria in mind. A burly-looking man, he seemed an excellent candidate from whom to feed. He was hanging out near the old and just about abandoned Linda Vista Community Hospital, where on any given day or night, movie and television production crews could often be found filming anything from medical dramas to horror movies.

Tonight, however, it seemed truly abandoned. It was a scary place, even for me. Though I do not believe in ghosts, and have been given no reason to believe they exist, there is malevolence about the place that seemed to affect just about anyone who visits it. Look up its history sometime. Once upon a time, they kept tuberculosis patients in tents on the front lawn of the building. It had ceased to function as a hospital in the early 1990's, but was kept very busy in its new incarnation as a filming location.

"Come over here with me, Nathaniel. You'll have a better place to watch him from up in this tree," I gestured at an old and stately magnolia tree a little behind us, and then suited words to action, quickly climbing up into its branches and concealing foliage. Nathaniel darted up behind me and perched, crouching, in front of me, though on a different limb. "Be careful not to make too much noise while you're up here. You don't want him to hear or see you."

I gave whispered but running instructions as the moment fast approached when Nathaniel would have his first human blood and truly enter his new life. He was distracted because of his hunger, but I knew that he was hearing at least part of what I was so desperately trying to impress upon him.

Perhaps it was my assumption that I understood his need to feed that clouded my judgment. Damn, but I was being foolish.

"See how the human is trying to keep to the shadows, Nathaniel? He is obviously up to no good. If you look more closely, you can see he has something in his right hand. It's not very shiny, so it is safe to assume that it is probably a gun."

"Gun?" I really should have been paying more attention, but I had put myself too deeply into instructor mode.

"Just because you are a vampire does not mean that gun cannot hurt you, and in certain instances, could even end you permanently. So while he is our target, we will have to get that weapon out of his hand so we will be safe."

Not yet having had the opportunity to learn control over such things, Nathaniel's fangs were already sliding out, and I could feel the keen pain that shot through him because of his extreme hunger. It went down into his very bones as his body slowly dehydrated and pulled every last little bit of moisture out of wherever it could. I wished more than anything that I could make this easier on him, but that was not to be.

I should have noticed when I stopped hearing him in my mind, but perhaps I was much too fascinated with the sound of my own voice. I have no excuse, nor should I attempt to even make one.

"Whatever you do, do not allow the human to taste any of your blood. That would be very dangerous for both you and me," I cautioned him. The last thing we needed was an accidental vampire, as I had been created all those many years ago. "Let's not turn this into any more involved a lesson than need be, okay?"

He turned as though he was listening to me, but the glance he gave was feral and downright scary. I wondered what I had gotten myself into, deciding to bring another vampire into the world.

Had I been too impulsive? Why had I waited so long for his first feeding? I felt like a fucking idiot. Would this end with me ending my own child?

"Hungry," he grated out through clenched fangs that were made more prominent due to his half-starved state. The feeding he had had from me upon first awakening was not something intended to nourish his starved tissues, but something to help create the connection that we had achieved in that dark communion. Thus, his skin was drawn tight to his skull, giving him a ghastly appearance I hoped no unfortunate innocent would ever see, as I was certain it could and would cause terrible long-term nightmares should they survive the encounter. Hell, I found myself quite happy that vampires do not dream.

"Blood," he said then, turning his head to look at me, those blue-gray eyes gleaming with an unholy light. "Need blood. So hungry."

I shivered with something other than cold at his sing-song tone. Did I look like that when I was desperate to feed? I was glad that I would never know, unless I was foolish enough to ask someone.

We have to be willing to accept these small blessings when we are creatures who visit terror in our victims as their final conscious experience. I would never welcome dreaming about the thousands of deaths I have visited upon humans over the past four hundred plus years. Perhaps there exist some vampires who might welcome that opportunity, but I would not be one of them.

"Just a few more minutes, Nathaniel," I told him, but it was for naught. My failing control over him suddenly snapped completely, due to the extremity of his condition. Nathaniel had had enough of waiting and with a guttural snarl, dashed for his victim, mouth already open, ready to bite and tear the human's tender flesh. I did not dare to call out, as that would have alerted the human to danger, which was certainly what I did *not* want to do. I ran after Nathaniel, but even his small head start, added to his extreme hunger, gave him too far a lead on me to intercept him.

The sudden shattering of our connection left me feeling a sense of aloneness I had never before experienced. It was like having part of my soul severed, the pain it caused me was almost tangible and it was all I could do not to scream out my agony. This was something that I, a vampire who had thrived on solitude for the past four hundred years, would recently have considered to be impossible.

Obviously, I was wrong, and I had to find some way to regain the bond we had, or face the real possibility of having to end Nathaniel, even if it took me with him. I could not bear the thought of a mindless rogue vampire terrorizing a metropolis like Los Angeles.

Still snarling, he grabbed the startled human and pulled him into the near-total darkness of nearby shadows, one hand over the man's mouth to muffle his high-pitched screams of terror. I watched with a kind of horror as Nathaniel brought the man's face around so that he could see his own death reflected in blue-gray eyes that seemed to glow, even in the absence of light. He smiled at his victim, revealing his ivory fangs, and the human rewarded his cruelty by wriggling madly in Nathaniel's iron grip, his eyes wild during his futile attempt to escape his executioner. The human made the mistake of looking to me for rescue, but I saw the vain hope shining in his eyes dashed with my next words.

"Do not torture your food, Nathaniel. Unless it's absolutely necessary, we do not make those who feed us suffer unduly," I told him softly. I did not want to aggravate the situation, and wanted to avoid any more messiness. "Give him some peace, please."

A muffled wail of abandonment made it past the flesh of Nathaniel's palm. I wondered what it must be like to have that last hope that someone will come to your rescue, and then suddenly discover that the perceived architect of your salvation has no interest in playing that role within the script you have created for yourself.

"Mommy!" I could hear the desperate word through Nathaniel's hand. Unless she had preternatural hearing, I seriously doubted the woman in question could hear him. I wondered if the human's mind had already descended into insanity and if the veil of confusion it brought would ease his path into death.

My child looked over at me at the last, still smiling, eyes glowing and half-crazed, and then turned his regard back to his victim. The human screamed once again into the chilly flesh of Nathaniel's palm. In that moment, I was so very glad I could not sense what Nathaniel was feeling. It was horrifying enough watching it all happen.

"Mine!" he said triumphantly as he bit into the sweaty flesh that throbbed over the human's carotid artery and began sucking down the hot, salty bounty that fountained forth into his mouth. All vampires seem born knowing where the best place from which to feed is located. If you doubt my assertion as to its quality, stand in front of a mirror sometime and watch the vein at the side of your throat throb with each beat of your heart.

To a vampire, that sight is well nigh hypnotic, and we can sometimes become fixated on that part of the human anatomy, even when we aren't necessarily hungry. It is like dangling a nice piece of steak in front of a well-fed dog that has already emptied his bowl, but is more than willing to entertain the idea of something more to eat.

The human's screams, though muffled, changed to sound like the pathetic squeals of a small mammal. I knew the sound well and thought of it as intelligence suddenly turned to raw instinct. My nostrils flared as I caught the sharp tang of the human's blood on the faint breeze. Though I could go for another day without feeding, the scent still thrilled through me like a rush of adrenaline.

In the midst of all this chaos, Nathaniel had somehow managed to wrest the gun from the man's hand and throw it across the darkened street and into a far wall, only breaking a few of the man's fingers in the process. Somehow he had managed to avoid getting shot, but I have no idea how. Perhaps the human had been so startled that he could not fire his gun, but I would never know.

I could hear his desperate slurping and saw that the human was fast losing consciousness as his blood was drawn away and down into the tissues of Nathaniel's starving body. The human's terrified squeals were quickly fading to become low animal-like moans.

When the human's blood loss was great enough that he no longer had the strength to fight, he stopped trying to break away from his single-minded captor and sagged against Nathaniel's arm. Once the human's desperate attempts to free himself had ceased, Nathaniel seemed to know that he no longer needed to cover his prey's mouth, and he let go. He snaked his now free hand around to his victim's back and pulled him closer, the human's limp body hanging like a broken marionette in the vampire's iron grip.

Believe it or not, it does not take much before a human will pass out from blood loss, actually not much more than one gives at the blood bank when one chooses to donate. That is only one of the reasons why blood banks require that humans hang around to drink juice and eat cookies. Blood bank staff become rather annoyed at those humans who insist they are perfectly fine and tries to leave early. I am certain they are tempted to allow those who are particularly insistent and stubborn to hit the proverbial deck, but safety policies would not allow them to let that happen.

Too bad. It would certainly make for quite the wake-up call. Pun intended.

I watched as the human's mouth opened and closed like a landed trout, his eyes wide but unseeing. It was as though his mind, his very thoughts, had left him at some time during the attack. Although I had no tolerance for thugs, I was glad that he was spared knowing exactly when he was going to die. His body was essentially on automatic pilot, but that would not last much longer.

I stood amazed as Nathaniel's face slowly filled out again with the addition of moisture to his dehydrated tissues. It really did not matter that I had seen it before, it was still like something magical. The human's body became paler as his blood was drained from his veins, slowly taking him from a toffee brown color to something wan and unhealthy-looking. At the same time, I could feel our connection slowly reasserting itself between us, and I was overcome with a wave of gratefulness that it had not been lost completely. My soul was once again becoming whole, and the pain I had been experienced lessened and then ceased completely.

Impatient for more of the inexorably dwindling blood as the human's heart began its downward spiral into true death, Nathaniel sat on the ground and turned the dying man upside down, methodically breaking the man's ribs and crushing his chest cavity. This brought more blood to the open wound on his throat, which Nathaniel greedily consumed. I had done something similar more than once during my existence, when I had gone too long without feeding, so from an outside vantage point, I found the process interesting to observe. I was also surprised that it appeared to be instinctual on Nathaniel's part to do so.

This was so very different from my own first feeding, where I had used my own body to distract my first victim. Vampires are very sensual creatures, and it is apparently second nature for us to use that aspect of ourselves to hunt. Of course, at that time, I did not know what I was. I had found the man looting the bodies of people I had known for years, and that had disturbed me greatly.

Unlike Nathaniel, I had not been starving when I fed for the first time. While hungry, I had not yet reached the point of mindless desperation. I had only awakened to my new existence a short time before and had no idea of what had happened to me. I also still appeared to be human when the thief first laid eyes upon me. Well, until he was close enough to me to notice the myriad changes my transformation had wrought. Poor Nathaniel had gone a full day before this, his first human feeding and it showed. I would have taken him to feed sooner, but this was a far different time than it had been when I had risen. These days, hunts needed far more consideration and planning before embarking.

Long past was the time when a vampire had carte blanche to feed in a truly random manner. Now it was a matter of much careful thought and preparation. I had decided early on that I would take him to feed on violent gang members, as their passing or outright disappearance, while it might catch the attention of their own families and loved ones, would generate little curiosity on the part of the rest of society beyond a sense of happiness that there was at least one fewer gang member out on the street.

When I heard the human finally get to the point that his heart was about to stop, I pulled Nathaniel's face away from the gaping wound he had created. It was too soon for him to learn what happens when a vampire drinks dead blood. He was filled full of blood like an engorged tick, so he did not fight me very hard, for which I was grateful. I made a mental note to myself to never allow him to go for so long without feeding again. It was entirely too dangerous and we had dodged the proverbial bullet this time. Tempting Fate was never a bright thing to do.

The skin of his face, chest and upper arms felt tight against my hands, full as his upper body was with the hot blood of the dying gangster. Over the next hour or so, the excess blood from those areas would move to his lower extremities and deeper tissues and the extremely tight appearance his skin now had would lessen considerably. For now, I had to get him off the street while that happened, as frankly, he would appear fairly grotesque until then. At least a fully sated vampire doesn't swell like a tick, but we do initially appear as though we've been taking a long sequence of steroids.

"Nathaniel, you must stop feeding now, or you will not like the consequences. Also, we need to dispose of this body. Neither of us wants forensics people to start wondering where all of this human's blood went, since there is very little of it either in his body or on the ground." I made him stand away from the body, and then began to clean up his mess. He was still too young to expect him to take care of all the potential forensic evidence himself.

If you did not know it already, the human heart can continue beating for hours after the brain ceases to function. However, that is not always the case, and better safe than ending up sorrier than you've ever felt in your entire previous existence. I preferred to stop drinking once I felt the life leave the body, regardless of the existence of a heartbeat, although there had been a few times where I had taken it to the very brink of even the heart's ability to keep pumping. There seems to be a point where you can actually feel the spirit, whatever it is that makes a living creature what they are, leave the body, and that's when I usually stop.

The feeding process had lasted no longer than five or ten minutes, from the capture of his prey to this moment. A vampire can drain a human's blood in a remarkably short period of time, which seems to be an instinctive desire to get it all over with and back under cover as quickly as possible. In order to drink more than just two or three pints of blood, a vampire actually must drink slowly, else they risk the death of the human from which they are feeding. Once that human is dead with not even a heartbeat, no self-respecting vampire will keep drinking, well, unless they are into some kind of horrific self-abuse.

A low, horrified moan got my attention.

Nathaniel was looking around as though he was only now realizing what had happened. He looked down at the cooling body in his arms and dropped it, a look of disgust on his face. I had explained what would happen as best I could, but nothing could really prepare you for the savagery of your first feeding as a vampire. His eyes had lost their glowing half-crazed appearance and he appeared to be open to reason once more.

"Oh my God, I did that! I killed him!"

"That is what normally happens when you feed, Nathaniel. Most times, there is no alternative." I told him. "I was horrified at what I had done, the first time I fed, but that feeling didn't last."

"But...I ate him!" he protested. "If I could have, I would have drained him completely dry."

"If you want to survive, you will do whatever is necessary to feed. You have no other choice. As for drinking him dry, however, you *never* want to keep feeding after your prey is dead, or your body will reject everything you just took in. Always stop feeding before the heart finally falters and stops," I grimaced in disgust. "You *really* do not want that to happen to you."

He stared at the body that lay on the blood-spattered ground, completely wordless, and I did what I had to do to bring him back to me. I didn't need him going down the path of a different kind of crazy now. I had to keep him focused on necessity and so avoided saying anything that might make him reject his new self.

"You must always take care of the remains and do everything you can to remove evidence. I know that the blood is almost impossible to eradicate completely, so we're not even going to try to do that. There isn't even enough on the ground to prove that he's dead."

"I drank that much blood?"

"Yes, you did, and that's fine. Now it's time to deal with the unpleasantness that comes at the end of these things. Our kind has worked very hard to keep our existence a secret, and violating that will lead to your permanent ending by the greater community. The humans would never get the chance to kill you themselves." I was doing all I could to make him understand how serious all of this was to his continued survival. "I know that, because I've helped end some of them, myself."

"All I wanted was blood. It was all I could think of, God help me," he said softly, as he gazed at the corpse at his feet. It was more like he was talking to himself, rather than to me. "So help me, I would do it again right now, if I had the chance! Even with all I just drank, I feel like I've been starving forever and that I haven't filled myself up yet."

"I know, and it will seem like that for awhile, but it won't be forever. You will gain more control as time goes on, you'll even start doing better and better over the next few weeks. It won't be a dramatic change at first, but you'll find yourself more in control of your own hunger."

"That just seems so hard to believe right now," he replied. He knelt next to the human and ran the tip of one finger down the man's face, lingering over the flesh on the unruined side of the man's throat.

He poked at the pale cafe au lait colored flesh at first softly, and then a bit harder. The flaccid body rocked a little, but nothing else. Watching his inspection of the corpse he had created was a bit strange, but I suppose it was natural for him to be curious about what he had done.

"I went through the same thing, Nathaniel. I've felt what you're feeling, and I know how powerful the desire to hunt and feed is right now for you, but we don't have time to hunt more. We need to cover our tracks to avoid the authorities. So, pick him up, and we will take the body someplace where he will not be found for a long while," I told him, breaking into his shocked thoughts. "Don't worry about the body leaking on you a little. I have some spare clothing for you in the backpack."

Running shorts and a tee shirt were not much, but if you are covered in gore, it is not generally a very good idea to walk around in public looking like you are a bloodthirsty fiend who has just left a fresh kill. I had purchased a few sets of such easy clothing for him, thanks to the prevalence of online retailers and cheap overnight shipping.

There was an abandoned 1940's era building I knew about in the area that had been visited by only a few, if any, humans in at least three years, so I felt fairly comfortable dumping it there. Plus, the building was so old and out of date that there were no inconvenient cameras to take notice of the process, so that was good.

It was a short run to the boarded up building, and then frighteningly easy to slip inside, even toting a limp body. I'd done this before a few times over the past several decades, even once while the building was still in use about fifty years earlier, when I had gone under a different name. It was good to know that the place was still accessible.

"Come with me," I told him, and took him to the basement of the place. Cobwebs and dust showed that no one had been through here in at least a month's time. That made it perfect for our needs. I didn't want to find myself answering inconvenient questions. We went to the furnace. I unlocked and pulled open the big round iron door of the thing. It creaked a bit, but that was natural, considering the age of the thing and how long it had gone without regular maintenance.

"Put it on the floor and we'll do what we must to make it disappear."

I made sure to roughly dismember the body before we put it in the decades old furnace. It would muddy the waters about his demise, when the time came that whatever remains the corpse might leave behind were discovered and perhaps even reported to the authorities.

The damage Nathaniel had done to the body actually made it easier to dismember, so I considered myself lucky. The slight edge that my vampiric strength offered during the process reminded me of a butcher matter-of-factly dismembering a fresh chicken.

I felt like a human mother taking care of her offspring as I pulled out a large packet of wipes and clean clothes for Nathaniel, once the body's components had been stuffed into the basement furnace with the stinking remains of a few others I had placed there over the years.

Nathaniel looked at me a bit oddly as I handed a fistful of wipes to him and gestured for him to start wiping his face and his front. It appeared that he had not even realized how gruesome his clothing had become while he was feeding, and his mouth gaped open when he saw the congealed blood that had stuck to the fabric of his now filthy tee shirt.

"Get those clothes off and you will be able to do a much better job of cleaning up, Nat," I told him, waving at him to do just that. He turned his back to remove his clothing, and when he removed his pants, and then his underwear, I was treated to a pale white butt with the vaguest suggestion of tan lines at Nathaniel's waist. Well, those tan lines would fade in a short time, and he would end up with a pale complexion similar to that of a homegrown member of my native country.

"Nice butt," I said. I just could not help myself, and trying to diffuse the seriousness of the situation seemed the best thing to do. I saw his backside tighten a bit and then he sighed softly. Apparently rethinking his modesty, he shrugged and turned around, so I saw the whole picture. "Well, it's not just the butt that is nice, I see. That will help you when you are on the hunt."

I think that he would have blushed, had he been able. Over the centuries I've found that men, both human and vampire, tend to become embarrassed when their gifts are commented upon by the females of both species. It was not as though I had not seen the whole package after he was turned, but this was the first time I had seen it with him standing and conscious, which does, after all, make a difference. I held out my hand for his ruined clothing. It was attractive, but since vampires make love differently than a human does, it did not create sexual feelings in me.

"Give me your old clothes, please. We need to be rid of them as quickly as possible," I told him, and he dutifully handed them to me for disposal. "Wipe your face, arms and hands, Nathaniel, especially your fingernails. They seem to have gotten the worst of things."

He did just that, with me stepping in to get to the areas he had either missed or not gone over completely. When we were finished, he looked reasonably presentable, so I handed him his change of clothing, which he quickly pulled on.

I put his ruined clothes and the used wipes into the furnace along with the body parts, and threw a small incendiary device in along with it all before quickly closing the door and firmly sliding the latch. As fast as I was, however, I still felt the *"fwoom!"* of the small explosion caused by the device against the furnace's door. While it might not completely destroy the body, as the fire in the furnace would need to get to a sustained temperature of between fourteen hundred and eighteen hundred degrees to completely consume a corpse, it would make it far more difficult to identify anything that did remain after the final embers cooled completely.

I was feeling comfortable until I heard the staccato thud of a quickly beating heart nearby, and as I turned to locate it, I heard it begin to race even faster.

Well, fuck!

"Who's there," I called out softly, making myself sound as non-threatening as I could. "Who are you?"

"Put your hands up! I have a gun!" came from a dark corner near the stairs.

Nathaniel struck a listening pose, but I whispered to him to remain still. I was famished and had this handled. One way or another, this human was not going to leave the basement alive, if at all. I knew what I had to do to regain control of the situation.

"Why would you want me to stay still," I asked him, speaking in a slightly higher tone of voice than I normally would use. It seemed to make me appear more juvenile, and thus, less of a threat. I slid into my seductive hunting routine as easily as a seal cuts through the water. I began to pull my tee shirt off, revealing my unbound, perfect breasts. When you're turned at the age of nineteen, your tits will never sag. "Don't you want to spend some time with me?"

Inside, I was kicking myself for missing his approach, but then, I hadn't seen a need to sniff the air. Also, I had been too distracted by Nathaniel's hunt and its aftermath to think of listening for heartbeats. Yes, I'd been a fool. Overconfidence can end a vampire quickly, especially when the human is armed, as was the case here.

"What are you doing," he demanded hoarsely. "Stop right there!"

He hadn't identified himself as a cop and now that I was sniffing the air, I couldn't smell a gun. Whoever he was, his bluff had failed and I was ready to eat. I continued my approach, hooking my thumb into the waist of my shorts over my crotch. I'd often seen it used as a suggestive position. Shirtless and shoeless, I had his undivided attention. He'd probably forgotten Nathaniel was in the room, too.

I can have that effect on people. It gives a whole new meaning to calling a woman a "vamp", a la a very famous silent film star. Nice woman, by the way. It was a time of wild abandon and endless possibilities, and anything could happen. She knew what I was and was fine with it. We hung out a lot during her early years in show business. How do you think she got so good at playing the femme fatale?

What can I say? She liked to watch. It was a little creepy, but I knew that no one would ever believe her, had she said anything to anyone else. She would be considered just another morphine-addled actress and her claims dismissed out of hand.

I miss those carefree days.

"Touch me," I crooned to the human. "I want to feel your hands on me. I want to feel your mouth on my skin."

I was now close enough to see that while he wore a guard's uniform, it was filthy. Good. He might not even be a legitimate guard. Most guard companies in town would not tolerate that kind of slovenly dress. I also did not see a gun. That was also good, as I had no desire to be seriously injured during what would shortly happen.

He was trying to continue to look me in the eye, but the distraction I had so thoughtfully provided kept yammering for his attention. I saw him glance at my breasts repeatedly and watched as he absently licked his lips nervously. . He was aroused and nervous. That was good.

He'd already pitched a tent in his trousers, so I knew I had him. The plan had been to go on the hunt myself after Nathaniel had fed, but crazy random happenstance had brought my meal to me like pizza delivery. I thanked the gods for my good fortune. It was still fresh and hot!

"Let me touch your face," I begged him, reaching out a hand to touch his cheek, running my hand along the line of his jaw and rubbing softly at the faint stubble I found there. I let my fingers linger around his lips and gently pushed at the slit that delineated his mouth with a fingertip. "So handsome."

His mouth worked, but no words emerged. Out of the corner of my eye, I watched as his left hand began to rise as though it had a mind of its own. It encircled my waist and gently but firmly pulled me close, and I could smell his cologne, something cheap with an underlying acrid quality that would have made my nose wrinkle in response if I had had a need to breathe.

"So muscular, so delicious," I breathed, running my hand down his face to cup his chin in the palm of my hand. "Kiss me!"

As he allowed me to gently guide his face closer to mine, enthralled by whatever makes vampires such sensuous creatures, I abruptly cut sideways and down to bite his throat and open the carotid artery there. He tried to jerk himself away, but by that time, I'd encircled the back of his head with my free hand and pulled him in close. With a small leap upward, I wrapped my legs around his waist and held on tight as he fought to break my hold on him and save himself. I clung like a giant tick as I gorged myself. The human's heart beat wildly as he fought to free himself and that made the thick crimson bounty a veritable fountain as it jetted forth from the wound I had created.

Being a small woman, I was also fairly light, so my weight did not overwhelm him. He kept to his feet until blood loss finally made his knees buckle, and suddenly, I was on my own two feet once again.

I took my time as I drank. I wanted to drain as much of the human's blood as was possible. It's kind of funny how the body will sustain itself awhile longer if blood loss is relatively slow. Truthfully, if a vampire has the time to linger, she'll take it, as that usually means more to drink.

Nathaniel stood and watched, and rather than feeling fear or disgust from him, I felt an excited kind of curiosity as I drank the man down. When the human began to sag in my arms, my Nathaniel came over and helped to support him to take some of the strain off of me.

What a sweet boy he was.

Yes, I had chosen very well indeed. Nathaniel would make a fine vampire.

"When I saw him, all I could think of was the man who shot me. I wanted revenge for what he had done to me. How he tried to kill me. And then it was all about the blood. I wanted it and I wanted it now," he told me softly as we walked back to the car, which we had parked far enough away that it would not be connected with the violence we had both committed. The second body had followed the first into the furnace, though not before it had cooled somewhat. "I could not think of anything else then."

"I understand, Nathaniel. I truly do. When you are still a young vampire, the bloodlust has a lot of control of you. With time, that will improve, I promise you, though it may not seem that way right now."

"I hope that's true. I don't like losing control of myself. The part of me that would have kept me from feeding felt as though it was trapped and helpless, screaming at me to stop, to be careful, but the stronger part of me just did not care. All it wanted was the blood."

"I know. It's like having another brain in your head, but a much simpler one that only considers basic needs, such as feeding and doing whatever it takes to survive. You'll learn to control it; it will just take some time for that to happen."

He shook his head, but I could feel that he understood what I was telling him and that he knew I was telling him the truth. Regardless, there is no point in lying when there is every chance that the person you're lying to will feel the falsehood.

"I still don't know who it was who killed me, but I remember that he knew my name," he continued on his original thought. "Why the hell was I important enough to kill? You know what? He never even asked me any questions before he shot me."

"He knew your name?" This brought me up short, literally and figuratively. I actually came to a stop. What had Nathaniel been involved with during his human life that might have ended with his murder? What in the world had I gotten myself into when I decided to turn Nathaniel instead of just letting him die?

"He called me and told me that he had to talk with me about something, but I have no idea what he was talking about. He said that we needed to meet near the pier, but once I got there, he flashed his gun and made me walk to where you found me." He glanced at me quickly and then looked away, as though he was embarrassed for some reason. "I don't remember being shot. The last thing I can remember is him pointing the pistol at me and then nothing. The next thing I can recall is seeing you when I opened my eyes again.

"He called you? So he had your phone number?" This was important. Who did I know who would be able to check call logs? I was sure I had at least one or two acquaintances that might fit that bill, but were they still in town?

"My cell phone number, which I don't give to anyone! Did you find my cellphone on me when you found me lying there?" He looked around wildly, as though it would somehow appear on the ground where we stood, even though we were miles and days from where he had died.

"No, I did not. Maybe he took it with him to hide evidence, but for now, he is long gone." Someone with enough presence of mind to take the cell phone with him suggested that this was something that had happened on a professional level. This was no random crime. This was something that had been thought out and executed with deliberate planning.

What would I find if and when I had someone look into it for me?

We had never really talked about what had happened to him, but I was glad that we were finally doing so. It would help my vampire child make peace with his transition and move on to the next stage of his new reality.

"I would like to find him sometime. I would like to give him a taste of dying, but I won't make him a vampire. He doesn't deserve anything this special," he told me with finality. "I will always remember his dark brown eyes and how he smelled like he worked in a bodega. He had an odd accent, though."

He smelled like a bodega, eh? Since Nathaniel had been able to pick up on that while still human, the man must fairly reek of the things that were common in such a location. That would help to narrow things down at least a little, anyway. Very likely, his clothing was kept in close quarters with whatever the incense might be. It was probably strong incense like *patchouli* or *nag champa*, then.

I decided then and there that it was not "if and when" I chose to investigate his murder, but simply "when". Nathaniel deserved some kind of closure, if only to help him move on with his new life as a vampire.

"I can't make any guarantees about being able to find him, Nathaniel, but I will do what I can to try to find out whatever information I can for you. It may take time, and it may take longer than the lifetime of the man who killed you, but I will do it for you." I knew as the words left my lips that I was not just trying to make him feel better. I knew that I meant every word I had just said and that I would do everything in my power to give him closure. Just because I was a vampire, it didn't mean I was an asshole. "For whatever reason, it appears you were a specific target. I wonder what you may have known or seen that made that the case. These things generally don't happen on a random basis."

I felt that I owed Nathaniel some kind of closure for his previous life. It is one thing to simply be attacked by a vampire and die that way, but to ultimately pass because of something so mysterious, it did not seem right to me. I had never given him a choice as to whether or not he wanted this kind of existence, but was glad that he had not cursed me for it.

"Thank you, Siofra," he told me, standing and then giving me a quick, shy hug. "And thank you for saving me, too."

Saving him? I did not think that turning someone into a vampire qualified as "saving" that someone, but if that was the way he felt about it, who was I to gainsay him?

"You're welcome, Nathaniel," I replied and squeezed him back. "Thank you for not hating me for what I did."

"I can't hate you for it, Siofra. I wasn't ready to die just yet. I know that this new life is going to take a lot of getting used to, but I know that if I want to survive, I can't be squeamish about what I need to do to make that happen."

"You have a remarkably open mind for this, Nathaniel," I said. "What did you do in life that might make you feel that way?"

"I don't know. Maybe it was one too many Discovery Channel shows about the circle of life and all that bullshit. If I can avoid taking innocent lives, it will obviously be a lot easier on me, I think. I'm no fool, though, to think that's going to be entirely possible."

How had I managed to find an enlightened human when I had created my first vampire? While I had long ago become convinced that the gods have a perverse sense of humor, I had not been aware they had anything like a sense of compassion for those of us who live on the fringes of society.

"It scared the shit out of me that I lost control back there. A tiny part of my mind was in there, knowing exactly what I was doing, but it couldn't do anything to stop what I was doing," he suddenly blurted out. "It wasn't that I didn't want to feed, because I did. I was starving, but I wish I could have done it without so much cruelty and violence."

"I guess it's a lesson to both of us to make sure that you don't go that long without feeding again, at least until you've got more control over yourself," I replied. "There will be times when that part of you will surface again, but the only thing we can do is to avoid situations where that would happen. I can go a little over a week before things get desperate, but then, I'm few hundred years old, too. It took a long time to develop that much self-restraint. Try not to beat yourself up about it. Remember, though, that violence is part of what we are as vampires. It's up to you to limit not if it will be violent, but how violent it will be."

We had reached the car and it was time to return to our small loft apartment and more discussions and lessons on what he was and what he could expect with his new life. I also needed to make a phone call to the one vampire I felt comfortable enough with to discuss the situation.

All in all, I felt pretty good about how Nathaniel's first feeding had gone. I had expected worse, but those fears had not been realized, which worked for me. As long as I remembered to keep him well-fed, things should be okay. At least, I hoped that would be the case.

Perhaps that relatively easy success was what led to our first real disagreement.

As accepting as he had seemed after his first feeding, Nathaniel had wanted to return to his family to try resuming his interrupted human life, pretending this had never happened. He had shouted at me. He had entreated me, crying, to relent, but no matter how his anguish tore at my heart, I had remained firm in my resolve. I told him that the media presentation of vampires was not anything like the truth. It could not be conveniently minimized as an unimportant personal quirk. There was no way he would be able to survive on what amounts to dead blood, and I told him so, including a graphic description of what had happened the only time I had been unwise enough to try to drink the stuff.

Once it happens to you, you will never forget the experience. No matter how hard you might try to do just that.

It must have been the bond formed by his first feeding upon my own blood that had made him obey me even though I knew—could *feel* —his overwhelming desire to disobey me and run back to his family and his human connections. I hated that I had so much control over him, but to be completely honest, I was grateful that it was there. He obeyed me just like a young conscript terrified to his core about what new horror lay over the next hill, but obey me he did. As long as I kept him fed, there was very little danger of a repeat performance of his breaking free of my control.

He had no choice, though I had done everything I could to show him that my concern was more than reasonable. I wanted him to know that I understood why he felt as he did. While he had been able to break through my control when he was starving, this was something entirely different that did not relate to hunger, which is why I think that in this thing I was successful. Even I knew what extreme hunger would do to the most self-possessed vampire. Apparently, the bond we had created was very strong indeed, but was not proof against disobedience, in the most extreme circumstances.

I remembered that self-important bastard of a vampire Andreas, proud old Austrian Nosferatu and not surprisingly, my own maker, and shuddered to imagine him ever having that kind of nearly unbreakable control over me. He must have been furious that I had been able to defy him as I had. Andreas had tried many times in my infancy to coax me into joining his kiss of then what consisted of about four Offspring, but I remained adamant that I would not do so. There were some solitary old ones, those usually at least four to five hundred years old, who generally kept to themselves and shunned contact with others of our kind. Many of them lived in the part of the world that once had been encompassed by the former Soviet Union, for whatever reason. Perhaps the regimented lifestyle common in some of those areas appealed to them. I did not know, and did not particularly care to ask.

I was clearly an exception to the self-imposed Luddite attitude often practiced by those of my longevity who had no affiliation to a kiss. I loved new things and embraced the new technologies that appeared on the horizon. What better way was there to keep up with what might someday be important? I hated surprises, so it made more sense to me to embrace the world.

That was what my longtime acquaintance who currently was the Master of a European Haven told me when I finally called to ask about the care and feeding of balky fledglings, once we returned from Nathaniel's first feeding. In hindsight, I felt like kicking myself, knowing I could have made this phone call days before now and saved myself the shock from some of the unwelcome things that had occurred during that hunt.

At my age, I really should have remembered the maxim "forewarned is forearmed".

The old bastard had been uncharacteristically amused when he discovered I was now a Sire. At the news, he had started laughing hysterically and then it took awhile for him to regain enough control over himself to tell me what I needed to know. That vampire had sired and successfully raised at least three or four vampire children in his six hundred years, so he had enough experience on the subject for me to feel comfortable asking for his advice.

Two

"You really went and finally did it, Siofra? Welcome to the joys of parenthood!"

"Fuck you, Janos."

The older vampire did not take offense in the least and only laughed harder. I could hear him beating the top of a wooden table with his fist as he was overcome with mirth. I waited silently until he once again established control of himself, though I could swear I heard the odd giggle periodically escape his lips.

"What is your child's name?" he asked once he was done beating his table into submission. Knowing Janos and his family, the table was an antique, and if he'd damaged it, his wife would knock the crap out of him. She liked fine things, and wouldn't have tolerated cheap furniture in her domain.

"Nathaniel. He is about twenty-eight or so. Nice kid, just really fucked up right now over all of this."

"Nathaniel? Nathaniel O'Se, if I remember correctly, and I usually do," he replied smugly. "That is a sweet name. You call him Nat, Nathan, Natty?"

"Either Nathaniel or Nat. If he has any other nickname he might like, he'll have to let me know. I'm not going to make assumptions," I told him. "Someone once made a very wise statement about the meaning and probable outcome of assumptions."

"My first child was a French girl called Natalie. Lovely child and a deadly hunter." Janos' heavy Slavic accent always brought a smile to my face, as it reminded me of the old classic Russian accents you would hear on television and in the movies where the bad guys spoke badly accented English amongst themselves, even when only their own countrymen were in the room.

In my mind's eye, I could just picture him purring to a captive that it were best he or she confess to whatever crime they had been accused of committing, as he already knew the fact of their guilt.

"At this time, I have four surviving children and even some grandchildren, although not all are good about visiting their grandpapa on a regular basis. I shall have to see about having discussions with them about their lack of respect."

He always reminded me of a great cat stalking diminutive and helpless prey, speaking sweetly to distract you while getting ready to attack. I would not want to be those recalcitrant grandchildren. "Grandpapa" had a temper on him.

Janos was originally from near Spain, although he had never told me exactly where he had been born. While he had been born in that part of the world however, he had obviously been raised somewhere in Eastern Europe, as his accent suggested. Of course, he also could be faking the accent, but that did not really matter. Vampires are consummate actors and often develop their own backstories to build more of a mystique in order to be more intimidating to the larger vampire community. It was considered very rude to ask a vampire about his or her actual origins.

He was tall, slender and fair skinned, even beyond normal vampiric paleness, with a glorious headful of long and wavy jet black hair which he often wore caught in a ribbon at the nape of his neck. On his face, he sported a slender but elegantly maintained mustache and Van Dyke-style beard. Janos had died with it, so it would always be there. At least he kept it all neatly combed and tidy. Nathaniel had been completely clean-shaven when he died, so he would never have facial hair of any sort.

There was something to be said for men who were attentive to good personal grooming standards. I'd always hated that five o'clock shadow look that so many human males had adopted since the days of the original "Miami Vice" television program. I could just barely feel the stubs of Nathaniel's beard when I ran my hand over his cheeks and chin.

Perfect.

What could have possessed the man to shave before going on the clandestine meeting which had ultimately resulted in his death? Well, at least he would not go through eternity looking like a bum, so there was that bright spot. No zits, either. Can you imagine existing for hundreds of years with an eternal blemish? I've seen it.

Ick.

There was usually a smile on Janos' face that appeared as though it had worked its way up into his eyes, making it almost impossible to look away from him when he glanced your way. It might have been real, but it was just as possible that it was not. Even as a vampire, it was tough to tell. It was not some kind of supernatural mesmerization, either. There really are humans out there who have the same ability to catch the eye and demand attention with nary a word. They tend to make either very popular actors or dare I say it, successful career politicians.

Janos had been married to his vampire wife, Estelle, for almost two hundred years, after an extended courtship that had lasted for nearly a hundred years. If you are planning to make a "forever" commitment, you had better make sure you truly love your partner, so that kind of extended engagement made a lot of sense in the vampire world. Janos' oldest surviving "son", an eighteenth century gentleman called Gregory, had met his beloved, a beautiful girl called Kathleen, while she was still human and although they were still together all these years later, they had never married. It was not that they did not love each other. Quite the contrary. Apparently, there was something else between them that made marriage irrelevant to their relationship.

I thought it was a sweet sentiment, despite my naturally cynical disposition.

Estelle had not been pleased with their decision to not marry, but that did not mean she did not love the woman who was essentially her daughter in law. Janos' wife was an old-fashioned vampire, and had come from a time when "decent" young women married and that was that. Too bad for her that Gregory's mate was a strong, independent-minded woman who was not afraid to stand her ground when necessary. I found that I liked Kathleen, and although we had never had a girls' night out to get to know one another better, so to speak, I always felt quite comfortable around her.

I had been fortunate enough to be invited to the eventual wedding of Janos and Estelle. It was the social event of the century, to hear the gossip thereafter. Everyone who was anyone had wrangled for an invitation, so there were some offended feelings here and there, but overall, it had all gone quite well for everyone concerned.

I had drawn the line at the rather frothy cream-colored bridesmaid gown Estelle had chosen, and instead wore a variant of the thing that excluded the frothy lace trimmings but kept the myriad natural pearls which had been sewn down in such a way that they appeared to pour down the front of the gown to the back around the hem, creating a miniature shining wake in the abbreviated train the thing had boasted. She had tried to insist on my wearing her own choice of dress, but Janos had stepped in and prevailed upon her with those dashingly good looks of his to allow me my little quirks.

Kathleen had not had that luxury. As his ostensibly dutiful daughter in law, she was expected to dress and play the part of the demure bridesmaid.

I always wondered how Gregory had been made to pay for the indignity Estelle had heaped upon his lady love, but I was not going to ask now. It was probably one of those couples' secrets anyway.

Janos and I had met while we were assigned to deal with a rogue vampire in Germany in the late seventeenth century. I was still relatively young as vampires are concerned, and he was at least a couple hundred years old at that time, and surprisingly patient with what to him was a mere child.

We had hit it off instantly, and made a very good team. He taught me aspects of hunting I had never before considered, and I used some of those techniques even now, when hunting humans instead of my own kind.

His beloved Estelle and I met a few decades thereafter, and once she was both assured and then convinced that I was not potential romantic competition, she had practically adopted me into their delightful little undead family. Had I ever been forced to join a kiss, theirs is the only one I ever would have considered worthy. Fortunately, Janos was not so Old World as some of his contemporaries. I am certain that I would have made a very difficult "daughter" for him anyway.

I could practically hear him bursting with pride about his Natalie, having heard a lot about her over the years. She had even given him a few vampire grandchildren over the centuries. His was a close family, as vampires reckoned it.

"His being 'really fucked up', as you so eloquently phrased it, is understandable, Siofra, but you are going to have to keep a very close eye on him. Do not let him get away with anything. Tell me, you did feed him yourself when he first woke, correct? Tell me that you did." The last sounded like a desperate plea, which was very unlike my otherwise self-assured and annoyingly confident friend.

"Yes, I did. Why?"

"That is what's going to help you have some level of control over him," he said, sounding immensely relieved, which suddenly made *me* tense. Why was this so very important? "From what you have told me about your own turning, Andreas did not feed you first.

If he had, you would have been in his power. I am sure that once Nathaniel drank from you, you discovered that you could feel what he was feeling."

"Yes, I could, and it confused me. I've never before experienced anything like it," I responded. "Why didn't you tell me about this before?"

"Quite frankly, I did not think that you would ever need to know. You have ever been a solitary vampire, and I could not see you making the decision to raise a child of your own. Color me surprised, my dear girl."

"Well, yes, I'll admit to being a bit surprised, myself," I replied grudgingly. He knew me too damned well and I told him so. "I think you know me better than I know myself, so your being surprised is almost funny."

"That sharing of blood is what makes that the case. Well, for a decade or so, anyway. That should be more than long enough to raise him to be a responsible member of our particular society. Once a vampire feeds on his or her own kill, that bond may not retroactively be created. The first feeding *must* be between Maker and child, or that bond will never be. Perhaps your own maker never realized that this was why his other children are bound to him. Wildly unlikely, perhaps, but still possible."

"Ten *years*? It didn't take that long for *me* to learn," I protested. "Are you telling me that it's going to take that long to teach him what he needs to know? It's not really all that difficult, as long as you're careful, Janos!"

"Siofra, remember that you became a vampire in a time and place where it would be far easier for you to survive your fledgling years. Humans were few and far between, except in the larger cities. Imagine what it is like for your Nathaniel, with all those beating hearts thrumming around him. Well, you should not have to imagine, as you can feel what he is feeling for now," he responded reasonably. "It's obvious that vampires are supposed to be raised by other vampires, else why would that bonding even be possible? Think of that first feeding as being like a new human mother breastfeeding her newborn. Think of it as vampire colostrum."

"Has anyone ever told you that you can be disgusting?"

He chuckled and I smiled automatically when I heard it. I just couldn't help myself.

"So my beloved Estelle has told me countless times."

Poor Estelle. However did she survive her husband's rather twisted sense of humor?

"Now," he continued. "That connection between you goes both ways, and you are going to feel downright maternal about the poor boy. Keep hold of yourself and do not be stupid with him. That would not be healthy for either of you. You are the parent, and thus must be the authority here. He is not too old to spank. Figuratively speaking, that is. I am sure you know how serious all of this is, but it is important that I stress this for you. What happened with his first feeding? Did he hunt on his own successfully, or did you have to subdue the prey for him?"

"I'm not sure that I'm up for this, Janos. How can I be responsible for a fledgling vampire when I screwed up so badly the first time Nathaniel fed?"

"I'm sure everything was fine, Siofra, since we're talking now and he's still with you," was Janos' more than reasonable reply. "You're crying over clotted blood, dear one."

"His first feeding was terrifying, Janos. He hunted and brought down the prey on his own, but it was such a near thing. I think I waited too long for it. He was like a wild animal! He actually frightened me a bit with his intensity, and I don't remember the last time I was truly frightened by much of anything."

"Sometimes it's for the best, Siofra. You got him past any initial squeamishness that could interfere with future feedings. Obviously you're back in control of things, or we would not be having this particular conversation."

"Did this happen to you with your turns, Janos?" I asked him quietly. "It was hard enough with taking Nathaniel out the first time. I can't imagine doing it multiple times if that always happens."

"With several of my children, yes. Not all of mine have been successful, and I'm not going to try to pretend that they were, Siofra. I had to end a few myself, and that's never something to do lightly. The last was only a few months ago, in fact." There was deep sadness in his voice with this startling revelation. "A new son to join the family. Estelle was devastated and called in all the children and kept them close for awhile, until she felt comfortable enough to allow them to return to their own existences. Kathleen was a dear and has stayed a bit longer while Gregory is away making more business contacts."

The thought that Janos had miscalculated a potential turn threw me for a loop. Janos had always seemed comfortable with the family he had. I had not known he was looking to expand it.

"What happened, or is that too personal a question?"

It took him a long time to answer, and I became afraid that I had overstepped. Finally, though I was rewarded with a long sigh, and then his uncharacteristically sober answer.

"I had high hopes for the boy, but he enjoyed the thrill of the kill entirely too much, and even in the most fortunate of circumstances, that cannot be allowed to happen. Not in this day and age, even in my own part of the world. So I killed him myself while he was deep in the throes of slaughtering an entire family. The bond we had between us made it all the more painful, as I felt his awful hatred at my betrayal of that bond. The subsequent cover-up exhausted a lot of the goodwill I had sown over the years in that part of the world. You may or may not have heard rumors of it over the grapevine, as we are all such terrible gossips."

I could tell that he was trying to lighten the mood and obligingly giggled at his last comment. I hated to see Janos at all unhappy.

"I don't want to see the same thing happen to you, child, so I must insist on this last thing. Siofra, you are going to have to get out of the country and off to somewhere it will be safer to raise your boy. I have an idea of a good place for that. Email me pictures of him and yourself. I will have all the proper documents prepared and in your hands by the end of the week," he said briskly. "Wait a minute, do you have a current passport?"

"My passport? Yes, I always keep it up to date. Why?"

"Siofra, you *cannot* stay in such a populated area right now, so the best place for you to teach your Nathaniel how to be a vampire is going to be somewhere with a lot of chaos going on. I know of an area that would be perfect for that, and have some contacts out there who will give you a place to stay as well. Trust me on this, kid. We have *family* in the State Department who will take care of what you will need, so do not worry about it and just take care of your local concerns."

"So are we going to have to stay in a hole in the ground, then? While I have done that more than once over the years, I just don't think that my boy is capable of that kind of roughing it. Nathaniel grew up in the States with the joys of the internet, cell phones and the like. He's probably never really been away from civilization for any appreciable length of time."

"Well, that 'hole in the ground', as you put it, may indeed be part of your future, but not for long, I am certain. I will also be sure to provide you with a satellite phone and small charging station so that you may contact the outside world. I will say this, my dear, you are one up on a lot of the other Old Ones out there," he said. "So many of them would simply shun such modern practicalities, even if it would be in their best interests to embrace them. It is a shame that advanced age makes so many of us into functioning Luddites. However did an ancient little girl like you avoid such myopic thinking?"

"Screw you, Janos; you are at least two hundred years older than I am!"

"True, Siofra, and you are certainly a lot prettier than I am, too. How *do* you keep your girlish figure?"

"I keep to a low carbohydrate diet, Janos. You should try it yourself, sometime."

"Ha, ha. There are still many upon whom that bit of snark would be lost, Siofra. Anyhow, so many of the One Ones seem to think that if they do not acknowledge the present, it does not exist or will not happen at all. They will not see that they must evolve with the times if they are to survive." His joviality vanished between one moment and the next, sadness entering his voice. "They refuse to embrace the ingenuity of the present and instead dwell in their own pasts. Overall, that way of thinking is not ending well for a great many of them."

"Yes, Janos, I know. I heard that Stephan was finally ended last year by the Russian strike force. It was only a matter of time, really. He seemed to think he could still feed with impunity." Stephan was a seven hundred year old vampire who had been the oldest vampire I could recall meeting. He had been aghast that I was not in the thrall of some master or at least loosely affiliated with a kiss. "What happened to his kiss?"

"Trust you to worry about them, child. The Powers That Be decided to give them a choice. They could join existing kisses with reliable and trustworthy masters, or they were ended as well. Only a few took the latter route, more the fool them," Janos replied. The vampire was as close to a friend as I had had when I brought Nathaniel over. "Fortunately, most of his kiss was wiser than he."

"Agatha?" Agatha was a German girl who was all of thirteen when she had been made a Child of Blood in the late 1600's. We had been thrown together for a while during one of the many invasions of the German Palatines a few centuries past, and I had found I rather liked the soft-spoken and unintentionally hilarious little girl. It would hurt me if she had been so stupid as to follow her foolish maker into true death.

"No, not our dainty little Agatha, although she almost went into the fire with Stephan, Fredrick and Isolde. However, my tenacious and beautiful Estelle managed to talk her out of that foolishness at nearly the last possible moment. Agatha is now part of Casius' small kiss in Australia. He will keep her out of trouble, bring her into the modern world and perhaps even teach her that it is okay to have a bit of fun."

I laughed. I had spent more than a little time with Casius in the past and so I was quite familiar with Agatha's new Master. It would be a good match, I think, even though it might seem unlikely.

"Janos, Casius is one of those who will yell 'Zombie!' in a crowded mausoleum. If Agatha does not learn to have fun, it will be through no fault of Casius," I replied. "The world is a better place because vampires like Casius are in it."

Janos laughed, but then quickly sobered.

"Stay away from the Old Ones, whenever you can, Siofra. There are some out there who do not like you and the even more progressive attitude you represent," he told me. "Two or three would gladly see you ended. Your success outside the *traditional* vampire social structure threatens all they hold dear, and they resent that. They fear what would happen if others of our kind decided they could be out on their own, without a Master over them."

"I will, Janos. I know you have not actually come out and said it before, but I am guessing that I will need to keep my eyes open. I number my own maker in my pile of detractors, though I do not think Andreas would go so far as supporting my demise." I was sure, at least, of my own maker. I might hate him, but knew he was entirely too egotistical to call for the death of one of his own children.

"No, Andreas wants you tied to a kiss, specifically his kiss. He is not one of those who are calling for your head on a pike. Let us just say that your current situation will lend itself well to steering clear of the more rabid of your detractors. You do have friends in the greater community, so those of us who appreciate you will be doing what we can to smooth things over while you are gone."

"How long am I supposed to stay away, Janos?" This was beginning to sound even more ominous to me and I did not like it a bit.

"I think you should plan on at least twenty to thirty years away from where you are now. I will get back to you with your paperwork, including new passports for the both of you, some one way tickets and the letter of introduction you will need once you get there," he explained. "I know you will do very well with your child, Siofra. You could not possibly do otherwise. You don't have it in you to fail."

"I still don't understand why I did it in the first place, Janos. I've never before even attempted to turn someone, and now, nearly four hundred years later, I do just that."

"It's natural, actually. I believe it's the vampire equivalent of a biological imperative. There is something that will drive you to reproduce at least once. It never seems to be just anyone, either. That first turn seems to look for just the right person," he said. "I'm not sure why it happens. My first child was a gentleman called Silvio. He was a sweet young man, but he finally decided to end things when his mortal lady love died. Poor Silvio was ever the romantic."

We were both quiet for a time as I am sure Janos was thinking about that loss. It cannot have been easy at all for him to lose his first child. I know that even considering the possibility of losing Nathaniel in such a way was downright painful.

"He fell for a mortal woman? How did that even work?"

"Oh, you'll love this. He was one for the sonnets, so she never even knew he yearned for her. She died an old woman, happily married to a devoted husband," he chuckled.

"I'd heard of people like that, it just seems strange to see it happen in our own community. Was he very old, then, when he ended himself?"

"He'd been a vampire for a hundred fifty years or so. He initially saw the woman while she was still a child, and became devoted to her the moment he laid eyes on her."

"That's creepy, Janos. Very creepy. Borderline pedophilia, I'm thinking. Overall, gross-out creepy."

"Creepy, yes," he laughed. "A good word to describe that kind of fatal fascination. I've never been particularly fond of sonnets, myself."

"Nor I, my friend. They've always just seemed a bit silly to me. Thank you for everything, Janos. You are a very good friend," I told him. "I'll miss you."

"Honeypot, I am your *only* friend, but I love you anyway. Now give me what I need and I will get the ball rolling on my end! Tell your Nathaniel 'hello' from his Uncle Janos!"

My Nathaniel.

"I will, Uncle Janos!" I assured him, allowing my smile to be caught in my tone. He chuckled again.

"Oh! Estelle has been after me to have you visit soon, but I think you will have your hands full awhile yet with my new nephew. Let us plan to spend the winter holidays together in a few decades, my dear. You should know that you and your Nathaniel will always be welcome under my roof!" His rich laughter warmed me and made me laugh in return.

I did know that I could trust Janos as I trusted no other vampire out there, so I thanked him, gave him my assent and my email address and then bid him adieu. I had promised my child that I would be taking him out to dinner tonight, and I did not break my promises to him.

I was glad that we had no pets to consider, as travel did not lend itself to bringing pets along, especially dogs. I had kept several dogs and a couple of cats as companions over the centuries, but even with the extended lifespan bestowed by a taste of my blood, they would eventually grow old and die. After all, they were not vampire animals. They were not undead. My first, a wonderful Irish wolfhound called Mathúin, had lived with me for at least forty years, until the day his strength failed him during a rather nasty fight and he was killed by a human wielding a sword when he leaped to my defense.

I promise you, that human died horribly shortly thereafter. Mathúin had been my protector and friend since before I had been turned, and was the last "family" I had from my days as a mortal girl. I remember feeling as though the last of my family had been ripped away from me, and that I was now truly alone.

It took me a long time to come to the point where I was comfortable making that kind of commitment with another animal. Before you ask, no, this odd bonding such as had existed between me and Mathúin was not possible between humans and vampires. While there may be "Renfields" in popular fiction, primates of any sort are beyond my ability to bestow extended longevity without my making them a vampire in truth. I had indeed attempted it a couple times in the past, and all had ended without success. The otherwise healthy humans had retched up the blood I shared with them and that was that.

I had not acquired a new animal companion since my last, an Abyssinian cat called Daisy, had passed away some five years ago. When you are essentially immortal, losing those with whom you have developed an attachment gets to you, and I had not felt myself yet ready to take on another eventual heartbreak. Also, it's hard to travel with a pet, sometimes, and I was not going to claim her as a service animal to get past the gatekeepers out there.

It turns out that was rather forward-thinking of me. Just in case, I had told Nathaniel to keep his blood to himself but glossed over why that was so important. We did not need any surprises at this late juncture.

"Really? My blood will make an animal live a lot longer? Does that work with any kind of animal?" I felt and heard his excitement, and knew I had to nip it in the blood quickly, before we had a curiously long-lived Boston terrier or Rottweiler on our hands. I had to be the bad guy here, and really didn't want that, but I had no choice in the matter. This was so much more of an issue than a nine year old human begging Mommy and Daddy for a puppy, as natural dogs only live about twenty years at most, and that's with regular veterinary care.

"It only appears to work with non-primate carnivores and it seems that you may only do it with one at a time. I've had dogs live to fifty when they've had a taste of my blood, although the size of the dog seems to have something to do with it, too. As with normal dogs, smaller breeds seem to live longer. Cats seem to live even longer than dogs, but I'm not sure why that is the case. In any event, we do not need any pets at this time, so don't make any."

"Yes, ma'am," he said meekly, and I felt his disappointment as his childlike curiosity was smashed into an imaginary wall. I only barely heard his parting comment as he walked down the hall toward the bedroom. "Someday, however..."

My vampire child had hated me for a time when first I told him that we were going to have to leave beautiful Southern California. Even a vampire can appreciate the gorgeous weather, the feel of warm sand between your toes and the soothing sound of the endless waves pounding up and down the beach. Nathaniel had been born in Los

Angeles and lived there his entire life. The thought of leaving the only home city he'd ever known must have been wrenching for him.

The day finally came, however, when he admitted that leaving was best for all concerned. Those first couple weeks of nearly constant hunger had proven to him that he probably would have killed those for whom he cared in his unending drive to sate his bottomless appetite.

His epiphany had occurred when I finally took drastic action in order to break through his ridiculous extended tantrum and get his attention. In order to drive the point home one night, I had made sure he was very well fed and then took him near to his old home. I allowed him to stand in the shadows and watch the silhouettes of his family behind their living room curtains for a time.

"Dad is home, and Christy, too." he breathed. I could feel his hunger growing, and only my control over him kept Nathaniel from losing himself and doing something I knew he would later regret. "They're all crying."

Glancing at him during that time of trial, I saw the blood tears running down his cheeks as he silently wept with the grief and realization that had suffused him. He was mourning a family who still lived, and knew he could never see again.

"It's only been a few days since you left them, Nathaniel. They are still grieving for you," I told him softly, putting a gentle hand on his forearm, not to hold him, but to try to give some kind of reassurance.

"Someone's in the back yard!" he suddenly muttered, dashing forward and leaping silently to the top of the fence. "Who—?"

"Natty?" Came a child's voice softly from the backyard. "Is that you? You're supposed to be dead."

Shit. How the hell were we going to fix this mess? He was as impulsive as a three year old, sometimes.

"Barbara!" he choked. "Oh, God."

I could hear the child's footsteps as she approached the fence where Nathaniel perched. This must be his fourteen year old sister, the one with Down's syndrome, who was a bit slow, but who Nat loved deeply about whom he was very protective.

"Can't you come in and let everyone know you're okay?" she asked him reasonably. There was no fear in her voice. "Daddy's been crying."

"No, Barb, I can't. I can't explain, either. Please don't tell anyone you saw me here!" he begged her. "It would only make things worse than they are already."

"But Natty! We all miss you!"

"I can't, Barb. I really can't!" he choked the words out, and I knew that his fangs had erupted in response to his small relation's proximity. "I can't explain why, Barb, but I wish I could. All I can tell you is that it's not safe for me to be around you!"

"You have blood on your face. What's wrong with your teeth?" she asked him, still sounding as though she trusted him completely. Human children seemed to be the most trusting creatures on this planet. "Your teeth look funny, kind of like the lion at the zoo."

Like a lion's fangs. What an interesting simile from her.

"I can't explain, Barb. I have to go now," he told her, fighting down the urge to leap, to seize and to drink deeply. "Maybe we'll see one another again, someday, but not now. I love you so much. Please, don't tell anyone you saw me. They wouldn't believe you, anyway."

I heard the sound of flesh hitting flesh as Barbara must have darted forward and embraced her brother. Perhaps she reasoned that if she could hold him, she could keep him with her.

I could feel the yearning of Nathaniel's vampire hunger as he struggled to control it in the face of his sister's unexpected contact. It rose inside him almost like the beginnings of an orgasm, and I expected disaster shortly thereafter.

"I can't stay here, Barbara. It's not safe for you!"

"But you need to stay! I need you to stay," she argued. "It's too hard with you gone."

"I love you, Barbara Jean, but I might hurt you by accident, and I'd hate myself forever if I did." I felt his hunger escalating as well as Nathaniel's nervousness. "I have to leave!"

His voice had roughened as his predator instincts began thrumming at the proximity of an easy meal. His sister, completely ignorant of the danger she was in, kept begging him to remain.

I prepared to intervene, but wondered what I'd do if he fed from her. With her disability, she would have trouble being a vampire. While she would probably make a good predator, as most vampires were, she would still be limited mentally by her disability. From everything Nathaniel had told me, she was high functioning, but would always need a caretaker, and that was something that was highly unlikely in the vampire community.

The next thing I heard was the sound of Barbara hitting the ground hard as Nathaniel shoved her away from him. His hunger was roaring in his head and it was all he could do to keep from savaging her. There was a reason why, in the past, that most vampires' first victims were family and friends. It was entirely too easy to make them feel perfectly safe before you drank them down. Teenaged Barbara could be easily taken, as she was as trusting as just about any human toddler.

"Natty!" She cried reproachfully, sitting on her backside in the dirt. I could smell her tears on the breeze as her hurt expressed itself in her eyes.

"No, Barbara! Stay away. I don't want to hurt you," he groaned in mental and physical agony. "I'm so sorry I even stopped here in the first place."

With a sob of despair, Nathaniel leaped back from the fence and ran away down the street, his feet never making a sound on the pavement.

"Nathaniel!" Young Barbara screamed into the darkness with a strength that surprised me. The terrific sense of loss and anguish in that cry tore at me more than I thought was even possible. She was only a human, after all. "Don't leave me!"

I ran after my fledgling, but not before hearing the sound of Barbara racing to the back door and throwing herself inside, yelling that she had just seen her dead brother. I caught the sounds of shock and raised voices inside the house, but tuned it out as I followed Nathaniel. Their upset was not my problem.

It ate at me to feel his grief, but I knew that this front and center lesson would be the only way to make him understand that I was really thinking of not only him, but of the safety of those he loved. I felt terrible that his sister would end up bearing the brunt of her family's disbelief, but I knew that was what would happen if something like this had happened in uncontrolled circumstances.

I had felt the war Nathaniel had fought as he battled his inner predator to keep himself from descending upon his mentally challenged younger sister and joyously draining her. It showed more restraint than I would have given him credit for possessing, but I also knew that he had been very lucky this time. Perhaps it had been his protective feelings toward her that had kept him from attacking her.

Using our curious connection, I tracked Nathaniel to the Santa Monica Pier, where he stood at the end of the long wooden structure, staring out over the darkly glittering ocean. He grunted an acknowledgment of my presence, not saying a word for about ten minutes. There were a few people in the parking lot atop the thing, and one or two closing up the arcade near the center of the pier, but it was pretty close to being deserted. That said, I knew very well that sound carries near water and hoped he knew the same.

"Fuck you, Siofra! Fuck you and what you did to me back there!" He kept his voice down, but his anger was still there and the force of it nearly rocked me backward. "I could have killed her, and you'd have just stood there and let it happen!"

"Nathaniel, I would have done everything possible to keep you from hurting your sister. You wouldn't listen to me earlier when I told you that staying here would be dangerous for the people you love and care about. This was the only way I could prove it to you."

He swore viciously again, head turned away from me as he watched the waves crashing against the pier's supports. Well, he had to get it out some way, but it was hard not to take it personally.

"I'm so very sorry, Nathaniel. Truly, I am. I know how much it hurts to have to say goodbye to the people you know and love," I told him softly. I carefully put one arm around his waist, ready to pull back if he flinched away from me, but he did not. Taking a chance, I cinched myself up close to him. "I had to do it the first time when my father couldn't afford to pay the rents he owed our landlord. He basically sold me to the lord as a servant. I never even had the chance to see them again."

"He what? He sold you as a slave?" Nathaniel responded, obviously shocked. He was so surprised that he probably spoke louder than he had intended, and he looked around quickly to see if anyone had overheard.

"I was essentially a slave, although not in name," I replied. Oh, the ignorance of modern western society. The English sold over two hundred thousand of my countrymen into slavery during the period in history from which I came, but that was something rarely taught to American schoolchildren. "Serfdom was a kind of slavery when I was still human. My father rented a few acres of land from a lord and paid him once a year from the crops he harvested. He didn't grow enough to do much more than feed us one year, and so I and whatever services I could render were taken in payment when the steward came to collect the rents."

People of all cultures and races have been subject to slavery at one time or another. Slavery's been an equal opportunity employer now for several thousand years. Don't ever let anyone tell you otherwise.

"How could a father do that to his own daughter?"

"People do the things they do for reasons that make sense to them, even when they don't make sense to anyone else."

"You're right. It doesn't make any sense to me at all."

"Nathaniel, my father had his reasons for what he did, and I didn't have any say in the matter. One, I was just a little girl, and two, I was a female child. I wasn't legally worth as much as one of his sons. When I was still a human child, a daughter was considered to be more of an expense to raise than a son. Unlike today, when a woman is no longer considered to be merely chattel, at least in the Western world."

"Chattel?" Apparently, Nathaniel was unfamiliar with the word.

"Until the relatively recent past, a daughter was considered to be more property than a person. She had to be obedient to anything her father demanded of her, as he would be expected to provide a dowry that is money or property of some tangible value, when she was married off into another family. That was the way things were in those days."

"It just doesn't seem right to me, Siofra."

"Again, Nathaniel, that's the way things were then. Any child of her body would be the property of her husband, who was not a part of her father's family. Those future children would add to the prestige of her future husband's family. A son could continue the family bloodline. A daughter married into another family to continue their own bloodline." I told him.

"It's barbaric!"

"Perhaps, but the circumstances of my human life are what allowed me to survive as I am now. Also it turns out; his trading me for his overdue rents was probably the best thing that could have happened to me, as my family was dead of some disease a few years later."

I could be philosophical about things, sometimes.

"So all of your family died, then? That's terrible."

"No, not quite. I found one of my brothers some years after I was made a vampire. I'd thought he was long dead with the rest of my family, so imagine my surprise at finding him mostly hale and hearty in Ireland."

"Did you eat him, too?" His tone was mocking, and I tried not to let it bother me. We hadn't made it through his anger at me.

"No. I was surprised to see him, though. I had thought him dead and suddenly there he was, right in front of me."

"How did he take it?" He sounded a little less angry, but still, I trod lightly. No sense in reminding him that he was pissed off at me, and conversation is usually much better than one sided bouts of profanity.

"Not well at all. I was certainly the last person from his past who he ever expected to see again, since as far as he knew, I was long dead. Apparently, someone had told him about the massacre, and he had gotten word that I was there when it all happened. I can't blame him for how he felt, and neither can I blame him for thinking me some haunt come to torment him. This was a very superstitious time, and in their religious fervor, people saw the devil and demonic possession all over the place. A son had a duty to his father to support the family, and my brother had not done that. Instead, he had tired of our father's casual brutality and ran off about six months after I was taken away."

"Did your reunion end badly?"

"Overall, yes it did. I'll share that story with you another time."

"That must have been hard for you," he pressed, but I wasn't ready to discuss the whole sordid business with him.

"Yes, it was. I had been a vampire for a few years by that time, but I was still too young to be completely trustworthy and thus it wasn't an option for me to constantly be around lots of humans."

"I don't know how you can tolerate all of this hunger without losing control of yourself, Siofra."

"Nathaniel, the urge to feed will always be there, but over time, as I said before, you'll learn to have greater control over it," I said. "I don't want you to end up hating yourself because you've done something you can't ever take back. Eternity is a long time to have regrets about something."

There were regrets aplenty in my own memories, but I didn't feel like sharing them with him right now, if ever. While they had never completely healed, there was no need to make them raw all over again.

Nathaniel seemed to think about this for awhile, as he stood there silently, but the echoes from his emotional turmoil in my mind gave the lie to his seeming quietude. His calm demeanor did not last, as I felt something like excitement from him.

"But I can just feed from the gangsters and rapists and those kind of people!" he tried to protest. I remember having those sorts of noble feelings myself, once upon a time. There was a hopeful grin on his face that I knew I had to dash quickly.

"Sweetheart, that's not going to work. It's simply not possible, as there just aren't enough of those kinds of people out there anymore. Well, at least those who won't be inconveniently missed. Between that and modern forensic medicine, a fledgling doesn't stand much of a chance in a scientifically advanced society."

"Is it really that bad?" he asked quietly, his grin now gone and his face expressionless.

"Once upon a time, when humans came across a body, it did not dawn on them to notice that the body was missing most of its blood. It was dead and it scared the shit out of them, but in most cases, they went on with their lives after disposing of it in whatever way they thought appropriate. Hell, these days, you can get fingerprints off a corpse! Until you have more control over yourself and can keep from thoughtlessly eating the neighbors, we can't live here anymore."

"You said 'in most cases'. What did that mean?"

"Once or twice, I've had to dissuade the wanna-be Sherlock Holmes types who just couldn't leave well enough alone. Those cases *never* ended well for the nosy human. Is that what you want to have happen here? Do you want to attack your sister Barbara some night when you are really hungry and that one part of your mind tells you that she will be easy prey because she trusts you?"

He was quiet for a long time before he spoke again.

"I'll never be able to see my family again, will I?"

"No, Nathaniel. You won't. I wish there was some other way, but that's how it is. By going away, you will be protecting them all."

"They're never going to believe whatever Barbara told them, either. I hate that I might have confused her and gotten her into trouble."

"I'm sorry about that, too, Nathaniel. I was hoping this all could have been accomplished without encountering anyone you knew, but the universe, I guess, had a twisted sense of humor tonight. All we can do is hope that they can convince her she didn't really see you and they can get on with their lives."

We stood together in a companionable silence for a long time. Several minutes later, to my surprise, Nathaniel reached out a hand and tentatively closed it over mine where it rested on the damp railing. I fed all the reassurance I could into my thoughts and feelings, as touch seemed to sharpen the bond we shared.

"It's not an easy existence we live, nor is it glamorous, all media depictions to the contrary. Not just anyone can hack being a vampire, but when I found you the other night, something told me you would be an exception to that rule. If at some point you feel that this is not for you, tell me and I'll end you myself, though it would break my heart, I think. I believe, however, that you are strong enough and canny enough to be a great vampire, you just have to survive your infancy and learn about what you are and where that could take you."

"For now, I don't want to die, Siofra. I'm not ready to leave. Maybe later that will change, but I guess I have to try to make it work for me," he said philosophically.

"That's good to hear, Nathaniel. I'm not ready to let you go."

"You told me that you were born in the early part of the seventieth century. Has it been hard for you to live this long?"

"I've known people from their infancy to when they died from very old age, and I've sometimes fed from children when there was no alternative. I do regret ending those completely innocent lives. Never think I don't. I've never been what you would call a social vampire, and keep to myself. I tend mostly to be a loner, and I like that. Bringing you over was quite a shock for me, as it was something I had never done before. It's something between marriage and parenthood, I guess you could say."

"What made you decide to turn me?"

"I couldn't say. It just happened," I replied. "It just seemed as though you weren't ready to go yet. Every time I thought your heart had stopped, it would beat again. Since I hadn't felt you leave your body, I knew you were somehow still there, fighting the inevitable."

"Leave my body?"

"Something like that. When whatever it is that makes a human who he is finally leaves, the body relaxes. It's like while your soul is still in there, your body keeps a certain amount of tension, a sense of warmth and presence. I've seen bad turns, where the human's heart was still beating when the vampire tried to bring them over, but the body had relaxed before the process could be completed. The revenant that rose three days later was mindless and had to be destroyed, since it was unable to think or reason. That's something you never ever want to have happen."

"Oh."

We returned to our comfortable silence once again, listening to the relaxing sound of the waves as they crashed into the pier supports and enjoying the feel of saltwater spraying onto our faces.

Finally, an hour (or was it two hours) later, one of the pier's security patrolmen came by and insisted that we leave, as it was actually very late and the pier was closing for the night. It was being used as a filming location, which had been a common occupation for the pier for several decades. Rather than argue with him, we decided to head back home.

On our way out, I politely declined when someone on the production crew suggested I be an extra for the night. Nathaniel teased me about it mercilessly all the way home. At least the distraction gave him an opportunity to think about something else.

It had taken this extreme act on my part to show Nathaniel that his two younger sisters and his widowed father would not be safe if he was in the vicinity, and I hated myself for it. The entire thing reminded me of old vampire lore which correctly stated that a vampire will often first feed on their loved ones before seeking blood elsewhere. The simple truth behind this fact is that family members rarely realize the danger they are facing until it is entirely too late to escape. The vampire might beat her breast and cry about it after the fact, but until a vampire has developed some measure of control over herself, if she cares about someone, she will stay completely away from them.

It was a miracle that things hadn't snowballed into something far worse when Nathaniel had inadvertently revealed himself to his younger sister. Fortunately, there was little chance of her being believed. I hated looking at things that way, but it was better that it had been Barbara than Christy the pre-law student. I decided that

I would find a way to send something to his family without telling him. Something that would provide for the two girls, especially as the youngest would need extra support for her entire life.

Yes, I do have a conscience in me; it's just that it doesn't come out very often anymore. I didn't need that small trove of valuables, anyway. They were just taking up space in my vault.

In talking about my own family and my surviving brother in particular, I realized I could do something to help Nathaniel's family and made a mental note to contact my solicitor. I would have him make all the arrangements for an unexpected bequest for his sisters from a hitherto unknown distant family member. It would, of course, be held in trust for the two girls, a trust that would also be overseen by my very capable solicitor.

I'd known his family for years now, and had in fact met his father during a stay in Nazi Germany. We'd kept in touch, and I'd eventually made sure that his children got only the best possible education. Klaus had shown a real knack for the law, so I had paid for his education at one of the best law schools in Europe.

In return, I was godmother to his oldest girl, Sonja, who was probably a teenager by now. Sweet kid, but she was entirely too "girlie" for me at this stage in her life, so I kept my distance. I don't do "girl stuff". I never grew up with it, so I just don't understand it at all.

Thinking about her age and then doing a little math, I suddenly realized something. It had been about five months since last I had heard from her, so I could expect that it would be another seven, at least, until I would hear from her again.

I'd have to send a belated congratulations card to the family.

Thus, a week and a half after my initial call to Janos, with the bequest taken care of and two very sincere looking but quasi-legal passports, first class airline tickets, et cetera, in hand, we moved overseas to one of the more tumultuous parts of the world, as that would be the best place to teach Nathaniel how to be a successful vampire. I knew that Janos had called in some fairly valuable favors to make it happen and that I was now indebted to him, but I had had no other choice in order to make this happen.

Janos probably knew that, too. I asked him why he had supplied me with a fake passport in a different name than my own, and he reminded me about some of the peculiarities of the part of the world to which we were moving. A moment's thought shut me up. He was right once again, damn his eyes!

He had worked his magic for us as only he could. Humans, vampires and others the world around either owed Janos favors or wanted to, and he was only too happy to utilize those opportunities whenever possible. No one would ever guess that the names on those passports were entirely false, especially as they had been issued by the United States government.

As I said before, lots of people owed him favors.

As I couldn't abandon my business and the dozens of clients I had so carefully nurtured over the past couple decades, simply disappearing was not in the cards for me. If I were to vanish, it would certainly get attention because of the money behind some of those very clients. So, I made my way through my old-fashioned Roll-A-Dex and called each and every one of my high-profile clients to explain what was going on, as far as the mortal world was concerned.

Only one client was particularly troublesome. We'd only recently done a huge server upgrade for her, and she was nervous that something might still go wrong, despite the fact that I had done it all myself and it was working perfectly.

"Ellen, I've had something come up, and I'm going to be away for the foreseeable future," I told the woman for whom I'd been maintaining internet servers for the past six years now. "Don't worry, though, I'm leaving you in very capable hands."

"I hope it's nothing terrible, Connie. Do you have any idea how long this will be? I rely on you, because you're the best out there!" Ellen Malone, CEO of AdorablePuppyPics.com responded. "Connie" was the name I'd been using for about ten years, since I'd set up shop in Los Angeles. I'd been working with her since the days when she'd just been chasing her own dog, a happily drooling and amiable Old English Bulldog called Mavis, around the yard with her cellphone camera. Now, APP was one of the biggest sites out there hosting puppy pictures from around the world. I could understand her concern at my absence. The puppy meme-verse was flighty, and would go elsewhere if they couldn't go to Ellen's site.

"For now, I don't have a return date, but Bruce will be stepping in while I'm gone. No worries there. I'm sending you an email with his after-hours contact number in case of any unforeseen issues that might need immediate attention," I reassured her.

"But what if something happens?"

"If it's something he absolutely cannot deal with, he'll get in touch with me," I lied. Bruce was a fucking genius with all things computer and internet, and I certainly paid him enough to keep him working for me. I also knew where all the virtual bodies were buried, and he knew I knew, so I would have no trouble from him if he wanted to stay out of a prison cell and near the computers and internet he loved so very much. As long as he had plenty of *hentai* and this particularly bloody vampire anime he'd been watching, he was a happy camper, the little freak. He did not know what I was, although if he had known, he probably would have begged me to turn him.

"But..." I cut her off, knowing that if I let her continue, I'd never get her off the phone.

"I knew you would be concerned, so I wanted to talk with you myself, to reassure you, Ellen. You'll be fine. I've never steered you wrong before, now have I?"

She grudgingly described herself as reassured, as long as I was "sure" about Bruce, and we hung up on more or less friendly terms. Ellen was the only client of the twenty or so that I called who practically became hysterical at the news of my sabbatical, which was no surprise. I was glad that my other calls had gone more smoothly. Hanging up after my call to Ellen, I sat for a moment and stared at the wall opposite my desk. I was glad I was successful enough that I did not have to contact all of my clients personally. I had people for that.

Everyone should have people, but few actually do.

Any other calls to less important clients would be made on a case by case basis via my manager, and not everyone would even know I was leaving.

My last calls were to my accountant and my lawyer. Frances, my longtime accountant, would keep an eye on the books and make sure that my life continued to run smoothly on the financial end of things. She'd been with me for about twenty years, though we had only ever met once, the day I'd engaged her services. Frances' family had been serving our community for at least the past hundred years, and had been "read in" to our peculiarities. This day, I would let her in on where the virtual bodies were buried, as well. It wouldn't do to have Bruce thinking he was finally free of me.

It also kept him from doing anything at all unpleasant to either my company or the clients for whom those in my company labored. They relied upon me, and I wasn't one to abandon them when I was forced to leave. I had always been good to my employees, at least when they followed my rules, and those rules were never too onerous to endure.

My lawyer, a Prussian vampire called Mattias, was audibly surprised to hear from me.

"My dear Siofra, what is so important that you must call me? Are you in trouble?" I imagined I could hear him straightening the cravat he had worn almost since the day I met him, so long ago. I'm sure it wasn't the same one, after all this time, but he kept them so immaculately, you could never be sure unless you employed a forensic investigator.

"Well, only trouble in the form of having my first fledgling. We are both leaving his home territory to avoid inadvertent encounters with family and friends, now that he is officially no longer among the living," I filled him in on what had happened and the next step in our journey together. "Someone else is working on his passport and other papers. I'm not really sure how long I'll be away, but I'm thinking at least a couple decades."

"Ah, congratulations! A new *nosferatu* in the family! I hope this is a happy and fortunate event for you!" he enthused. "I despaired of your ever sharing yourself with another in such an intimate relationship. It is never good to be completely alone."

"Yes, it's happy, Mattias, which I must admit surprises me more than I can say. So, I need you to set him up as a member of my Trust. I'm sure you can handle everything that needs doing to make that happen, as I don't have the time to see to every little thing. I probably won't be dipping into the Trust very often, if at all, for the first decade or so, but I want to be able to do just that if it turns out I can't avoid it."

"But of course, my dear. That is why you have engaged my services for the past two hundred years," I could hear the smile in his voice. "What is his name? At least, the name he must now use?"

"His human name was Nathaniel Bock, but his new name for the Trust is Nathaniel O'Se. That, I believe, is the proper form for tracing parentage in our community. I'll email you with the other pertinent information, including the names that we choose before we leave the country. Those passports are supposed to be here shortly."

"I have not heard that patronymic in a long time, Siofra. It seems strange to hear it," he said.

"It feels odd to even say it, Mattias," I admitted. Vampires very rarely use their patronymics on a daily basis, unless they were particularly full of themselves. "Currently, I'm known amongst the humans as Connie Bodhran, although that is about to change because of our need to relocate."

"I know the patronymic of your sire, Siofra. Is there any particular reason you do not use his family name, as is tradition?" he asked. "If I am being nosy, I apologize."

"Its fine, Mattias, and you're not being nosy. I don't use his patronymic because I was turned by accident, and he did not raise me himself," I explained. "Also, I think he is a pompous ass and really don't want to admit to even a fleeting familial relationship with that walking ego."

Mattias chuckled.

"Yes, this is true. I have had passing acquaintance with that vampire, and he does seem to think he is the epitome of vampire culture," he admitted. "I must ask, however, how were you turned by accident? Such situations are quite rare and rarely end well at all."

"He took advantage of civil unrest and invaded the castle where I was living at the time. When he grabbed me to feed from me, I bit him while I was trying to break free and kept chewing on his arm. I don't think he noticed me doing it during all the chaos. In the process, I accidentally swallowed some of his blood. So, when he had just about drained me and left me to die, the blood I'd swallowed was already making changes. Andreas' senses were so overwhelmed with what was happening around him that he didn't realize that he'd just created a new fledgling, so he left me behind. By the time he realized something had happened, I'd already had my first feeding and he could no longer bond with me. I have never asked him how he figured it out. Perhaps I should, someday."

"Did he not try to bring you back to his kiss anyway," Mattias asked, with something like pity in his voice. "That he would leave you behind to fend for yourself is unforgivable!"

"He did, but his misogynistic attitude put me off immediately and I told him to go hang," I replied with some asperity. "He's wanted me in his kiss ever since, but I have never given in. His attitude toward women is disgusting."

"I am sure that your iron willed reticence has not pleased the powers that be who rule us all. Be careful in your dealings with those who wield that power, Miss O'Se. There are some who would embrace violence to enforce their beliefs on the rest of our community, and I would hate to see you harmed," he said solemnly. "I try to stay away from all of the political wrangling. I find it draining."

I laughed obediently at his lame attempt at vampire humor and then, after making sure he would ensure that the Trust continued to operate smoothly, disconnected. There were other things to take care of before we left and wouldn't wait for a more "convenient" time.

First, though, I had to take my fledgling out to eat again. If I had to fill him to the point his skin split, I'd do it, if it would keep him from eating the other passengers and flight crew. A hungry fledgling vampire is a very dangerous vampire.

Three

We arrived at the airport about three hours before our flight time, because of all the security measures that had been put in place in recent years, and discovered in the process that I wasn't being hyper-cautious after all. The stupid kiosk wasn't working when I tried to get our boarding passes that way, so we had to join a very long line of other annoyed passengers who needed to do the same thing.

"I guess it was good, then, that we left as early as we did," Nathaniel opined on the heels of my thinking just about the same thing. "Good that we had a hearty dinner last night."

We had spent several hours hunting last night and ultimately feasted upon three humans in a final orgy of feeding. Although I had planned to hunt during our layover, I knew there was no guarantee that we would be able to do so once we arrived, due upon factors beyond our control. Plans are one thing, but anything could happen to ruin them beyond recovery.

With each hunt, I had become more and more impressed with my fledgling. Since he had been turned, Nathaniel had accomplished twelve kills of his own, and his hunting skills improved with each kill. For now, he was feeding just about every other night, so he'd had a lot of practice. Last night, he had managed to take his first target down without the woman even knowing what had happened to her. Those were the kinds of kills I preferred for myself when I wasn't in a pissy mood.

All was not perfect, however, as I had had to chastise him for toying with his second target, this time a human male. Nathaniel had come upon the human smearing his own feces on bus benches near skid row. Maybe Nathaniel had used public transportation a lot, while he was still human, but the subject had never before come up.

"It was a good meal and I liked that it was very filling, but I would prefer that you don't make a habit of playing with your food."

"Yes, ma'am," he replied meekly. I smacked him on the arm. He faked a penitent expression, but I knew his apparent submission was made out of whole cloth.

"'Ma'am me again and I'll kick you," I ground out, glaring at him. I hated that word.

I restrained myself from smacking him again when I saw him quirk his eyebrow at me and give me one of his funny little smiles. Nathaniel definitely knew how to get a rise out of me, as he had already shown over the weeks since he first awoke a vampire.

"Payback's a bitch," I told him. "At least for now, knock it off, okay?"

He feigned a hurt expression, but stopped teasing me. I shook my head and faced forward, willing the line to move quickly. That had never before worked in my long history of airline flights, but I could still hope.

"Sorry." He actually sounded as though he really meant it. "Probably nerves, on my part."

"It's okay. This is just a tough time for the both of us right now, so it's better to concentrate on that and we can address being playful once we've reached our destination and are settled in," I responded, giving a fleeting kiss to the back of his right hand. "I promise."

I continued to hold Nathaniel's hand tightly as we stood in line and had my other hand on my carry-on bag, not wanting to let him go in a place so tightly stuffed with humanity. When I felt his mind begin to wander toward thoughts of feeding, I squeezed his hand hard to bring him back to the here and now, which appeared to work fairly well.

It was begging trouble to even consider letting him loose. I knew the situation on the plane would be far worse and found myself nearly crushing Nathaniel's fingers. I instantly felt terrible for hurting him. The look on his face as he stared at me was far more telling than anything he could have said in response to the torture I was putting him through right now. If he could have wept tears, I think I'd have seen tears brimming.

Trying to make my handholding look romantic rather than punitive was difficult, and I forced myself to relax my fingers enough to lose their white-knuckled appearance, while still having a strong grasp of his fingers. I saw relief cross his face and knew that he wasn't going to have to feed to repair any damage I might inadvertently do.

It took us about a half hour to make it through that line, and I lost track of the times the woman in front of us had to send her older child off to chase down her toddler while we waited. I couldn't understand why she didn't just have them sit down somewhere and wait for her, but perhaps that just made too much sense. Young humans have the attention span of a gerbil, and making them stand in line like this wasn't fair to them or to the others who had to listen to the child's parent repeatedly yelling at said child to come back. In this case, it always ended with the older child, who appeared to be a young teenager, darting off to collect the diminutive human child.

"Where are you headed? We're on a trip to my parent's place in Wyoming."

I was brought up short by the sudden and unwanted curiosity of the woman in front of us. She was perky at an hour when no one should be perky, which meant she was either on amphetamines or she had drank the contents of an entire Starbucks. I couldn't smell the distinctive odor of drugs emanating from her pores, so it was probably the latter. Neither was a good thing. Maybe she had a good reason, but I wasn't in any mood to be any more sociable than necessary. Whether it was legal or illegal stay-awake, I could still see dark circles under her eyes.

"Vacation," I responded shortly. I hoped she would pick up on my reticence, but her emotional radar seemed to be missing.

"The kids are so excited to be going! They're going to go white water rafting for the first time!" She wouldn't shut up and leave me alone. "Where are you going? Somewhere romantic?"

At first, I couldn't decide if I should elaborate. She was being painfully nosy, but some people, both vampire and human, are like that, annoying as that might be to someone like me. I really just wanted to tell her to bug off and leave me alone, but that probably would not be the best response under the circumstances.

Thinking about it further, I decided that it was probably best to answer, since I didn't need any issues with someone thinking we were suspicious and passing those suspicions on to someone who might make things more difficult for us.

"Overseas. It's something we've wanted to do for a long time now, so we're doing it," I said, not giving any more information than that. I really did not want to have a conversation with this woman, and tried to dissuade from her talking further by looking off in another direction, with no success. She seemed determined to keep me talking, and I really did not like it.

"Overseas? To where?" Her face was all rapt fascination.

I'm surprised I wasn't grinding my teeth; I was becoming so frustrated with her brainless nattering. There really was no need to fill up the empty space with conversation. I'd never even said "hello" to the woman.

"We don't really have much of a planned destination; we're pretty much playing it by ear. Sort of like the whole youth hostel thing in Europe." That seemed to be a safe reference. When was she going to shut up?

"Oh, that sounds like it'll be fun. My ex and I had kids too soon, so we could never do that, ourselves." Lovely, there was an ex. This was exactly what I didn't want to hear about at all. "I don't think he would have wanted to do it, anyway. He was a bit of a bastard."

Relative silence reigned for about five minutes before she just couldn't stay quiet any longer.

"Sorry, I'm probably over-sharing. It's pretty fresh for all of us, especially for Brad, my oldest boy," she piped up, her eyes sad. Yes, she was over-sharing, but it was like watching a train wreck. I just couldn't look away. Damn it, I didn't need this. "The little one's too young to remember most of it, which is good, but my oldest got caught in the middle of it."

I couldn't help it. She had my attention and I resented it. Nathaniel had been listening, too, I guess. It wasn't as though we could even do anything about it, either.

"Middle of what?" He asked her directly. I knew where this was going and wished that Nathaniel had kept quiet. But then, there was something about Nathaniel that made you want to answer his questions. His face was so open and honest, that you felt you could trust him with whatever secret you might have, which was a perfect impression for any human to have of a vampire. It usually kept them quiet and at ease until it was time to eat.

The human seemed honestly surprised that he had responded, and told her older son to take the little one to the bathroom before she answered Nathaniel's question. I saw a haunted look in the boy's eyes and knew I was in for something terrible to hear.

The sound of Brad's heartbeat increasing did nothing to disabuse me of that notion. It probably would have been better if his mother had kept her mouth shut, as it appeared he would now be reliving part of something that truly terrified him.

"Roy liked to hit me when I didn't do things fast enough for him. I let him get away with it for a long time, since it was just me. I only took a stand once he started beating Brad," she said in a whisper, but both Nathaniel and I were able to hear her clearly. "I really don't know why I'm sharing all this with you."

"Sometimes, it just helps to talk about it. I'm happy to listen, if you want to share your story," Nathaniel offered. Again, he looked so innocent, and she almost tumbled over her own words as she continued.

"I haven't really talked about this with much of anyone except the police, my attorney and in Family Court. Not even my parents know how bad it really was for all of us. I wouldn't let them come to the proceedings."

I don't understand abusers, and never will. For some reason, she sounded as though she felt ashamed for what happened, even though something like that wasn't her own fault. Abusers are very good at making their victims feel that they are responsible for the abuse they suffer, and that perception can last for years even after the physical abuse had ended.

"What did you do?" Nathaniel asked her, almost as quietly. He put his free hand on her shoulder and just kept it there. Maybe he was trying to feed her some of his strength, but I don't know. I could feel his genuine interest, and felt something like bloodlust rising in him, but it wasn't directed at the human woman. "Did you call the police?"

"Well, the first time, I didn't, but I did hit him over the head with his bowling trophy," she said. "He took it away from me and beat me up again, but at least Brad wasn't his target that time."

"Did your parents know what was going on?" I was surprised to hear myself participating in the conversation. Why should I get myself involved in human troubles? They weren't mine.

The woman shook her head. I was starting to feel like a world-class asshole for instantly hating on her. Now how did I end up being the bad guy here, when I wasn't even on the hunt? It didn't seem quite fair.

"No, I didn't want them to know I'd married a monster, so I kept it all to myself. They hadn't seen me in years; we just spoke on the phone or exchanged emails. We lived in a very rural area, so I didn't spend a lot of time around other people who might notice. He even insisted that the Lord Himself had told him that the kids should be homeschooled."

I wasn't surprised. It's funny how religion often seems to find itself tightly wound into an abuser's mad plans. When one puts the intent of the Divine into the fabric of their personal fiefdom, anything can happen and usually does. Rarely is there a good outcome with such a tapestry.

"Sounds like a real control freak," Nathaniel interjected. "Did you know anything about what he was like before you married him?"

"He hid it really well. I knew him for almost a year before he finally proposed. He wined and dined me, and said all the right things to make me say 'yes'. He even had my folks fooled, thinking he was such a nice guy. I didn't find out what he was really like until he'd moved me from the city in which I'd grown up to another city almost an entire continent away. Once I was isolated from everyone I used to know, he could get away with things that my friends and family might have otherwise noticed." The look on her face was full of regret. "He was really good at playing his little games."

I couldn't help myself. I had to know what the outcome had been for this human's family. Yes, the train wreck had my attention, damn it.

"So, what finally happened?"

"The next time he went after my boy, I took out the little Mossberg .410 shotgun we sometimes used for hunting quail and used it on him. He saw what I was going to do before I fired, and ran away, but I did manage to get some buckshot lodged in his ass on his way out. Fortunately it distracted him enough that we were able to get out of the house." Her face grew hard. "The cops picked him up at the hospital. I was afraid he might be released, but the judge denied him bail."

I was glad to hear that. So many abusers seem to be turned loose entirely too soon, and then things end very badly for everyone involved.

"Where is he now?"

"He's about to finish his first year in jail for beating Bradley, and I just want to be as far away as possible from him before he does get out. He's only got another year after this. There is something monumentally stupid about abusers getting so little time in jail," she told us. "I'm afraid that he might try to come after us, even with a restraining order against him."

She was right. Using a restraining order to stay safe is like using a piece of tissue paper to hold an anvil. In her place, I'd have run as far away as I was able. I could feel that odd bloodlust in Nathaniel rising, and I realized what it was all about. Sadly, we would not be remaining in Los Angeles long enough for him to act on the strong emotions the woman's plight was causing him.

"Well, you keep safe and if you need help, you call this number and tell them that Ms. Bodhran sent you and that you need help." I scrawled a number on an old business card I no longer needed and handed it to her. The person at the other end of that number would do whatever was necessary to help her out. "I'll let him know that you might someday call him."

She stared at the card in her hand for a long time before she looked up at me again. I didn't know if she understood what I was obliquely telling her, but I wasn't going to spell it out for her, either. Plausible deniability and all that, don'tcha know.

"Thanks. I hope I won't need it."

I guess she did understand, after all.

At some unseen signal from their mother, the two boys rejoined their mother in the line.

"I don't know why I shared all of that, but you're right. Talking about it did help a little," she told us. She assayed a weak smile and reached out to quickly squeeze Nathaniel's free hand. "Thank you."

Then, in the manner of lines everywhere, it was their turn at the counter, and they were off on their journey. I silently wished them well, and hoped she would never have to call the number I'd written on that card. She'd be safe from the person on the other end. He'd never hurt her, especially as I had as much as given her my protection by sending her his way.

Nathaniel's eyes stayed on her until she finally turned the corner on her way to her boarding gate. Once she was gone, he looked at me with a dead expression.

"If I could have, I'd have..."

"I know, Nathaniel. I know. I'd probably do the same thing, but as that's not in our immediate future, the person at the other end of that phone number will be happy to help her out."

"I could almost taste his blood," Nathaniel whispered hoarsely, and I stepped in close to give him a hug and distract him. We needed to get out of the airport and into our plane as quickly as possible. I felt bad for the woman and her kids, but why had she felt the need to share her situation with total strangers at the airport? Vampires tend to be much more circumspect, I've found.

"Hold on, Nathaniel. You'll get through this, I promise. I've done everything I can to help her. Now it's up to her as to what she does, but having heard what she did when her boy was attacked, I don't think she's going to leave anything to chance," I hissed in his ear as I pretended to kiss him. Damn the woman's chatty nature and my offspring's naturally gallant personality! "I was taking a big chance, but since I'm no longer 'Ms. Bodhran' I think we'll be okay."

I was distracted by a commotion behind me, and turned to see another mother, this one looking harried, trying to keep control of her two children, one a rambunctious toddler. She must have noticed me noticing her. I prayed to all the gods that might be that this human would keep her troubles to herself, at least the ones that weren't immediate, anyway.

"Kids," the mother said to me at one point, while her older child, a gangly boy with hair almost as red as my own, was off chasing her other little bundle of joy around the airport's lobby. Airport security seemed to be pointedly ignoring the whole thing. "I swear, my littlest one can be across a room before I know it!"

"I always find it's best to keep a tight hand on them, so they don't get distracted and then do something unpleasant," was my reply. I gave her a tight little smile and watched her gaze falter a little as she suddenly could not meet my eyes. Taking this as her recognition of my absolute disinterest in her situation, I looked ahead of me to the airline's counter.

"Kyle! Bring Chris here and just hold his hand!" Out of the corner of my eye, I saw Kyle grab his dark haired little brother's hand and then swing him up into his arms before walking back to their mother. However, instead of just standing there, holding the toddler's hand, he very pointedly handed his little brother to his mother and then walked away to sit on one of the benches that lined the far wall.

He never said a word to his mother, either. He was probably as tired of things as I was now. When Kyle pulled out his little music player and jammed his earbuds into his ears, I knew he had drawn his line in the sand where his mother was concerned.

Problem solved. Little Christopher wasn't happy with his new limitations but it reduced the noise and chaos by at least one level, so that was good. Even Kyle, back on his bench, eyes closed, one foot unconsciously waving in time with the beat to which he now listened, looked a lot happier at no longer having to drag his little brother back once again. Their mother, on the other hand, now had her hands full, and was too busy to keep yapping at me. I had no desire to become involved in any more drama.

I was so very happy when we finally got our boarding passes, and was pleased that we were also able to get the boarding passes for our subsequent flight as well. One thing I must say for air travel is that it was getting as streamlined as possible, if only to keep the lines at the ticketing counters are short as possible. It was one less thing for us to worry about, which allowed me to stress a little less.

The line to get through security was even longer, as it involved not only processing passengers from multiple airlines, but also had to deal with the extra precautions taken for international travel. I was glad that Janos' people were good at their work, as the security people barely blinked when we handed them our papers.

Our carry-on bags and their contents were fairly boring, so they caused no comment, but not everything, it appeared, was destined to go smoothly.

I was about to heave a mental sigh of relief at how well things were going, when the powers that be threw a monkey wrench into the works. For whatever reason, it was decided that Nathaniel would be subjected to more in-depth screening before he would be permitted to proceed.

When I automatically attempted to follow them, my way was barred as agent grabbed my arm to stop me. It was all I could do not to hiss at her and then rip my arm out of her grip to follow Nathaniel anyway. It was a real effort on my part to keep my fangs retracted, as their natural state in such a situation would have been to slide out, ready for battle. I did not want Nathaniel to pick up on my distress, but knew that any such attempt to dampen it would be futile at best.

He looked back at me as he was taken by one arm and walked to the private search area. The stricken look on his face bothered me, and there was nothing at all that I could do to make it better.

"I am sorry, miss, but you need to stay here," said one of the other agents, an imposing bald man who seemed wear his uniform like armor. "Please finish the screening process and you can wait for your traveling companion on the other side. It shouldn't be long."

Feeling a bit out of sorts and very uncomfortable at the situation, I did as I was bid. Not for the first time, I wished that vampires did indeed have the power to mesmerize humans and escape situations such as this, but that wasn't in the cards.

All the while, I tried to listen for any sign of trouble. I wondered what I would do if things got out of hand, and unbidden, my imagination thoughtfully provided several rather bloody and terrible possibilities. Abandoning Nathaniel and making good my own escape was not one of them, I noticed.

I could feel Nathaniel's hunger rising and I almost forced my way back to the area where he was being detained, but held back as I felt him mentally beat the hunger down himself. How he had managed to do that, I do not know, but I was relieved that he had been able to do so.

It was another few minutes before they finally came back out with him, and I saw what may have delayed things, as the security officer who walked him back was a middle-aged woman with too-bright eyes. Nathaniel was chatting her up and putting on his friendly, affable face. I knew that his seeming friendliness was a lie, since I could sense what he was feeling, and I knew that things had been resolved just in time.

"That's a good story, Steven! I hope I'm on shift the next time you come through here," the woman was gushing at him as she helped him through the rest of his own security check. When she laid eyes on me, her gaze became almost hostile, obviously thinking me to be some kind of rival, for whatever reason. I restrained myself from laughing at her illusions. It's not as though he could ever look at her as more than a meal, but she didn't know that.

"I'll be sure to look for you, Karen," Nathaniel told her, smiling broadly. "I hope things settle down with your son."

"Thanks for taking such good care of him," I gushed at her, taking Nathaniel by the hand and turning to leave. The wash of relief I felt from Nathaniel as he rejoined me enfolded me like a psychic hug and I felt a lot better. I didn't wait for the human to reply. "Come on, honey, we have a plane to catch!"

Nathaniel and I sat in the airline's passenger lounge for about an hour and a half, before they finally called pre-boarding for our flight and we could start the next part of our journey. We each had a laptop computer to distract us, so the time went more quickly than it might have, otherwise. I think that Nathaniel spent his time trying to see if he could find any news items that would describe what had happened to the young woman and her family, but if he was, he never said anything to me about it.

Janos had gotten us seats in First Class to give us a bit more room on the long flight. The VIP lounge to which we were thus entitled was sparsely populated, so that was going to help the waiting go a little more easily. Several thousand dollars for an airline ticket had its benefits. If the lounge had been jammed with humanity, things might have once again turned as dicey as they had been while Nathaniel was being felt up by the oversexed woman in the security line.

I don't know if he knew that he was already turning on the charm when he was in close contact with humans, but like me, he had picked up on it very quickly as a handy tactic for keeping them emotionally disarmed. By the time we left the lounge area to board the aircraft, the helpful lounge attendant who was obviously smitten with my fledgling would probably have happily allowed Nathaniel to drink all of his blood and would then have apologized for not having any more to give.

Pre-boarding was a blessing in disguise, as it got us aboard the plane with as little distraction as possible. I mentally uttered hosannas when I saw that there would be no children in the area in which we would pass the flight. In my experience, children rarely did well staying in their seats during a long airline flight.

The seating arrangements in First Class were fantastic, with lots of leg and elbow room available and free satellite-based internet. Passengers were seated in pairs, and the seats had enough room before and behind to allow us to lie nearly flat if we so desired. I was happy to see that there were not many humans who were also seated in our section, but the downside of that was that the flight crew assigned to this area had a chance of being extra-solicitous.

I didn't want anything like that kind of attention. I wanted to be left alone as much as possible.

In fact, I hoped the wealthy-looking Middle Eastern gentleman in the crisp white head scarf would monopolize most of their attention. It appeared he had one or two of his wives with him, so anything could happen. Both of the women were modestly veiled, but I knew that during the security check, they would have had to unveil themselves to a female security agent to verify that their identification documents agreed with their appearance.

A week earlier, I had contacted the airline to let them know that we had very special dietary requirements, so they did not need to supply us with meals. We would take care of our own needs in that regard. I had received a kind offer from the young man at the other end of the phone to try to meet those mysterious needs, but I just as politely declined his generous offer.

It was better to let that be the case than to leave entire trays of food untouched. Some people get a little touchy about wasted food, even when it's nearly as unpalatable to humans as it is to vampires. Funny, isn't it?

The first leg of our flight was fairly uneventful, except for Rachel, the pretty and rather solicitous blonde female flight attendant who was assigned to our side of the First Class seating area. She had laid eyes on Nathaniel as we boarded and practically fallen all over herself to direct us to where we would be seated. Rachel appeared a bit disappointed when I put myself into the aisle seat, which placed Nathaniel at the window.

Too bad, little human. I'm trying to keep you alive, but you'll never know that.

Takeoff was uneventful, and Nathaniel stared out the window during the whole process, watching as he was torn away from Los Angeles, not knowing if or when he would be able to return. I thought of when I left Ireland, and squeezed his hand in sympathy.

Young Ms. Rachel apparently believed that the very pale Nathaniel was suffering from a fear of flying that would somehow be assuaged with the liberal internal application of complimentary alcohol and the sight of an attractively heaving bosom. Little did the innocent child know that Nathaniel's white-knuckled grip on the arms of his seat were in part due to his determination not to eat the passengers or crew.

"Here, sir, take this! Sometimes a little nip will help you to relax enough to forget about things," she urged him, dropping three bottles of vodka into his lap. Considering that she had to lean over me to get to him where he sat next to the window, her attentiveness was annoying to me, but I kept my mouth shut. With so much extreme airline security, I did not want to catch the attention of any plainclothes air marshal that might be aboard. "Don't let the other attendants see them, or I'll get in trouble!"

Well, drinks were free in First Class, but multiple little bottles all at once probably broke the rules, anyway.

"Thanks!" he responded curtly, cutting his eyes toward her throat before resuming his staring contest with the back of the seat in front of him. I could feel his distress, as he smelled the blood rushing through her carotid artery. It was all he could do to keep from taking "a little nip", to use her vernacular.

Obviously disappointed that her flirting was not working, Rachel wished him well and went back about her duties. She had probably decided that my boy played the other side of the field, else how could he have resisted her ample feminine wiles.

Or maybe she had a flotation device hidden in her uniform blouse. What do I know?

Foolish humans were everywhere today, thinking with their gonads instead of their brains. I could smell her pheromones as they swirled in the otherwise stale air of the airplane, but it was not that natural human odor that had grabbed his attention. For Nathaniel, Ms Rachel's allure was something much more base than sex and had all the potential for violence you might imagine.

It would have been nice to actually close my eyes and rest, but I had to keep my attention on the vampire next to me. I was certain that I would end this flight in a particularly bad mood, but that was how things were. I hoped things became easier after we got someone to eat during the layover. This was not a vampire airline, so there were no contracted donors available to assuage our hunger.

Coffee, tea or A positive?

Yes, you read that right. A vampire airline. I'll leave you to wonder about that one. I knew it threw me for a loop the first time I heard about them, too. They're so expensive that only the highest ranking members of vampire society can afford to engage their services. I'm not anywhere near that high ranking, and don't ever want to be. Who in their right mind would ever want to be caught up in that layer of vampire politics, beside Janos, who seemed to thrive on it?

Not me.

"Siofra, it's overwhelming!" he muttered under his breath, still staring fixedly out over the landscape below. Now where had I heard that refrain before? He moved his right hand from the armrest and clutched at my arm, the force of it making me squeak a bit until he loosened his iron grip enough to make it stop hurting me. "I don't know if I can do this!"

"Yes, you can, Nathaniel. I know you can. It will be easier for you to survive this if you inhale through your mouth in order to speak, instead of your nose. Once the flight attendants say you can use electronics, pull out your laptop to mess around with or your e-reader and find something to read. I've preloaded it with the stuff I know you like. I am sure you can find something there to grab your attention," I told him. "I will stay awake and make sure that you don't forget yourself."

I had slept as long as possible before we had abandoned my apartment this morning, knowing that this would be the case.

Yes, vampires get tired, too, and need to sleep. We may not get a tiredness of the body, but we can and do become mentally exhausted. If you've ever become exhausted by a long day of protracted thinking on weighty subjects, you'll understand what I mean when I say that. It wouldn't be a good idea to sleep on the plane, anyway, because we would both appear dead and that was something I wouldn't want to have to explain to anyone when we suddenly and inexplicably sat up again.

Yes, that had happened to me before, and ended in what could only be referred to as a surprise Continental Breakfast. Fortunately, the other members of our party had already gone ahead of us, as they had an appointment to meet, so I had not had to kill them all.

That was some two hundred years ago, and I have been much more careful since that time. Why waste food if it's not necessary?

I spent some time going over the preparations I had made for our departure, second guessing only a few, and surreptitiously sending out text messages as a result. If the stewardess had discovered me on my cell phone, I'm sure it could have gotten ugly, but I'd gotten pretty good at hiding what I was doing over the years. I'd only been caught once or twice in the course of several dozen airline flights in the time since cell phones became such a necessary part of our lives, but had always been able to talk myself out of trouble.

My cleaning woman would be more than a little shocked when she showed up later today to clean my place and found a note on the refrigerator telling her that everything in the loft apartment was hers for the taking, along with supporting paperwork to verify that she was the new owner of the items in question. Anything I truly cared about had been put into storage, so although many of the items I was giving her were fairly expensive, they weren't anything that could not be replaced.

I had only a few truly personal items that were traveling with me, but my treasured boot knives, which I had had almost since I had first become a vampire, were packed up and would be delivered to me once we reached our destination. I had no desire to lose them to a nosy and acquisitive luggage handler anywhere between Los Angeles and Iraq. They were part of some of the few happy memories I had of my time in Ireland, and so they had special meaning for me.

Already wearing the soft high boots I would need, it would only be a matter of slipping them into place once the knives were in my hands, where they belonged. It felt very strange to not have their familiar weight along my calves.

Ever practical, I slipped the little plastic bottles of unusable but otherwise expensive booze into my carry-on luggage. We wouldn't be able to take them into Saudi legally, so they would need to be disposed of before we boarded our second flight.

I missed the days when those three little bottles might have been suitable for use as bribes in a country that frowned on alcoholic beverages. I had done that during Prohibition in the 1930's in the United States with excellent results. Just because neither Nathaniel nor I could drink, it did not make it a complete waste. Before so many of the Middle Eastern countries had nationalized around the oil companies that had engaged in sucking the precious crude oil out of their sands, I would have been able to bring those three little bottles with me and perhaps had some felicitous results for having done so.

That was no longer the case, as with the advent of nationalism, the infidels had been thrown out of positions of power and those countries had changed their laws to more closely reflect their religious cultures. I was fairly certain we would lose them completely at Saudi Customs, but that was to be expected.

Janos had been the one who had thoughtfully provided us our new laptops, which had arrived the evening before our departure. While Nathaniel had not been as excited about his new toy, I was all over my own, and went through every little bit of it as thoroughly as I could before I slept.

When I had expressed a concern about having to lead a completely unconnected existence for the foreseeable future, he had offered me the best laptops he could procure on short notice, and I wasn't disappointed. As an aside, if these were the "best" he could provide "on short notice", then I'd love to see what he could manage with a long time to plan things.

He promised me they would come preloaded with all the programs I wanted and he had even gone so far as to arrange for an ongoing annual payment for my favorite MMO, for at least as long as it was still playable. Janos often teased me about my being so involved in something that was pure fantasy, but I think part of him understood my need to have some connection with the "normal" outside world where I could be myself, but hide it by playing on a role-playing server. People I'd met playing the game often thought that my vampiric alter-ego was "charming" and "fun".

I'm usually only "charming" shortly before I eat you, never forget that fact. However, I did stick to the genuinely accepted rule that states "Never eat your guild mates". I will admit to thinking that I was "fun", however. Maybe not *your* idea of fun, but certainly fun in the vampiric sense.

Janos had also promised me that our destination already had electricity and internet available, but I could not, for the life of me, understand how that was even possible. If I thought about it at the time, I would have realized that where Janos was concerned, anything was possible and that I should never question even the most unlikely of his kind of miracles.

Now seemed to be the time for stories, since Nathaniel had been forced to put away his laptop until the pilot said it would be okay to pull electronic devices out again. Anything that would distract Nathaniel and keep him from breaking the furniture was a good thing. Airlines tended to look down on such behavior. It made them testy and sometimes even a bit shrill.

"Did I ever tell you about what happened to me up until the point where I first left Ireland? Of course, most of this all happened after I was turned." I said quietly enough that I would not draw unwanted attention to our discussion, but just loud enough that he could still hear me.

I knew that I had not, but if I could distract him, all the better.

"Uh, no. You haven't," was his startled reply. "I know a little bit about you, but I was afraid to ask you too many questions. I don't like seeming like a nosy little kid."

At that moment, I realized that Nathaniel knew me much better than I thought he did. I had to wonder if that was a good or a bad thing.

"Well, like you, I was leaving everything I knew. Yes, it had been a good three decades since I was turned, but until then, that was the only world I had known. I would have remained there longer, but people were beginning to notice me more often, so it was much easier to notice that natural changes that should have been occurring were not. So it was no longer safe for me to remain in Ireland, even though I would have given my left arm to be able to stay. I would have been about fifty human years old by then."

"Fifty years?" His eyes were wide and his jaw actually dropped. I could understand it. He was looking at someone who appeared to be a young woman who was maybe only in her late teens or early twenties. Even knowing what I was, how do you reconcile something like that?

Yes, I had his attention. Good.

"As I've said before, I was born in Ireland, and was human until I was about seventeen or eighteen years old, first with my parents, and then as a servant with a succession of households belonging to the gentry."

"Why did you leave your family? Didn't you want to stay with them?"

"My father sold me off to pay a debt to our landlord." I responded.

"He did what?" He really must have been distracted now, because I thought I'd mentioned something along those lines before.

Was that the sound of metal giving way? It probably was, but I didn't want to bring attention to it. I saw a small amount of blood oozing from his right hand, but he didn't appear to notice that he had damaged himself while crushing the armrest. Well, Janos wasn't going to be happy at having to pay for the damage, but that's how it is, sometimes. I'd probably hear about it later, too.

"While slavery within Ireland wasn't necessarily legal, it wasn't unheard of for something like that to happen. It turns out that I lived longer than most of the members of my family. Most of them died from some illness about a year after I was taken away, so I guess in a way, it was a blessing of sorts."

"But to pay off...you hear about that in school when they talk about African Americans during the days of slavery, but to hear about it with...wow. I'm just shocked," he said. "How many families did you work for before...?"

"Only two, but I worked for them for about seven years, between the two of them. I became a woman during that time, but I'm still rather amazed that they did not try to marry me off to one of the bondsmen who also served the household."

"You were never married?"

"Oh, I had a fiancé for a time, but that relationship ended very badly."

"Badly? What happened?"

"He fell off a roof while he was trying to fix it," I told him. "It seemed as though any time I was close to having happiness as a human, something happened to tear it all away from me."

"Well, I'm not going anywhere, Siofra. I think I'm at least a little harder to kill."

His smile was disarming and I couldn't help smiling in response to his expression. He was still young and didn't yet know much about his new self. Yes, we're hard to kill, but we still have limitations.

"It wasn't too long thereafter that I met my maker." I couldn't help giving a wry smile at my unintentional pun. I heard Nathaniel snort as he caught the reference. "Since after the battle and his personal attacks, I was the only 'living' thing remaining, I was forced to leave. There was not one left to eat, after I drank the one remaining human on the grounds into his grave."

I received a long look from Nathaniel as he digested this new information.

"Why didn't your maker take you in? You didn't leave me alone after you turned me. What made it different between you and your maker?"

"He didn't realize that he'd turned me. I was an accident. When he finally figured out what had happened and eventually found me, it was too late for him to create that kind of connection with me. He and I never had the bond that you and I share, that was made when you drank from me before you made your first kill. If he had, we probably would not be having this conversation now, and I would be somewhere in the general vicinity of Eastern Europe." I said, and covered his hand with mine. "He was an ass then, and he's an ass even now, although he still wants me to join his kiss."

"His kiss?"

"That's what you call a group of our kind. He's got a small one, mostly made up of women he's turned over the centuries. He's one of those Old World chauvinists who still lives in his own little world, in which he is King. I don't believe that he has any modern women in his kiss now. I think they're all from about 1850 and earlier."

Nathaniel shook his head at my description of my maker, Andreas. All these years later, I was still doing the same. How do you keep your people in thrall when they can see that the world has matured while you remain in social stasis?

"So you say you worked for other people for about seven years. How old were you when you were turned, then?" It was a reasonable question, and I didn't have a specific answer for him.

"I've never been clear on my exact age, that's why I made that earlier guess of seventeen or eighteen. I was pretty much forced to leave my home and travel to the nearest big city I could find, just so I could survive. My first stop was Dublin, at least for a time. After that, I traveled the length and breadth of the land while I learned about myself. Overall, for a woman, it was a pretty rough place, although as you can see, I survived the experience."

We were quiet for a time before I spoke again, remembering my original subject and wanting to keep Nathaniel's attention focused on something other than the passengers on the plane. I could not afford to let him even come close to forgetting himself again.

Four

I stayed about five miles outside Dublin for nearly a decade, before I decided it was time to move on. I hid in the ruins of an old stone farmhouse, barricaded in the cellar for safety. It was the only thing that really remained in nearly perfect condition. I still had to do some brickwork and weatherize it, but even if I hadn't, it still would have been perfectly livable for a vampire with few needs. It wasn't as though I had to keep a stock of food on hand or build fires to keep warm, so I had a lot of freedom. You already know that we don't feel weather changes the same way a human does, so keeping warm or cool isn't something we even have to consider.

Over time, I installed some simple furniture in my hideaway, and with my dog to help keep it safe, I was as happy as I could have been during that time. As far as a vampire would be concerned, you could almost call it an "idyllic" time for me.

Food that I could safely and happily consume was fairly plentiful, as there was plenty of traffic from traders and highwaymen, so I rarely had to exert myself in order to find a meal. I would often allow myself to be mistaken as a solitary and therefore vulnerable traveler, as that would make many men less careful in their actions. I took easy advantage of their foolishness. They were guarding their purses and always made sure I put my daggers on the table before we got companionable. Of course, they didn't realize that my fangs and talons were even more deadly than those two long pieces of steel. Well, not until it was too late for it too matter anymore.

Surprisingly, I only resorted to using my daggers a few dozen times, when I wasn't all that hungry and wanted to dissuade a human from something that might end very badly for him. In the event that the human did not get the hint and continued their unwanted advances, my knives were pointed and sharp enough to slide up under the chin, through the human's throat and then into his skull without much effort at all.

I've still got those knives, and I thank Whomever may be listening that I encountered him when I did, as we each did the other a service that day. I had never returned to the swordsmith who had made them, but always think of him when I have to use my knives.

I had still been young when I met him, and had been more open about myself than perhaps I should have been at the time. Of course, I had saved his life using my unique talents, so it would have been difficult to pretend it had not happened.

My audience remained silent, simply sitting and listening to my tale. I decided that if it would keep Nathaniel's attention on something other than the gallons of human blood that surrounded him right now, I'd talk until we landed. His oozing wound appeared to have healed on its own, so it hadn't been serious enough to require him to eat someone before it could do so. I already knew that if someone tested the blood on the seat's arm, it would appear to be at least a full day old, so they would not be able to trace it back to Nathaniel.

I wasn't actually alone, as I had both my dog and my perpetually irritable and unpredictable horse. But, other than that, I usually only spoke with humans if I was going to have them for dinner. I did not feel a great urge to interact with my fellow beings, which could have been because I had spent so many years before that jammed in with stinking humanity in the manses in which I labored before I was turned.

Once or twice, my horse brought home dinner, too. That generally happened when some idiot saw the big horse and thought it would be smart to steal him. Of course, the would-be thief did not know that with few exceptions, the animal would not let anyone but me near him. There were always bad consequences when they tried. He was never so far from where I was staying that I didn't hear the screams of the thief, once he'd had at least one of his legs broken. The thief's reward was invariably the sharing of a very long drink with me.

Some might expect that the lack of human contact might make me lonely, but I had long before learned that life is sadness, as you may recall. When everything you have ever experienced ends in tragedy, why would you want to bring that on yourself all over again?

The first five years went by far more quickly than I would have thought possible, but that could have been because the world was a brand new place for me. For one, I had stayed close to home for my entire human life previous to that, so I had no worldly experience. For two, as you now know, vampires experience the world in a much more different way than humans do.

I know that you've seen that we hear things at a much wider range than we did as humans. We are able to see when there is little to no light present. Not even bats can actually see in the dark, and have to rely on sonar to get around when they fly.

Really, vampires are just about the perfect predator, as we can hear a human's heart beating in his chest, smell his scent on the breeze, and we can see them when it's so dark, a normal human can't see her own hand, even when she holds it up in front of her face. It's nearly impossible to hide from a hunting vampire and escape becoming his next meal, but still they try.

It was like being a toddler and learning about the world all over again.

Over time, I started to venture further out from my home base, and explore my homeland a bit more. I'd be gone for a month or two at a time, but would always eventually return to the familiarity of my basement home.

On those adventures, I would try to meet as many humans as possible, my goal being to meet them, get to know them, and then leave them as healthy as they had been when first I met them. I was not always successful, as I'm sure you can already understand, but I certainly made the effort.

I wanted to learn about the world outside Ireland, as even then, I knew that I would not be able to remain there for too much longer. Thus, I made the acquaintance of English, Scottish, French and even a few German travelers during that time. I would pepper them with questions about their homelands and even try to learn some of their language and accents. I found all of it fascinating, and loved the freedom that my vampirism offered me.

It was the best of all possible holidays, and an amazing learning experience.

I only left my hideaway behind permanently after it become flooded during a very bad storm that lasted for several days time. I had been gone for at least a week, as I recall, on an extended hunt, so when I came back, it was to find my home doing a very good impression of a modern swimming pool. It was obvious that even attempting to bail it out wasn't going to be an option for me. There was very little that I was able to salvage, so I chose that time to go on my way and resolved to only use a basement again in the most extreme circumstances.

This meant that I would have to rejoin civilization on a more permanent basis, something I had hoped to avoid as long as possible. While humans could be delicious, that didn't mean I wanted to be near them any longer or more often than necessary. Even whilst on my extended holidays, I rarely stayed in one city or village longer than a week, if I could at all avoid it, as I did not want to establish that kind of familiarity with the locals.

Despite all my misgivings, I took up residence for a short time in one of the seedier inns in town, and my horse got the chance for decent meals that included good hay, grain and a roof over his head. I enjoyed the luxury of a feather bed and the services of the inn's housekeeper while we stayed there. I knew we wouldn't be staying there permanently, but we would remain until we found a more attractive situation.

Mathúin endeared himself to the cook, and was often found gnawing on a toothsome bone from the kitchen that was all that remained of the night's roast. He became even more popular the night he attacked the robber who attempted to hold up the place.

We were sitting in the tavern portion of the building when a masked man holding a brace of pistols entered the place. It was about one in the morning, so things were quieting down, but not so much that there wasn't the potential for a nice haul.

He was a bit wild-eyed, and swung his pistols around the room, trying to intimidate the tavern's patrons into obedience. Although he tried to disguise his voice, I knew from his scent that he was one of a small party of hooligans who had passed through only a few days ago. The proprietor had kicked them out when they broke a wooden serving platter over the head of one of their party. He was not one to tolerate bad behavior in his establishment, even with the seedy reputation it enjoyed.

He had not seen Mathúin behind the bar, where the wolfhound was prone to hide in order to avoid the attentions of overfriendly patrons. He stayed out of the barkeep's way, so there was no argument about it.

The robber had a pistol trained on one of the serving wenches and was bellowing orders when Mathúin, rudely wakened from his nap, came soaring over the top of the bar and tackled him. Both of the pistols went flying as the human, faced with a snarling dog the size of a small pony, screamed and turned to run. The enormous wolfhound's fangs were perfect shining ivory, and glittered in the light of the oil lamps.

It all got a lot bloodier and much more unpleasant from there. The wolfhound savaged the human's forearms and hands as the robber tried to protect his tender throat from those gleaming fangs and the dog's murderous intent. Mathúin may even have swallowed one or two of the human's fingers, but I don't remember specifics. I only called him off once the human was shrieking with terror.

After the constable arrived and dragged the bleeding miscreant to the local lockup, Mathúin was feted with the remains of the night's roast and a heaping bowlful of cold stew. Drinks were offered to me by the other patrons as the owner of the night's hero, but of course I politely declined. As it was, the owner told me later in private that my room was on the house for the remainder of the month.

The hanging the next day was nearly the event of the season, as far as the townsfolk were concerned. The would-be robber's pleas for mercy fell on deaf ears as the hangman sent the human on to meet his own maker.

From that point on, the proprietor made sure the dog received more than just leftovers for his meals. Mathúin, smart as he was, knew a good thing when he saw it. It was also obvious that he did not mind the overstuffed pillow by the fire that the place's proprietor placed there for his use.

I was often out and about, looking for a new place, but hadn't found anything suitable. I wanted to avoid anything that required considerable maintenance, and I wasn't interested in setting myself up with anything that would require ridiculous amounts of rent. I worked my way through a month's worth of room and board, even after the generosity of the proprietor, before I finally found a relatively permanent place to stay, but it wasn't due to any of my own active searching. Only crazy random happenstance brought me together with my future accommodations.

FIACH FOLA

Due to an unexpected encounter, I finally chose to stay with a local granny midwife and give her my protection during that time. This was in the days when midwives tended to women's issues, and a granny midwife was often a widow who had shown some skill in helping pregnant women to deliver their offspring. At that time, physicians rarely involved themselves in such domestic activities as childbirth. A midwife would bring her tools and perhaps a few charms to ease the birthing, and when a successful birth occurred, she might go back home with a chicken or two and if she was lucky, even a few new coins in her purse.

I remember that we met late one rainy night while she, mounted on an ancient mule, was being set upon by a single and obviously horseless highwayman. What he thought to steal from an old woman on a mule still evades my comprehension, and unless he was particularly fleet of foot, he would have trouble accomplishing his escape.

It was not as though the old woman's mule was worth much of anything alive, and its meat was probably much too tough to chew. I'd had mule meat when times were tough, and I wasn't impressed, even though I knew I might not have meat again for a long time. Maybe he was new to the highwayman business and hadn't gotten a handle on the ins and outs of the profession.

I did not react immediately, but just stood back to watch for a short time, entirely entertained by the spectacle before me. The granny was swearing sulfurously at her assailant, and amongst her many other accusations regarding his character, suggested that his ancestry was undoubtedly perhaps of infernal origins.

I was rather impressed at her command of profanity and was surprised to hear it coming from her wrinkled and pale old lips. I wondered how she had collected such a treasure trove of obscenities. Perhaps it was one of the benefits of having lived a very long life. If that was the case, by the time I finally ended myself in one way or another, I should have quite the collection of them as well.

I saw him blanch at a particularly vile declamation, but he kept on with his attempts to knock her from the mule. I could see that he was not at all dissuaded from his intent and probably felt more than a bit antagonized by the woman he had thought helpless. That was when he completely lost control of the situation and finally swung at her with his sword. Anger and frustration make poor companions when you are trying to succeed at much of anything, and in this, the brigand was no exception.

He missed her, but instead startled her gallant steed when his sword flew from his fingers and disappeared into the weeds along the side of the road. The night's comedy was not yet complete, however. There was yet another Act remaining.

Apparently unused to such rude behavior, the gallant steed in question, surprisingly athletic despite its obvious age, reared up, dislodging its passenger, and then brought one of its great rock-hard hooves down on the assailant's booted foot. Once it resumed its four-legged stance, the mule stood absolutely still, like a statue stands on its pedestal, although in this case, that pedestal was the brigand's foot.

The man's screams were impressive as his toes were crushed by the angry mule's hoof, and he took that moment to try to skewer the animal with a dagger he seemed to produce from nowhere. That was a bad idea, as my own companion decided it was time to act. I never had to say a word. Instead a snarl cut through the air and I was suddenly involved in the drama before me.

Leaping forward, my dog, Mathúin, quickly divested the brigand of first his knife hand and then took out his throat, spilling all that hot blood across the ruts in the road. It did not take the highwayman long to die. Once the throat is opened up, it is only a matter of moments. Perhaps he did not deserve such a quick death, but at least he was dead and would trouble no one else.

Don't think that I didn't care about what was happening when I first came upon the scene, but my longstanding policy is to keep to myself and not interfere with human activities. It was not as though I was hungry then, having drunk a sailor under the table only a few hours earlier. However, once Mathúin showed that he had no tolerance for what was happening, I was forced to come to her aid as well.

Being a pack animal and having been raised with them, Mathúin seemed to have more of an emotional connection to humanity than I did anymore. I do believe he missed having more of a human connection, but as he was a dog, I couldn't ask and he certainly could not answer.

Yes, with time, you, too, will become more emotionally isolated from humanity. It's like a kind of necessary coldness. You can care about them, but it is rarely in the same way you might care as one human cares for another.

As someone I knew for a very long time once said to me:

"Angels we may wish to be, but that we are actually demons is our only reality. To love a vampire is to love a predator. To love a human is to love your prey. Neither situation will end well when the hunger rises and one is left with no choice."

In speaking with other vampires on the subject, they have also found this to be true. It seems to be a natural progression for us, as we slowly lose what made us human in the first place. It took me a little over a decade to start becoming the way I am now, but I don't know if that time frame has been different for other vampires. I don't believe I've ever asked.

But I should get back to my story...

In retrospect, it was a good thing that Mathúin had chosen to do the dirty work, as it would allow me to keep my human guise unless it became absolutely necessary to reveal myself at some later date. He was a good and loyal companion, and I still miss him, although for now, another such companion is not in the cards for either of us.

Surprisingly, she wasn't hysterical over what had happened, and even spat on his rapidly cooling body as it passed. It was obvious that she was more angry than afraid. This was a formidable human I had found, so maybe it was a good thing that Mathúin had decided she was worthy of a rescue.

After I got the old woman reseated on her miraculous mule, I rode with her to her client's farm a few miles further and stayed to return her safely home. Perhaps I was feeling lonely, and that was why I decided to hang around. That's something I'm unable to recall. I do recall that she delivered a healthy infant, even after the delay the brigand had caused.

So I have no idea what went through my mind that night. Was it loneliness? Kindness? Momentary insanity? I really couldn't tell you. I can tell you that over the years, I learned that babies seem to arrive when the weather is wet and unpleasant. If the journey to the laboring mother-to-be could possibly be damp and unpleasant, well, that's what I could expect on those nights when I was her companion.

All these years later, my sharpest memories are of things that had a strong and direct effect on me. I can say that my apparent thoughtfulness led to her offering me a place in front of her fire for as long as I desired, so that, by definition, had one of those strong and direct effects I was talking about just now.

My own mount, a big bay Andalusian stallion called Ádhamh, did not like her mule at all, and I had to keep him far enough away from the animal that he could not bite or kick the thing. I did not like having to keep him so tightly reined in, and he fought me the entire way, but that was what I had to do to keep the peace.

It made the ride back a bit of a challenge, as the mule moved slowly, as compared to the horse's long strides, making Ádhamh more than a little frustrated by the time we arrived at her cottage. I told him that it was his own fault, but he was a horse, so he didn't understand what I was telling him.

As I had no intention of sleeping on a pallet in the main room of the cottage, within the next few weeks of my stay, I endeavored to construct another room onto the cottage, using some of the money I had hoarded to fund the venture. The room I built was actually larger than the cell the old woman used as her own room, and she was very surprised when, at completion, I insisted she take the larger room and I her former bedroom. She tried to object, but I would not hear it and so I prevailed.

While Mathúin had the freedom of the cottage and its surroundings, the same could not be said of Ádhamh. If the situation had been different, I would have allowed him to roam in order to graze on his own, but I was forced to build a corral in which to house him and consequently had to keep him supplied with food. I don't know what it was that he had against mules, but I later discovered that he felt this way about all members of that species. Eventually, the two animals developed something that, while not a friendship, was instead a kind of detente that consisted of pointedly ignoring one another whenever possible.

Despite my attempted concealment, the old woman knew I was different, but never really said anything about it. She suggested that she knew I was not what I appeared to be, but it never came down to direct questions. At least she didn't try to chase me away or reject me entirely. I was with her until the night she finally passed away, some seven or eight years after we first met. She had caught some illness from one of the women she had attended in childbed, and was, at her advanced age, was unable to shake it. I thought about leaving her to die on her own, but could not bring myself to do that to the human who had taken me in on only a few hours' acquaintance. Thus, I stayed and cared for her until she took her last rattling breath, and then I buried her in the tiny burial plot she kept a dozen yards from her cottage. I remained in her cottage for nearly a decade after she passed on.

Before she passed on, she told me that her cottage was now mine, and that she hoped that before I moved on myself, that I would find the right tenant for the property and cottage. She told me that she knew she could trust me to follow her wishes, and told me that I would find the legal paperwork to the property in the enormous iron-strapped chest in her bedroom.

I don't know when she had found the time to visit a solicitor, but it appeared that she had done so. For my name, she had caused to be entered "Sorcha Miller". I had never shared a last name with her while she lived, so she had pulled that one out of the air, if only to make the document legal. I think I only remember the last name she gave me because it was such a shock that she had gone to those lengths to be sure my ownership was not contested. Maybe it was her own last name, but I truly do not remember if that was the case.

So as I said earlier, I stayed in her cottage for about a decade after she passed on, but there came a time when I realized that I had to move on. My life or unlife, whatever you want to call it, was continuing, and to stay in the cottage would be to stagnate, which I've never liked to do. Also, the possibilities for prey were diminishing and it made no sense to hunt further away from the place when it made far more sense to move closer to populated areas.

In the modern world, if you live in or know of an area that has had more than its share of crime, and then, over a period of time, the number of crimes diminishes, there is a good chance you've got a vampire hunting in that place. He or she will continue to hut there until prey is too difficult to find, and then will move on to a more suitable hunting range.

Well, when I was still young, I did not necessarily discriminate between criminal and innocent when I fed, but I also knew enough not to completely empty an area of its inhabitants, either. Something like that will always attract the wrong kind of attention. Remember that.

It made no sense to completely abandon the cottage, especially as she was childless and had no other heirs, so her decision made perfect sense. Before you ask, yes, if someone had come forward with a legitimate claim on the property, I would have left on the spot, but that never happened. I knew, though, that as she had set the deed on me before she died that there was little chance such an heir existed. That is, of course, not to say that attempts were not made to swindle me out of the place. Those people were delicious.

It's funny, but even spending all those years together, we were never what I would call friends. I could not tell her what I truly was, because if I had, I don't think our relationship could have continued. She brought lives into the world, while I took them away, often long before they would have died a natural death. How do you justify and accept that kind of dichotomy? Despite what I had seen the night we met, she was too gentle a soul to be able to understand me and what I was forced to do in order to survive.

Perhaps she had some inkling, because she had to have noticed that over my time with her, we were accosted by fewer and fewer brigands, but she said nothing about it. Perhaps by ignoring it, she felt that it would not be anything she would ever have to seriously address.

Over the centuries, I have had acquaintances here and there, but not many I would consider to be friends, and only one or two of those were human. Mostly, I've had what could be called close acquaintances. You, Nathaniel, are the first truly close friend, well, family, really, that I have had since the night I died.

The realization of this fact suddenly hit me a little hard, and I found that Nathaniel had moved one hand off its armrest and was gently rubbing my back. When had I hunched forward? I didn't remember. I found his touch soothing, and as the tension I was holding released, I slowly began to lean back toward the back of my seat, at which point he moved his hand to my shoulder, continuing to gently rub muscles that I had not realized had become so tense. The bond between us had obviously helped him to pick up on my distress, and he had been moved to act accordingly.

I know I mentioned my brother to you earlier, and promised I'd tell you what happened when I found him.

There was no reason I should have expected to find him alive, as from everything I had been told, he had perished with our parents on the small farm my family had worked for generations. He didn't even look much different than I remembered, only his pale red beard was heavier and sported two gray stripes going from his bottom lip to his chin.

Well, the graying beard and his several missing teeth were different, but then he hadn't had the advantage of the wise cook into whose care I had first been placed when I was taken from my family. The one who had insisted I keep my teeth clean so they would stay healthy and whole longer than they did for the average human at that time.

Have I ever told you about the old world vampires who only have their fangs left and no other teeth in their mouths? They became toothless before they were turned, and a vampire doesn't grow anything back that wasn't there before they were turned. The fangs are essential, but beyond that, you don't use your human teeth to feed, so they're not necessary to your continued existence. It's actually kind of funny to see, but don't tell them I said that to you. It won't end well, believe me.

My brother's eyes were what caught my attention that night. They were still the same pale blue I remembered from my childhood, a blue so striking that they doubtless invited conversation. I could easily see someone with those eyes being quite accomplished at coaxing a reluctant maiden into a compromising position.

I found him one night as I was hunting along the docks. Sailors were either safely drinking in the local taverns, or they were already abed in their shipboard hammocks. I was beginning to think I would have to hunt elsewhere, when I saw a slight figure limping down the docks. He might easily have become my next meal but there was something about him that made me pause long enough to realize who was in front of me. Only my enhanced vision enabled me to see those unforgettable eyes before I did something terrible. I was rendered speechless, as I had thought him long dead.

He turned to look me in the eye, and I finally found my voice.

"I can't believe it's you!" I exclaimed, taking him by the hand and feeling him stiffen in response. I had forgotten how very cold my hands could be when I had not yet fed. It's a different kind of cold than how a human's flesh feels when they have been exposed to cooler weather, and I knew it made people uncomfortable to experience my touch.

"Who...who are you?" he demanded, trying to pull his hand out of my own. His heartbeat began to race and I felt him tense in anticipation of running as far away as he possibly could from the apparition I must have presented to him.

"I'm your little sister, Siofra. They took me away when I was a little girl," I explained, allowing him to pull his hand from mine. "When Da couldn't pay the rents. I thought you were dead. They told me that all of you had died from the plague."

"Siofra? I can't believe it! They said you were killed when that one Lord's lands were pillaged. H-how...?" he stammered. Gingerly taking my hand once more, he raised my hand to his face, so he could get a better look at it, and I knew that he had noticed its very visible oddities. Then his eyes grew wide as a draft horse's iron shoes and he backed into the rotting timbers of the wall behind him, clearly terrified. "You should be an old woman! You can't be alive! Get away from me!"

His fear cut through me like a dagger and I staggered backward, barely keeping my balance. It might have hurt less if he had stabbed me with his belt knife.

I remember feeling terribly hurt at this rejection, as I hadn't yet thought things through about whether or not I could reconnect with my family. I stepped forward to reassure him, and he tried to press himself further into the wooden wall, which made crackling sounds under the increased pressure of his body against it.

"It's me. I'm here!" I exclaimed. "I'm not gone!"

His mind had essentially turned off, however, and it seemed he could no longer hear my words of reassurance. I was something terrible in his mind, and nothing would disabuse him of that notion.

"Oh God, please deliver me from this demon and I'll go back to church every Sabbath once more!" he whimpered to the sky. "I repent my wicked ways! Just get this evil thing away from me!"

"Evil thing?" Yes, that's what he called me, and I found that it hurt me far more than I might have thought before. I dropped his hand and fled, hating myself for unintentionally terrorizing him, even though that had not been my intent at all.

I remember sobbing as I ran away into the night, his words continuing to stab at me like well-honed daggers. While I had not fantasized about a family reunion since the days when I had thought them still alive, this outcome was something I had never envisioned in my wildest daydreams. I ran for miles, until Mathúin finally went so far as to knock me down and keep me on the ground until my weeping ceased. He had chased me until his paws were bloody and kept going until they were actually raw. I think only his blood-bonded loyalty to me kept him going that night. A normal dog would have broken off the chase as soon as the pain got to be too much to bear.

I found out later through the grapevine that my brother was found in the morning, still up against the wall of the building where I had left him, but was huddled in a puddle of his own shit and urine, too terrified to move from the spot. Feeling terrible for the horror and agony I had created for my brother, I arranged to have a solicitor I trusted present him with a large purse of money for him and his family, with the wish for a full and happy life. The solicitor had brought the purse twice before my brother accepted it, but not until the solicitor had to threaten him with my return if he did not do so.

As I said earlier, I did not attempt to recreate our family bond. My brother was obviously terrified of me, but he still eventually accepted the monetary gift I made to him, albeit only when the solicitor visited him for the second time, and then under threat of my reappearance.

Perhaps he has been afraid to insult me by refusing, I couldn't say. There was a part of me that felt terrible that he was frightened of me, but another part that told me that this fear would keep him from trying to stay in contact.

Fate has a strange sense of humor, as even though we had been reunited, we could not remain so. If we had kept in touch, he would eventually notice that I wasn't behaving as a normal human would. I would never eat with him or his family, I certainly would not age, and what would I say to distract him from those inconsistencies? I couldn't bring myself to lie to him, so the best thing I could do was to disown him completely, for his and his family's own safety.

You know what, Nathaniel? I could have avoided all of his and my distress by choosing not to address him in the first place. It isn't as though he had recognized me when first he saw me. I had gone from being a gangly kid to a grown woman in the intervening years, even paler now than I had been when I was still a child. Deathly pale skin and hair a stunningly dark red. I had been a child with slightly darker skin than I had now, and hair that had been bleached by the sun to a strawberry blonde.

To this day, I hate that I even made his acquaintance, since it was something we could never expand upon. I probably could have found a way to give him the money through intermediaries, but I wasn't thinking clearly, since I had thought he was dead with the rest of my family.

As it was, I couldn't get away from him fast enough, because even though he was my brother, in addition to the pain his words caused me, the mere scent of his blood was nearly undeniable. My hunger was still too much for me to trust myself around him. If I left him alone, he had the opportunity to keep our family going, but as I wanted to completely break that connection, I have never looked to see if my brother's descendants are still around today.

Oddly, I have forgotten his name. Although I know that I remembered it when I found him then. You would think that because he was a member of my immediate family that it would be lodged in my brain, but for whatever reason, it's gone. Perhaps it's because we did not share much together while I still lived with my family, and once I was gone, he was something from my past that was too painful to explore further. I was, after all, the lost sister who spent most of her infrequent "free" time perched in a tree.

After nearly ten years, I decided it was time to do more exploring and perhaps broaden my horizons. So, after finding someone to maintain my land, I spent my time traveling in and around the country. I had been contacted by more than one prospective tenant about the cottage, the one I finally decided upon was another midwife, as that seemed to make sense. The old granny midwife would likely have approved of my choice. I left all the details in the hands of my then-solicitor, and knew he would take care of things and make sure that any rents would be kept against my return. There was also to be an inspection of the entire property and its equipment every six months, to be sure it remained in good repair.

The new midwife was a relatively young one and I knew that the tools of my deceased benefactress' trade would be more than passing useful to her for many years to come. I also knew that the small kitchen garden the granny midwife had kept to supplement her meager diet would help to fill the new midwife's empty belly. I had done what I could to keep it alive during my own tenancy, but the new tenant had a job ahead of her to undo the damage I had wrought through inexperience.

I had moved my hoard of trinkets and other valuables to another secure location before I left, taking a few items with me to trade in another city. I also was careful to have a goodly amount of money secreted about my person. It became a bit of a game with me to be able to carry my money and other valuables, but not allow it to jingle as I moved.

In my travels, my goal was to learn as much about the English invaders as I could, since I knew that eventually, I would have to leave Ireland. To my great surprise, I even found another vampire who was traveling through the country, researching ancient sites, from what I can recall. We did not spend much time together, really. It wasn't that I didn't like the other vampire, it was just that I felt no need to become long-term traveling companions. We probably traveled together for only a month or two, but I don't remember exactly. I believe we were traveling companions only through my time exploring Counties Cork and Kerry.

He was familiar with my maker and it seemed he held a poor opinion of him. From what I could gather, he felt that Andreas was a bit of an old world snob, and considering that this was the late middle 1600's, old world meant something entirely different at that time. The other vampire and I parted about six year later on a friendly basis, but I don't believe I ever met up with him again, so I don't even know if he still exists. I couldn't even tell you his name, but I don't share that kind of information, anyway.

Everyone is entitled to keep their secrets, if keeping them won't make things worse.

As I at least implied earlier, in the time before and since the granny midwife passed on, I had pretty much cleared most of the riffraff out of the area. I certainly couldn't eat them all, as that would cause too much conjecture and possibly even an investigation, which I did not want in the least.

After I had explored nearly the whole of Ireland, I decided it was time to finally go to England and see what I could learn and do there. I had amassed a small fortune during my hunting across the country, as the people from whom I fed no longer needed their money and possessions. I kept my treasure buried in a few places in and around the old granny midwife's cottage, keeping only a few pennies with me most of the time, so I did not appear completely destitute.

Now, all these years later, I had more than enough money to buy passage across the water and establish myself in England. I had been practicing my English accent full-time for the past few years, and to my own ear, it seemed to be fairly good. My former traveling companion had said that I seemed to have an ear for dialects, so that seemed to be a good sign as well.

My move would actually require very little extended planning, as I had no living baggage to bring along with me. My horse, Ádhamh, had passed on about twenty years after I acquired him, and in the time since his passing, I had chosen to lease an animal from local livery stables, rather than take up the expense of keeping my own.

Mathúin, the dog who had been my companion for the past thirty two years had finally died, as the drink of my blood he had inadvertently taken so long ago had not granted immortality, but merely a greatly extended lifespan. Mathúin had been my best friend since long before I was turned, so it was a terrible loss for me. Thirty two years might not seem like much time to you, but as he was an enormous Irish Wolfhound, that is a very long lifespan for a dog of his size. I had known him for nearly six years while I was still human, and then over twenty three after Andreas turned me.

I'll tell you the whole story of Mathúin's and my history at another time. He died bravely, always trying to protect me as he had during our time together. I'm sorry that it is too long to tell in the time we have available right now.

Even when you spend most of your time traveling, the humans around you are going to begin to notice that you're different, especially when you live in such a relatively small country as Ireland. Any number of things can lead to a vampire's potential unmasking, and for me, it took about twenty years before it started happening to me.

As I recall, I started getting a lot of questions that seemed to be engineered to make me err and give answers that would show that I was not what I appeared to be. Somehow, I managed to avoid stepping into that trap with all but one of my would-be interrogators. The last, however, did not have quite such a fortunate outcome for the questioner.

I was riding along with the wine merchant, who had offered to give me a lift to the inn at which I was staying during my time in Belfast, and as is perfectly natural he engaged me in conversation. I was so lulled into complacency that I made a fateful error in a response to one of his gently probing questions about some moment in history to which I should have feigned ignorance.

I regret having to do what came next, but I truly had no alternative. He had been traveling all over two or three counties for at least the past ten years, so it was inevitable that my oddness would eventually gain his attention. Unlike the other women my purported age, I still had all my teeth and not a single gray hair on my head. I dressed in such a way as to appear older, but that can only accomplish so much. He probably he thought me a witch kept young by a deal with the Christian devil.

The human screamed loud and long when I turned to face him, my fangs out and right there for him to see. He tried to jump from the wagon's seat, but I held him fast by his upper arm, preventing his escape. There was no one nearby to hear or help him, and I told him so. I was angrier at myself for my mistake than at him for discovering my secret, but I took my anger out on him. I was hungry, anyway, and he was a convenient and very easy target for me.

I ate him and then threw his corpse into an old spent well a few miles out of town before unharnessing his animals and turning them loose. There was little chance that someone would find him in there, as according to local lore, it had dried out about forty years earlier. The rodents and other creepy-crawlies who live in the dark probably made quite the feast from his remains.

Anyhow, I knew that this final event was my cue to get the hell out of Ireland. Who knew with what other people he might have gossiped with his wildest flights of fancy, and while I was fairly certain he had no real friends in Dublin, it was foolish to think he might not be missed by his co-conspirators. It was readily apparent that I was the subject of conjecture, as no less than half a dozen had asked me their loaded questions. So, as soon as he hit the bottom of the well, I left Sorcha Cooper behind, became Chastity Fitzwilliam, and remained Chastity for the next twenty years or so.

Believe it or not, no one recognized me, either.

The late, unlamented Sorcha was an Irish girl with a thick brogue who leaned to leather leggings, snugly laced tunics and a mouth like a longshoreman. She kept her hair braided close to her head and under a tight cap, and today might be called a 'tomboy'.

Her successor was nothing like her.

Chastity was a frail little feminine thing who wore her very long hair plaited into a loose braid that hung down her back and tied with a bright green satin ribbon. She dressed herself up in satin and lace, and was not averse to hiring men to carry her trunks to the wharf and about ship whilst cooling herself coquettishly with a dainty fan.

It was an excellent way to appear harmless and vulnerable when you want your prey to not suspect that he or she is actually taking on a wildcat when they try to take advantage of you. They think they are the wolves, when in fact they are the lambs.

Remember that you are now a creature who survives by dissembling. You pretend to be something you are not, in order to lull your prey into a false sense of security so that you can feed. Pretending to be someone else is easy and you will discover it is actually second-nature to you.

Nathaniel looked a little doubtful, but I knew that in time he would learn that what I now shared with him was the truth. It did seem to be something wildly unlikely, but I had been doing this for hundreds of years now, so it was nothing to me anymore.

I spent my first few days in town completing the creation and person of Chastity Fitzwilliam, daughter of a member of the English gentry and an Irish noblewoman. First, I engaged the services of a dressmaker, who was not well pleased that she was under a deadline to create two good formal gowns and a pair of bed gowns, but who became more amenable to her situation with a healthy purse of coin and the promise of a bonus upon completion, especially if she was ahead of schedule. In the end, she made them both barely on time, with one for everyday use, and another for more formal occasions.

Decorum required that I stay in a local inn that wasn't quite as raucous as one I might have patronized before this time. I needed to start that change in appearance with a change of personality. I dug some of the nicer jewelry I had collected over the years out and hung pearl ear bobs in my ears and other fripperies that would make people see Chastity and not have even the most fleeting thought of Sorcha when they saw me.

Being a vampire, since my ears had never been pierced while I was human, the holes would have immediately closed if the ear bobs were removed. Happily, as long as the ear bobs remained where they dangled, there they would stay. There are clear benefits to being a vampire.

I had been practicing the speech of the English occupiers and was fairly good at it, I thought, although I still had a slight Irish accent. It was faint enough that I could pretend to be mostly English, with the truth that I had been raised in Ireland. That would help me in my travels through England. Once I traveled from England to France, there was little chance my Irish accent would be noticed, so my origins would fall even further into the murky past.

The first time I put on those dresses, I felt like an overwrapped package. I had never been comfortable in fancy clothing, and losing my trousers did not make me very happy at all. I had worn gowns out of necessity, but they were never my first choice in clothing if I had that liberty. Trousers gave me a range of movement that a gown could not; however, I didn't want to be taken as some strumpet by whomever I engaged for transportation.

So, the day before I left Ireland, I went down to the docks in my second-best formal gown and found a willing captain who would not charge me a usurious price to sail for England. I brought a couple traveling trunks with me to complete the illusion of a well-to-do human woman on her way to England. As I had hoped, a couple of the local captains practically fell all over themselves trying to get me to hire their ships, so I obviously had done something right.

The voyage was relatively short taking only about a full day, and as I recall, it went fairly smoothly. I can remember that I 'accidentally' knocked a sailor overboard who was attempting to put one of his hands up my skirts. I babbled and apologized to the captain for my error, but I think now that he knew what had happened, and allowed me the pretense of having accidentally knocked his crewman into the ocean. I was certainly paying him enough to overlook that fact.

I found that talking about my history with Nathaniel had seemed to help to clear up some of the blank spaces in my memory. Vampires live so long that they don't always remember everything that has gone on over the centuries. It's much like learning a foreign language and then ceasing to use it at some later point. While you may at one time have been fluent, you will eventually forget that other language because you're not keeping in practice using it.

Five

After about three hours of my rambling storytelling, Nathaniel had loosened his death grip on the arm of his chair and could look at me without the whites of his eyes being quite so prominent. I was glad that I had been able to distract him and keep his mind off things.

"No more storytelling for now, my dear. We have a long time ahead of us where I'll be able to share the rest of my story with you," I smiled at Nathaniel and laughed softly. "A very long time, indeed."

Turning off the overhead lighting, we each pulled out our e-readers again, and we kept to ourselves for a time. My new e-reader had its own lighting, so I wasn't forced to use the plane's bulbs to read. I was just about done with my current novel and was eagerly awaiting my opportunity to dive right into the next one in the series. The author had taken what seemed like forever to finish and then publish the next book, and my patience had worn thin.

Yes, I'm that kind of reader.

I think that after a while, Nathaniel had started pretending to read whatever he had pulled up on his e-reader. At some point, it seemed Nathaniel had finally decided he'd rather talk than keep up the pretense of reading. He waited politely, as though it was perfectly natural for him to do so.

"Thank you for sharing all that you did, Siofra. I really appreciate it."

"No problem. I'm just happy you look a lot more comfortable now." I don't know if I'd have been quite so patient, but then, I've never really been a patient person. Rather funny, isn't it, when you consider that I'm effectively immortal.

As I said earlier, I had been reading the second most recently published novel in a fantasy series I enjoyed, but put it down to look back at him. If he was in the mood for talking, I should pay attention, right?

I was trying hard to be a good maker. Very hard.

"Are you okay?" I asked him, even though I knew from our connection that his stress level had lessened considerably. "Do you want to talk about it?"

"Have you taken a lot of trips where you were so close to...humans... for a long period of time?" He kept his voice very low, but my enhanced hearing let me hear him just fine. Vampirism has its benefits beyond an extended lifespan. "This is maddening."

"You want close? Imagine crossing the ocean from England to the New World in the 1700's. It normally took about four weeks in close quarters before we made landfall. Trust me; there were many potential meals I dared not touch during that time. I took that trip at least four times."

"Four *times*? So eight times across the ocean and no guaranteed way to feed?" He still managed to make his voice squeak with shock at such a low volume. I squeezed his hand to remind him to control himself. "I think I'd have lost my mind, Siofra."

"At least this is just a twelve-hour flight to Istanbul. We have a nearly eight-hour layover where we can find someone to eat, and then we're off again to Riyadh. Fortunately, the last leg of the trip is less than four hours long." I found myself feeling like one of those stereotypical parents with the "are we there yet" kid in the back seat of the car. However, in my case, I could not threaten to leave him at the side of the road and keep driving to grandma's place.

"So it took four weeks to cross the ocean each time? Even as old as you are *(I hit him on the arm when he said that)* you would not have been able to wait that long. So, how did you feed?" Now that

I had distracted him, I was happier. Perhaps this would be an easier trip than I had originally expected.

"One, I am not "old', I am 'experienced'. Never tell a woman that she is 'old', unless you want a knuckle sandwich. Keep in mind that those are inedible for multiple reasons, Nathaniel. Two, I kept an eye out for those who were ill and near death. Every voyage would lose passengers during the trip. They could and would die due to starvation, disease, or any combination thereof. If I was lucky, I would find them before they died, so I could feed from them."

"How did you feed from them without it being obvious that..." his voice trailed off.

"There are ways, they can just be more difficult to accomplish. You also did not want to drink them anywhere near dry, because it would be much more likely that someone would notice."

"What was the longest you went without feeding?" His eyes were wide as he hung on my every word. It sounded as though he was expecting a tale of violence and a hell of a lot of blood. Typical kid, just taller. "What happens when you do not feed often enough?"

"One time, I went for about a week and a half without feeding on a trip. I started to dry out, so I looked like a starving human, only worse. It was all I could do not to attack someone in the open. At that time, I could comfortably go without feeding for perhaps a week's time, but that was pushing it. That time, I was fortunate enough to have had a servant with me who knew what I was, so he was beside himself and afraid of what might happen. It grew so desperate that he eventually offered to feed me his own blood, and I had to accept his gift. It was terrifying for me, too, as I had to be careful that I did not drain him."

"You can do that? You can feed without killing someone? Maybe..."

"No! This was a special situation where this person had known about our kind for his entire life. He came from one of those Havens

131

I told you about earlier. Our agreement was that he would serve me while I crossed the ocean and I would set him up in a certain business when I left to continue my land journey across the country. I was also paying for his immediate family to come along for the voyage, so I was also responsible for their welfare. His contract did not include feeding me in the event of an emergency, so this truly was something selfless for him to do," I gave Nat a hard look before I continued. "When this happened, I was already over a hundred years old, so I had more control over myself at that time."

He stared at me for a long time before he spoke again.

"How did you only take a small amount from him?"

"He cut himself deeply on the fold of his elbow and I drank from there. He slapped me with his free hand when he started feeling a bit dizzy. Before you ask, I actually told him to do that. It knew it was the best way to get my attention if lost myself in the blood."

"You allowed him to slap you?" He seemed genuinely surprised that I would allow a human to strike me. "I was thinking that you would never allow a human to do something like that to you."

"Oh, there are humans out there whose families have longtime standing in the greater community. They serve a special purpose that I will explain to you when we have more time," I told him. Better to explain havens to him when we were in a more relaxed atmosphere. You never knew when you might need one in a hurry. "In time, you will likely find them as personable and useful as I do, beyond merely being a source of food."

"So you were lucky that time. Were there any other close calls?"

"On one trip, I ate the passengers and crew. There was already pox aboard, and three quarters of the passengers had died of it before I did what I did."

"Three quarters?"

"Yes. I don't remember if I knew where it came from, but it was something that was always a possibility in ocean travel with the humans. I had a servant with me, but this wasn't a situation where I could necessarily feed from him to keep from feeding on the other humans."

"Why not?"

"Because the captain was afraid of who would get the pox next, and I was concerned that he might find me sleeping and think me dead. He had already started throwing dead and barely living human bodies overboard. I could not chance him thinking I was dead or dying as well if he came upon me while I was asleep."

I sighed.

"I took the passengers and crew one by one in the dark of night. I couldn't risk discovery, but I had to feed. The vessel had become a death ship, and it was unlikely that it would have even been allowed to land in the New World with so much death aboard."

"Why was that?"

"The humans already knew that the pox was something potentially deadly, so they did everything they could to avoid it. If the ship had actually encountered another ship, it would probably have been set afire and the passengers and crew prevented from escaping. At the time, it was the only way to keep the infection restrained."

"It sounds as though the ship didn't make landfall then. How did you get there?"

"The ship was about two miles from the port when I made the decision to jump overboard and swim for shore. I left behind most of my belongings, which pained me, but I was careful to bring my coins and baubles with me, concealed within my bodice."

"My servant had finally perished from the pox a day before it all came to an end. I even wept for his passing, which was unusual for me. He had been a good man in the twelve years we'd been acquainted and I missed him for more than just the services he could no longer perform. While not a friend, he was an excellent companion."

"The captain was the last one from whom I fed. He was a jackass and seemed to think that he was impervious to the sickness on the boat, but I could smell it on him. It was only a matter of time before he too sickened and died. It would have been foolish to have allowed him to survive long enough to infect the colonists in the New World."

"Didn't he realize that something was wrong, since it was just you and him at that point?"

"Oh yes, he knew something was up, and after tying the sheets in such a way that the boat meandered in the general direction of shore, he bolted himself into his quarters with all the food he could carry. I don't think he suspected what I was, but it was obvious that he distrusted me."

"What finally happened?"

"The night before, I waited until I heard him fall into a restless sleep. He had been awake for a full three days and nights and could no longer stay awake, no matter how hard he tried. I remember that I ached from hunger and through sheer determination, I broke down the door to his cabin and attacked him where he lay on his back across the bed, crumbs and unhappy weevils from his last meal of hard tack spread across his chest."

"He pulled his primed and cocked pistol from under his pillow and shot me point-blank in the chest, but to a vampire, that's nothing beyond an inconvenience. I jumped on him, holding on for all I was worth, and opened his throat so I could feed."

"He threw himself around the cabin, screaming where no one but me could hear him, and I wasn't going to rescue him from his fate. I felt him begin to plunge his belt knife into my flesh repeatedly, but I clung to him, refusing to let go. There was no way he was going to survive this encounter, but it was clear he intended to take me with him."

I remembered the fight and how crazy it had gotten. He had clawed at me with his manicured fingers, to no effect. His fingernails were like the nails of a frog, so they were barely able to leave a scratch behind. He had tried religious invocations and the like, but they had no effect on me. I was no imaginary Hell spawn who would be repelled by such references.

My arms were wrapped around his neck, my face and fangs pushed against his throat, and I wasn't going to let go. His blood was mine and mine alone. I imagined I could again feel the possessiveness I had experienced that night as he battled and I drank. It still felt good.

"When I had finally drunk enough of his blood that he passed out, my wounds began to heal with the blood I continued to ingest. When I was done, I threw him overboard to join his crew and the passengers he had failed. Then I gathered what I could carry easily and jumped overboard to begin my swim to the New World."

Nathaniel said nothing after that for a long time, choosing instead to look out the window into the blue sky. I knew that his improved vision allowed him to see more than a human could, but if there was something he wanted me to know about, he'd tell me. Until that happened, I'd leave him be.

Finally, in order to pass the time in a more stimulating fashion, I pulled out a pack of playing cards and resumed our extended game of gin. For shits and giggles, we were keeping score of what each "owed" the other, but knew that there would never be a point where either would demand repayment.

The game ledger was a continuation of one we had started a few nights after Nathaniel first woke as a vampire. Currently, Nathaniel had the upper hand, points-wise, but only time would tell if that lucky streak would continue.

We had a lot of time before us, but an hour or two playing cards would help to while the time away and distract us from the press of humans all around us. Yes, I felt them, too. I'd just had more experience in controlling my hunger for a longer period of time.

The numbers in the ledger we kept to keep track of our wins and losses shifted around a bit as we played, but a few hours later, we finally reached a point where playing cards got old and decided to find something else with which to amuse ourselves.. We put the deck away about the time that Ahmed the flight attendant came by offering extra blankets against the unnaturally cold atmosphere of the airplane cabin. Accepting two each, with an appropriate bribe surreptitiously passed on to the waiting flight attendant, we bundled up under them and feigned sleep. We did not particularly feel the cold, but it made more sense to accept the blankets to preserve our appearance of normality as much as possible.

Earbuds jammed into our ears, Nathaniel and I closed our eyes and did our best to ignore the almost overwhelming proximity of so much food. I would periodically feel Nathaniel twitch as he lay, pretending sleep, and would reach out a hand to soothe him as best I could.

We landed in Istanbul as the sun was just beginning to set, bathing the horizon in yellow and orange fire. It was breathtaking, well, if I breathed, anyway, and I could not help taking out my camera and getting a shot of it.

Yes, vampires can also be touristy types and be impressed by nature's beauty. Just don't tell anyone I said that. We vampires have a cold and heartless reputation we need to support.

I had stayed here for a time in the early part of the twentieth century, and had had the misfortune of being around just before the infamous roundup of the feral dogs that had once been a ubiquitous part of the city, howling long into the night. Tens of thousands of dogs had been transported to an uninhabited island where they eventually either died violently or ultimately died of starvation. I was a dog lover, and if I had known what was planned, I probably would at least have attempted to intervene.

Nathaniel and I would need to wait until nearly one a.m. for our next flight, so we had to find somewhere to amuse ourselves until it was safe enough to venture out and feed. It had been a few decades since I had last been in this part of the world, but I remembered a particular area where the pickings had been good when one needed a meal on the go, as it were, so we stowed as much of our carry-on luggage as we dared in a locker at the airport and then hailed a cab for a certain part of the city.

The cabdriver, a man who identified himself as "Hassan", seemed to limit his conversation to Nathaniel as though a woman's conversation was unimportant. He picked us up and took us to our destination. Along the way, he kept trying to get Nathaniel to buy one or another of some trinkets he had stashed in a small box next to him in the front seat, but my child politely declined all offers. I could feel his anger at the cabbie's dismissive attitude toward me, and whispered to him to try to not let it bother him.

"Will you be staying in Istanbul long?" The cabbie asked Nathaniel, as though trying to find yet another way to part him from his money. "I would be happy to take you on a tour of our city's fine sights. For a small retainer, of course."

Of course.

"No, thank you, Hassan," Nathaniel responded politely. "We have already arranged for that. Just take us to Taksim Square and we will go from there."

So Hassan the cabdriver spent the next twenty minutes trying to sell his services to us as "superior", but we finally reached our destination and he dropped us off, but not before trying to get us to pay for him to wait for our return. As it was, he tried to overcharge us for the taxi ride, but Nathaniel stood adamant against the cabbie's demands and he instead went away with the correct fare plus a meager tip.

Taksim Square was notorious for shady dealings, and thus I knew it would be an excellent place to find someone to eat. The bars were rife with prostitutes and thugs who worked in league with the bartenders who would grossly overcharge naïve tourists and then strong-arm them into paying the money they demanded.

The scents of the city were nearly as I remembered them, but with the stink of industrialization fouling what had once been enticing in its spiciness. It made me a bit sad to see what modernization and commercialization was doing to what had been an exotic country seemingly lost in a time long gone.

I spent at least an hour pretending to look over textiles hanging in the open-air market, and eventually had Nathaniel haggle a merchant down to a reasonable price for a gauzy scarf to which I had taken a liking. It was lovely shades of green, gold and red, and for some reason, it made me a bit homesick for the land of my birth, something that did not happen very often at all anymore. Nathaniel looked at me a bit oddly when the purchase was completed, but apparently decided not to ask why the scarf had struck me so. Perhaps he could feel the slight sadness that had overtaken me when I saw it.

"That looks lovely on you, Siofra," he said to me as we walked away. I wrapped it around my head and shoulders, sniffing at the scents of the silk, dyes and humans who had been involved in creating it. "It really suits you."

"Thank you, Nathaniel."

Once it was late enough that we felt more comfortable and thus safe, we visited a bar that was situated near the end of a dark alley, knowing that would be the best place to find what we needed. The equally darkly-lit bar was sparsely populated with what appeared to be employees, rather than customers, and the in-house prostitutes glanced hungrily at Nathaniel. One of them started toward him, but another of her number, a scrawny girl with badly bleached hair and enormous beaded hoop earrings, noticed that I was with him, and grabbed the other's arm, pulling her back with a curt admonition. The first girl fixed her gaze on me as though only just now seeing me, then shrugged, turned back toward the bar and fixed her attention back onto her watered down drink, as Nathaniel clearly would not be available.

"This looks like a good place to sit and wait. I think the hunting will be good tonight."

Choosing a small table about midway into the place, where the shadows would helpfully conceal how pale we really were, we waited for the waiter to come for our orders. I played with the fronds of the potted palm that abutted the table, enjoying the texture of the individual green spears. One of the benefits of being a vampire is a much more sensitive sense of touch. It makes tactile experiences almost sensuous.

When the waiter finally arrived, I took a moment to take in his appearance and scent. He was a skinny man with a swarthy and heavily pockmarked face, with a dirty dishrag clutched in one hand, and he made it quite obvious that he was going to be our best friend while we drank at "his" bar. He also smelled as though he should have had a bath the week before, but had somehow forgotten that water was for more than rinsing out glasses. His shoulder-length hair was slicked back with stinking pomade that seemed to be used to disguise the fact that his hair was filthy, rather than making his hair look well-groomed. Health-wise, he was clean, but physically, he was more than a little distasteful. He would be someone from whom I would feed only under extreme circumstances, and that because in those sorts of situations, I am probably not going to be thinking very clearly anyway.

"What drink are you wanting?" he asked in heavily accented English, perhaps being brusquer than he intended to be with us. Language differences can and do make for some interesting misunderstandings. I often found myself wondering where people learned other languages as well. I remember one young German vampire who, I discovered, had learned English by watching old episodes of "The Honeymooners". It made for some interesting discussions.

Bang. Zoom.

We made a big deal over what the local specialty drinks were, and finally settled on a pair of something exotic sounding that of course we had no chance of drinking. When they arrived, they looked rather pathetic, with silly looking little paper umbrellas in them, perhaps intended to obscure the fact that they were overfilled with ice. That was also the moment when I realized that the waiter had not actually figured out that water could be used to rinse out dirty glasses, which did not help my perception of the place at all.

The plant beside us was the unhappy recipient of our drinks. I wondered how often that was the case with other dissatisfied customers. We certainly could not have been the first to immediately dislike the unattractive fluid that was presented as something worthy of consumption.

We ordered two more of the terrible things, and finally asked for our tab so we might pay it. That was when it got uglier.

The bill came to something like eight hundred dollars. Nathaniel's eyes became huge in his head, and I realized that I had forgotten to tell him what he could expect here. I had only told him that we were going to an area I knew and that he should follow my lead. Overcharging in this part of Istanbul was standard operating procedure, it seemed.

"What the fuck? What kind of total is this?" Nathaniel demanded. "Eight hundred dollars for four drinks? I don't think so!"

Two rather burly men materialized from the shadows of the back room and came to stand at our table. One of them put a hand on my shoulder and squeezed hard, and I faked a squeal of pain, to which he smiled.

"That is what you need to pay, if you want to keep your woman from being raped. This man likes them little like yours. I wonder how well she would like two men." The second man smiled an ugly smile at Nathaniel.

"I do not have that kind of money on me!" he protested. "This is robbery!"

The man who had a hold of me swung me around and held me against his chest with one arm, burying his nose in the top of my head. I could feel his throbbing erection from behind me, and knew that he probably planned to rape me, whether or not Nathaniel produced the ransom they demanded. I squeaked again, and I could sense his smile as it oozed across his face, buried though it was in the top of my head, in addition to hearing his pulse quicken in anticipation of the violence to come.

I played the part of the terrified damsel in distress and proceeded to struggle ineffectually, pretending to try to escape his grip. If I had really wanted to, I could have torn his forearm from his upper arm and fed it to him, but I had a role to play in this farce, and my reward would be satiation, at least for long enough to get us safely to our destination.

"Tell you what, fuckhead. How about we four all go to the cashpoint machine and get the money you owe and we might let you go at that," the thug who held me suggested in quite capable English, albeit with a thick accent. I felt him squeeze me to him just a bit tighter. "Or we could just take it out in trade."

"Oh please, Jeff, just do what he says! I am so scared!" I lied. I could hear the thug who held me's heartbeat increase at my words. I hate men who get their jollies terrorizing innocent people.

"It's okay, Sarah. Just hold on and everything will be fine," he replied, following suit. I could feel his hunger, and was glad that I had had us feed heavily before we left Los Angeles. I had learned my lesson well with his first feeding and never wanted a repeat of the difficulties of that encounter.

We were bundled out the rear door and shoved into a tiny old banged up Fiat which had probably seen much better days at least twenty years earlier. It smoked like a pile of flaming rubber tires and smelled worse, and I wished I could stop pretending to breathe so I could avoid it entirely, but our ruse required that we seem like helpless humans, at least for now.

I sat in the back of the wreck with the man who wanted to rape me, and Nathaniel was up front with the seeming "brains" of the operation. I tried slapping away the hands of my attacker as he took my necklace off me and yanked the rings from my fingers, but as I was attempting to appear helpless, I let my blows fall very softly indeed. My apparently ineffectual attempts to defend my belongings and my honor appeared to cheer him all the more and he laughed in my face loudly.

We waited until they were deep into a dark alley before we revealed ourselves to our attackers. I turned to my would-be rapist and put out a hand, resting it on his arm, looking into his eyes.

"You are not playing the game properly. You need to hold me and try to force me," I purred at him. I heard a startled grunt from the driver's seat, and the next thing I knew, the car had come to an abrupt halt. "Why did you stop?"

Running my small hand up his arm, I squeezed gently at the oversized bicep that bulged beneath the fabric of his pressed cotton shirt. I took my other hand and ran it over his jawbone, petting him gently.

I felt, rather than saw, the driver staring at me, having apparently forgotten that Nathaniel sat next to him, staring at him and planning his next move. I knew that when I used seduction during my own hunt, my movements were very nearly hypnotic, and that that effect would not simply be for my intended meal. That was true here as well.

I leaned in and kissed my prey lightly on the lips, tasting him with the tip of my tongue and appreciating that he apparently thought well of regular oral hygiene. Perhaps the same would be true of the rest of his body. While vampirism is proof against human diseases, one still does not normally choose to sit particularly close to them if it is at possible to avoid them.

He unconsciously leaned into the kiss and I kissed him back, leaning in ever closer, yearning toward his throat and the bounty that lurked therein. It was so very close, but his heart was not beating hard enough yet to make it all completely worth my while. It would take just a little bit longer before I could feed satisfactorily.

"What are you doing? Ali, what..." and those were the last words the driver spoke, as I chose that moment to make my attack and feed at the font that beckoned to me with its pulsing siren's song. Nathaniel took his own foolish victim while that worthy was distracted by the horror that met his eyes.

The car became a vehicle of certain death as we both gorged ourselves on the bounty that had voluntarily trapped itself in the vehicle with us. They initially tried fighting us off, but that was when they learned that we were much stronger than we appeared to be.

I felt a sharp pain in my gut and found a short bone-handled dagger protruding from my stomach. Stopping a moment to pull it out and throw it to the floor of the car, I returned to feeding, which allowed the wound to heal to invisibility. That was the last bit of fight I had from the human, as he shortly thereafter lost consciousness and stayed that way until he was so close to dying that I knew it was time to stop feeding entirely.

Looking at Nathaniel in the front seat, I saw that he had his victim pressed against the back of the front seat and was latched onto his throat, sucking the blood from his human's shredded throat with abandon. I took a moment to simply watch him enjoying his vampire self, something far more deadly than most any other of the planet's predators. I could not let him revel in his blood meal forever, though, and finally had to call a halt to his excesses.

"Nathaniel, he is nearly dead. Pull back now before you drink dead blood. You'll hate yourself if you do," I called softly to him. "It would undo all the feeding you have just accomplished and we do not have the time to go and find another human from whom you might feed."

I gently pushed at him with my mind and was rewarded with his acquiescence as he pulled away from the dying human and sat back against the passenger-side door. I had taught him to be more careful with his feedings with the five he had had before we left the States, so he was nowhere near as messy as he had been after his first feeding, but a change of shirt for the both of us would be in order.

Looking at him, I could see that he looked a bit more robust, with a slight blush to his cheeks, though that would soon fade. I also knew that for a little while, at least, the hot blood he had taken in would make his skin feel warmer to anyone who touched it. A fully fed and sated vampire almost always looks disturbingly healthy and thus much more attractive to unsuspecting humans.

Climbing out of the car after cleaning out their pockets for anything of value (but leaving their wallets behind in their pockets, just in case), we took our belongings out of the trunk of the car and I dug around inside my soft sided bag for what I needed.

Having some idea of what would likely transpire and knowing that I had to be prepared even before the charade had begun, I had taken a moment before we left in the taxi to pick up a bottle of rubbing alcohol. Now that we had fed and there was more evidence lying around than I was comfortable with, I poured nearly all of it onto a clean rag I had taken along with us. I took the resulting impromptu wicking and stuffed it into the fuel intake area of the car. Nathaniel struck a match on the bottom of his hiking boot and lit the thing, stepping back about ten yards to watch the show safely.

The gas tank gave a satisfying *thwoom* sound as the contents ignited, and shortly thereafter, the car itself was engulfed, hopefully destroying enough of the evidence that the true means of the men's deaths would be obscured. I did not know how much fuel the ancient automobile had contained, but it seemed to be burning merrily, so I did not worry too much.

As the corpses' flesh was further dehydrated from the flames and extensive heat, the bodies began to writhe in the car, their muscles contracting as what little moisture remained was pulled out of them and dissipated into the air around them. It made for a macabre little dance of death which I found strangely satisfying. How many people had suffered at the hands of these thugs over the years? Would anyone truly miss them? How could anyone truly love a monster?

The bartender was clearly in on the scam, how could he not be? Thus, he would soon be wondering what had happened to his cohorts, but it would likely never occur to him that it was their latest victims who had done them in. Most likely, he would believe these two had found the mother lode of ransoms and had absconded with his "rightful" share.

I shared this thought with Nathaniel and he chuckled blackly.

"It's too bad we don't have the time to take care of him, as well," he growled and I chuckled along with him. So-called "black humor" was a common way to get through life when you exist as we do.

As we both wore black jeans, any blood spatter was almost invisible, and fortunately, little to none had splashed there. Our shirts, as I had noted earlier, were stained, so they had become part of the contents of the now-engulfed Fiat. We wore twins to those shirts now, so should anyone care to check on our location and condition at any particular time, we should cause little to no suspicion to the casual observer.

We had used the remaining rubbing alcohol to clean the last of any blood residue from our faces, hands and arms, once we had exhausted our supply of hygienic wipes. All of our garbage was thrown into the car to be immolated with the bodies.

I preferred to do things this way, as it generally left very little for identification. It was also generally effective for obliterating whatever fingerprints I had either been unable to or simply had forgotten to wipe from the car's surfaces.

We walked for at least a couple miles, keeping to the shadows whenever and wherever possible, before we felt comfortable enough to hail a cab. We wanted to be far enough away from the scene of our feeding so as not to attract attention. The cab driver was apparently a fairly honest sort, and he took us to the airport terminal, as we had requested. This cabdriver actually took the time to speak with me, and was even respectful about it.

He asked us politely about our trip, gently pressed us for information on our experiences, to which I had already developed a few little white lies in order to cover ourselves. The cabdriver was saddened to hear that we had only been able to spend a few hours in town while we waited for our next plane. When he dropped us off at the terminal, he wished us well and said he hoped we would come back again to visit as soon as we were able and to spend at least a week's time in the safer areas of Istanbul.

His words. He was visibly shocked that we would even have considered visiting the Square and scolded us for taking such a terrible chance at not only losing our belongings, but maybe even our lives. He looked a bit sideways at Nathaniel, apparently shocked that he would have brought his delicate flower of a wife to such a rough part of town.

"Surely you would never deliberately take such a dainty and demure young woman to such a dangerous place. I beg you to reconsider doing that ever again!" He protested Nathaniel's apparently unconcern for me, his wife.

Naturally, the cabdriver did not realize that *this* delicate flower had fangs in addition to her thorns, but his attitude was sweet, rather than off-putting to me. I believe that if he had daughters, he was probably very protective of them.

What a nice man, and the complete opposite of the fool who had driven us to the Square and what he had to have known would be an unhappy time there. I made sure that Nathaniel tipped this driver the entire amount of the fare. He smiled shyly in return, gave me a blessing of some sort and hopped back into his taxi and sped away, looking for his next fare.

I was glad I had already fed, as it really would have been a shame to eat this guy. Either he was truly an open-minded sort, or he was intelligent enough to know that you never bite the hand that feeds you. Whatever it was, it was what made him someone I would gladly deal with again.

We arrived at the airport with about two and a half hours before our next flight would leave, but I wanted to find our gate and be able to rest a bit before we went on the next leg of our journey, short as it was. Plus, it was an excellent opportunity to use the restrooms to wash up a bit before we took off for sunny and affluent Riyadh.

Six

J anos had wisely decided that we should land in a city that bordered our destination country, as there was no way we would be announcing our arrival to any of the authorities where we would be staying. Foreigners were most often looked upon with suspicion, and we wanted to avoid any of that if at all possible. This part of the world was a powder keg where strangers were concerned, and xenophobia ran rampant throughout it.

For safety's sake, Nathaniel and I were identified as husband and wife, as a woman's ability to do things on her own in that country was carefully circumscribed. It pissed me off that women in Saudi Arabia needed the permission of a male family member to do things, frequently in the company of a male chaperone and that I would not be allowed to drive myself anywhere.

I could not get to our destination quickly enough. While I may have grown up in a time and place where women were limited by society in what they were able to do, that does not mean that I accepted it then or now. I've always been a stubborn broad.

It was a relatively short hop between Istanbul and Riyadh, a matter of only a couple hours. The flight attendants on this flight were all male, and were obviously doing their best to avoid staring at me. It very suddenly dawned on me what the fuss was all about, and knew I would have to address it as quickly as possible.

Thus, when the "fasten seatbelt" sign went off, I went to the airplane's restroom, where I pulled my hair into a loose bun, then covered my head in a simple light headscarf with a random pattern in lavender and pink. When I returned to my seat, there was an immediately sense of relaxation from the flight attendants, who from that point on, did not give me a second glance.

No sense in antagonizing the locals unless it was completely necessary.

So now, we were Mr. and Mrs. Steven Greene. Nathaniel knew that this was simply for form's sake, as I had made him learn everything possible about the area we would be staying in for the foreseeable future. He also knew and accepted me as his senior, even though to look at the two of us, I looked as though I was just barely an adult and he an older brother or what we pretended at this time, my husband.

It took us awhile to get our luggage from the baggage claim area and then to make our way through to customs. Heavily armed and uniformed military types were ranged around the enormous room, keeping an eye out for illicit activities.

The line of exhausted travelers waiting for inspection snaked around four or five times from where we first entered it until we finally reached the customs inspector. His face was expressionless as first he requested our papers, after which he rifled through all of our bags, looking for contraband.

The tiny bottles of alcohol in our carry-on bags were confiscated with a stern warning about its illegality in that country and an oblique request for a bribe to keep the agent from taking the issue further up the food chain. Apparently he felt he was being a friend by letting it slide, as it were, but friends do not hold you up for money when they do something like that. I noted to myself that the bottles were not immediately deposited in the waste bin. Rather, the customs inspector slipped the bottles, along with a few midrange American greenbacks into his coat pocket while he thought none of his superiors were looking.

I saw that his respect for the rule of law only went so far, but I chose not to press the subject. When you're a female in Saudi Arabia, pushing it with a man is not the brightest thing one can do.

After finishing the ransacking of our luggage, the customs inspector zipped up our bags and put an adhesive tag over the handles, motioning us away. He eyed the humans behind us, obviously judging their potential worth to his wallet by their dress and absently licked his lips in anticipation.

"Welcome to Saudi Arabia. Enjoy your visit," he said. He was done with us and we were now entirely uninteresting to him. He had bigger fish to fry with his next victims.

"It's been forever since I was last here," I told Nathaniel as we joined the larger mass of travelers moving toward the doors. "I'm trying to remember where we can get out of this zoo and find our guides."

"Okay, do we have all of our bags? I see the carry-on's..." Nat's voice trailed off as he made note of all of our bags. "Yes, they're all here, thank goodness!"

"This is one of those times I miss the guys from U.S. airports who can haul—"I broke off as our conversation was suddenly interrupted.

"Surely you do not wish to carry those bags on your own! For a small fee, I would be happy to help you with them!" A boy's high thin voice piped from the wall just beyond the customs area. I looked in the direction from which it came to see a young boy in barely serviceable robes with one hand on the main tool of his trade. He spoke surprisingly good English for a foreign kid, but I supposed that you learned the language of those who wished to impress.

"We don't have much money to spend, boy," Nathaniel replied cautiously. I had warned him about being careful with his wallet before we had even left my old loft. "How much did you have in mind?"

A calculating look came into the boy's eyes, as we had a large number of bags with us. It seemed that avarice was about to win out, but then he appeared to come to a decision and shrugged.

"I leave it to you, Mister. Pay me what you believe is fair once we have your bags loaded into your vehicle," the child said magnanimously. I suspect he was usually paid very well, as he was not insisting on payment up front or a set amount. He caught my eye and winked at me outrageously. The boy certainly had enough personality on him and more to spare. He obviously liked the push the social rules of his country, since he could have gotten at the very least a beating for his temerity.

An agreement was shaken upon and the boy, whose name it turned out was Fadi, wrestled our bags onto his trolley. It was apparent that he had had lot of experience doing it, as he managed to get every single one of our bags on board the thing, and nothing wobbled dangerously when he did.

Nathaniel took my arm and we made our way to the front of the terminal. Our enterprising baggage handler traveled in our wake, lugging our bags on his small but sturdy trolley and whistling tunelessly as we worked our way through the crowd to the main entrance where our guides would meet us.

We had obtained contact lenses to obscure the appearance of our eyes once we reached our destination. My green eyes and Nathaniel's blue-gray eyes were different enough in color than what the locals would have that they might invite more attention than I was willing to risk. A quick stop in the restroom allowed me the opportunity to install my contacts, and after I returned, Nathaniel went to do the same in the men's facilities. It was easier to do it now, rather than when we might have wind blowing sand hither and thither. While it would do no lasting harm, sand in your eye still hurts, even when you are a vampire.

The boy gave us both odd looks, as though he realized that something was different about us, but did not say a word about it. Perhaps he was accustomed to the strange behavior of the foreigners who came to visit his country.

When we eventually exited the terminal and came out into the cool air of the Saudi morning, I saw all manner of greetings and farewells on the sidewalk. There were tears of joy and sorrow, laughter, stoic expressions and more. Each person there had their own story, and we likely would never find out what those stories were, as opposed to the chatty humans at the Los Angeles airport. It was fun, though, to put my own fantasies in place over their realities.

Around me, I could see everything from the long-separated brother or sister, the family reunion at a close, and everyone going their separate ways. Life, hell, even unlife, is something that is always moving.

Unlike humans, however, vampires are physically static. We will always be as we were when we were turned. Age will never touch us, and that is what keeps us away from so much of humanity. If we did not remain as careful as we did, humans would at some point notice our difference and we would become targets for medical study and eventual extermination, once they decided we were too dangerous to be permitted to exist as more than lab rats.

I shook my head as I realized how very dark my thoughts had become. Nathaniel was looking at me with an odd look on his face, obviously feeling the dark turn my thoughts had taken. If I could have blushed, I would have at that moment.

"Sorry Steven. Sometimes my thoughts get away from me." I put a smile on my face as I called him by his alias and hoped the expression reached my eyes. A silly thing to hope when your offspring can read your feelings as though they were his own. "Let's find our guides and we can be on our way!"

The look he gave me in return let me know I was going to be having a discussion once we were in a more private venue. This time, I had brought it on myself.

Our guides had been secured before our arrival and knew full well who and what we were. They would also be able to keep up with us as we traveled, so that made them doubly useful and thus welcome. I had discovered their kind less than a century earlier, but I had learned all I could about them after I did. They were from a very old race, indeed, and their history is one of tragedy and an enormous will to survive and prosper.

They met us outside the airport in a beat up old Volkswagen bus that had more rust on it than paint. A notably tall older man and a younger man, also quite tall, who bore a strong resemblance to his elder, came forward to greet us. There were a couple of youngsters along as well, both boys of maybe about nine or ten (I have trouble, sometimes, judging human ages, but I was probably close) very likely to help socialize them before they hit puberty, when some things might change for them. The Leone did not often mix with humans unless it was absolutely necessary or completely by accident.

"Look what crawled in the doorway," said one of the Leone in Arabic. "Fadi, why are you out on the street? You should be in school."

"Oh! Hello Hamzah!" The boy exclaimed, tugging his forelock respectfully. He replied in his own language (which I understood) when he saw the eldest of our guides. I wondered how they knew one another, but did not ask. Sometimes it was better to pretend ignorance, as often one could gain more information that way. Another part of me wondered why I should be surprised at all. "You are here to take care of these infidel foreigners?"

"Yes, Fadi, but be polite. These are friends, and you do not call friends by such a term. Allah watches over them as well as Muslims such as us. We must leave immediately, if we are to escape the heat of the day." Hamzah continued in the same language. "How is your mother? We have not seen her in a few months. Is she well?"

"She died last month, Hamzah, and has gone on to Paradise. We could not afford the medicine the doctor prescribed," he replied. "When she died, I was left with a choice. I could go to school, or I could eat, but not both. I chose to eat."

"I am so very sorry to hear that, Fadi. Where are you living now?"

"The landlord chased me out the day after I buried my mother, so I have been living in an alley near here. I found the trolley and have been making a little money every day here at the airport. The security guards here take about half of what I make each day, in exchange for letting me in the building," he finished matter-of-factly. "The funeral took all of what little savings we had left."

"Oh! That will not do!" exclaimed Hamzah, stepping forward and going down on one knee to be closer to eye level with the child. "Come with us boy, and we will help you. Our school is not perfect, but we have very good teachers there."

The boy appeared startled, and I heard his pulse speed up in response to the offer. I am sure our guides sensed the same thing. This was clearly something the child had not expected. Family was important to the Leone, and they were letting this child know he was welcome in theirs.

Hamzah rose and turned to me, holding out a thick but otherwise nondescript envelope, which I took without a word. I knew what was in it, but would not open it until we were in the relative safety of the van.

"Madam, I understand that your errand is important, but we have known this child and his family for many years. He has lost his mother and now has no one and no real home. Humanity, if not common courtesy requires that we bring him with us. Have you any objection?" The leader, Hamzah, speaking now in English, looked me in the eye and waited expectantly for my response. I think he knew I could understand the conversation he had had with the boy, but respected my need to continue our illusion.

"I understand the import of the situation and would think less of you if you left him on the streets. Your care and thoughtfulness are laudable in this cynical world. Certainly bring him along," I replied, letting him know that I was no savage.

Everything was quickly and securely tied to the rack on the top of the van, and we all clambered inside, with the three children stuffed into the rear third of the microbus. Nathaniel and I sat in the center bench seat, and Hamzah and his oldest son in the two front seats. We had not yet been introduced by name, so it was considered bad form to engage him in conversation until the formalities were observed. Nathaniel kept things interesting by engaging young Fadi in conversation.

"Where did you learn to speak English so well, Fadi?"

"I used to watch American television shows at a friend's house. They had a satellite dish and were able to find American television stations," was his reasonable explanation. I'd stupidly forgotten how easy it was to use satellite dishes for more than spying on your friends and enemies.

"What shows did you like the best?"

"I liked to watch, what do you call them? Cops and robbers shows. Are all American women so immodest," he asked bluntly. I heard a dull thump as one of the Leone boys hit him upside the head as a rebuke for his rudeness. "They leave their heads uncovered and paint their faces like prostitutes!"

"That's just television. It's not real. Most women don't dress so provocatively in America," Nathaniel replied calmly. "I can imagine that seeing shows like that put Americans in a very bad light with people in this part of the world."

"We are always hearing that you hate us and want to change us," the boy continued. "They say you want to kill us all with bombs."

"There are those who might wish to do something like that, Fadi, but that is not the case with the majority of Americans. Most of us want peace between and understanding between our peoples. I know that there are those here who talk people into doing terrible things, and they will even lie and tell you that you won't be hurt when you do these terrible things. Don't let anyone talk you into hurting other people; I don't think that's something Allah wants any of us to do."

The conversation quieted for a time after that. I suspect young Fadi was processing the information he had been given, and was weighing the words for their truth. I hoped that he believed Nathaniel, as I believed the same things he did.

The two lanky Leone boys eventually dragged Fadi into some sort of a game in the rear of the VW bus, and we were serenaded with the sound of whispered conversations and giggling boys. Happy sounds were almost always a good thing in my book.

We drove for several hours, stopping twice to refuel the bus before going onward. I don't know if Fadi realized that while he and the Leone ate, neither Nathaniel nor I did so. I was pleased to notice that Nathaniel seemed calm, and I wasn't feeling his hunger pangs, which meant that his system was finally beginning to settle in to its changes.

We finally pulled into our destination some six hours later, with the sun long down and the stars glittering in the night sky. It was glorious. I had not seen starlight that bright in a long time, but then, the cultures I had lived within most recently lent a large amount of light pollution to the night.

Nathaniel and I were escorted to the cottage we would call home for the foreseeable future, and Fadi went off to the home of one of our host's sons for safekeeping. If he did not know it already, he would soon learn the secret of the Leone, and it would be an interesting diversion to see how he handled the surprise.

Our lives in this part of the world were about to be very different. I had lived in Western society for a long time, so I had become accustomed to certain freedoms. As Nathaniel had never gone further north than Calgary or south of Tijuana, this was going to be an upward learning curve for him as well. I had tried to give him as much information beforehand as I could, and had purchased books on conservative Middle Eastern society in order to prepare him and myself.

It was bad enough that I would have to walk fully veiled once we crossed the border, though I drew the line at a complete burqa. I was no glutton for punishment. All those who looked at me would see would be a pair of hazel eyes staring out from the concealing folds of my veil. Nathaniel would have a head dress to keep the sun off his head and his dark brown contact lenses in place. As a male in a country that embraced the idea of restricted female movements, he would have far more freedom than I would legally enjoy.

Overall, our being Westerners would always put us in a certain amount of danger. Nathaniel more so than myself, as his Arabic was currently almost nil. We were working on it, but it would take time, which fortunately we had plenty of at the moment. His and my forays out into the world would need to occur after nightfall, when we could conceal ourselves in the shadows and move more quickly than a human could ever hope.

Seven

It turned out that Fadi was aware of the wonderful peculiarity of the Leone. His mother had been the cousin of one of the Leone with whom we were now living. Although she was Leone, she was not a shifter, so she did not have to worry about keeping away from humanity. She had not suffered from the predator's need to hunt for fresh bloody meat or the feline's apparently irresistible desire to play with one's prey before bringing it to a hopefully merciful end.

There was a chance that Fadi might have inherited his race's heritage, but as I had not recognized his scent as being Leone, that chance was very remote. He smelled fully human to me. I could feel the faint stirring of Nathaniel's hunger as he, too reacted to the aroma of the boy's humanity. I was momentarily concerned, but then realized that what he felt was only stirrings, like someone considering a snack, rather than the intensity brought on by full-blown hunger. It made me glad that I had thought to have us feed during our layover in Istanbul.

As a relation, he would always be welcome with his people here in the mountains, but he would likely never achieve much status if he remained there much past adulthood. Most likely, he would eventually be sent to one of the larger cities with an endowment to allow him to open a business beneficial to those of his relations who remained in the relative safety of the mountains. As long as he continued to provide at least some measure of support, whether it was financial or in kind, they would look out for him.

That was the way things were in this part of the world.

The Leone, who were essentially ethnic Kurds, lived up in the heavily wooded mountains in Northern Iraq. It really reminded me of Aspen, Colorado, with the climate and the trees. There were even trees there that flowered in the spring, perfuming the air with a spicy, cinnamon-like scent. The Leone would sometimes roll in the fallen blossoms while they were shifted, giving them a kittenish appearance, which was something you did not want to ever do. Like felines everywhere, they were ever on the alert, and when distraction came, they would immediately focus on the perceived threat.

I'd seen it happen, and it even scared me a bit.

We waited quite some time before we were comfortable enough to reveal our true selves. Yes, Hamzah and Fatima knew who and what we were before we arrived, but they understood and respected our need to be cautious to not reveal too much at once. The Leone children knew that we smelled odd and nothing like prey would, but we waited until their parents were comfortable enough with the idea of such familiarity before we shared our own kind of uniqueness. The Leone, like the human Kurds who also lived in the area, were standoffish people, and one had to prove herself to the community before trust was offered. As most civilizations open relationships with the sharing of food, and we as vampires did not partake of conventional victuals, we were hampered in that regard, thus we would need to find other methods with which to build that trust.

"Here, have a human full of O negative," just isn't going to be in the local lexicon, for some reason.

Interestingly, while there were livestock, there were no horses or other normal beasts of burden to be found in the Leone village. I had kept horses during most of my time as a vampire, from my first, the Andalusian stallion called Ádhamh who I acquired in the mid-1600's and then dozens more in between until my last, a sturdy Morgan mare called Pooka, who passed away in about 1915 from some sort of equine plague. I had decided at that time that I did not want to get another horse, as this was the age of the automobile, and it seemed foolish to take on a mouth to feed when it was no longer necessary to rely on an animal for transportation.

I'd bought myself a 1915 Ford Model T Speedster, had it painted a gloriously shining blood red, and enjoyed the thing immensely. The gentleman who had built the thing for me once it arrived had seemed a bit horrified by my choice of color, but enough presidents' faces laid across his palm allayed his reluctance and he performed admirably. He had seemed to think I should keep it the stock "black" color, but I was never one for fitting in with the crowd, at least not in that time.

It confused me that it seemed the greater Leone community had not taken Fadi's mother into their care while she was ill. The Leone were very particular about looking out for family members in need, and I would have thought they would at least have taken in Fadi's mother because of her son. One day I finally gathered up enough courage to ask Hamzah's wife Fatima why that was the case.

For a moment, I thought I had overstepped the bounds of curiosity, because she never looked at me when I asked my question. Instead, she thought for a bit before pausing in her bread making long enough to provide what answer she had.

"Sarah always had the opportunity to come to us, but long ago made the decision that she wanted Fadi to live in the world of men. She herself had never shifted, so while she could have stayed here, Sarah would have few opportunities to find a mate of her own amongst the Leone. As you well know, our family ties are bound together in such a way as to ensure the best opportunity to bring more full Leone into the world. So she left our village and moved to the human city, where she found a human male and took him as her life mate. Yuri made some bad business decisions and was dead before Fadi saw his second year."

Yuri? That didn't sound much like a Middle Eastern name to me. Sarah's family, being fairly clannish, must have been scandalized. I wondered if the human had been a holdover from the war with the

Russians decades before. Either that, or Yuri was the son of a soldier, but I'd probably never know the truth of that.

"We went to Sarah and offered her a home with us here in her home village, but she would not listen to our entreaties. It was her own selfishness that ultimately put the boy in such a bad place when she finally died," she told me. She shook her head sadly. "Self-pride is not always a good thing to have. Sarah's overweening self-assurance could have left her son dead or worse."

"Worse? What is worse than death, Fatima?"

"He could have been forced to become a soldier or a slave. Death would be terrible, but it would have spared him the indignity of such a terrible fate as a living death."

"So she could have come here anytime she wanted. Does Fadi know that?"

"It was not our place to interfere while she lived. While human society here is patriarchal, the Leone are matriarchal. Our males posture and fight for their mates and position in our society, but our females do not behave that way." She gave a soft snort and put three slashes into each of the six loaves she was preparing. "More human societies would be better if the women ran things and left the men to primp and prance around."

Now that was interesting. In the wild, the male lion is the ruler of his pride. Apparently, that was not the issue with the Leone. It seemed to make a lot of sense to me, but then maybe that's because I'm female, so I could be a bit biased.

"While Hamzah is the male for our village who deals with the human world, here I am the Pridemother. I make the day to day decisions and make the final arrangements for the matings between our young ones." She swatted the backside of a presumptuous youngster who came into her kitchen at a run and tried to run off with handful of fresh, warm cookies. "Khalid! You know better than that! Get outside before I give you a real beating!"

Rather than being intimidated by the threat, Khalid giggled and caromed out of the cottage, one cookie jammed in his mouth and two others clutched in his right hand.

"He probably has some compatriots he will share those others with," she told me complacently. "Khalid has always been very good about sharing, which is something that more than a few of our males have not yet figured out. Now, we were speaking of Fadi's mother, yes?"

"You have a good point about what it would be like if females ran the world. It seems a very wise decision for the Leone, Fatima," I replied. "Has it always been so?"

"At first, the males thought they were best chosen to oversee the Pride, but over time, even they realized that they were much too mercurial to make rational and sometimes hard decisions. Males are creatures of the moment. Females are much more thoughtful." Her words collided strongly with Muslim beliefs, but I had no idea how the Leone reconciled those differences. However they did it, it did appear to be working. "Still, it was a decision that caused no end of strife with some members of the Pride, and the stories say that those who would not change were killed. The Leone must look to the welfare of the many. If some will not embrace necessary change, they are removed from the community."

She fell silent and finished shaping her loaves before leaving them for their final rising. I could almost remember the taste of fresh hot bread, and found that I missed it. Fatima's children and grandchildren certainly behaved as though it was ambrosia itself when it was fresh out of the oven and she served it steaming hot and slathered with clotted cream and honey.

I had only tasted honey a few times while I was human, and then only after I was taken from my family. Mistress Fairworth had pressed some on me after the death of my fiancé, feeling that something sweet would help to alleviate my sour mood. I remember that I had liked it a lot. I had always considered it to be a kind of miracle that bees could essentially turn flowers into something so wonderful.

"Is there anything I can do to help out, Fatima? It will be another day or two before Nathaniel and I must go out to feed again. For now, I'm teaching him restraint. However, it's always good to have something with which to occupy myself and I thought you might like some assistance."

"As I am sure you are aware, in the next few days, we will have some new cubs getting ready to go up higher into the mountains for their time away from the rest of us. We will need meat, and while the males could certainly go and collect fresh meat, perhaps you and your child would be willing to go and collect some few animals as well. Fat ones would be best, if you can find them. Let us see if you can hunt beasts as well as you hunt the humans," and she smiled at me, a twinkle in her eye. "I have work to do, so get out of my kitchen and make yourself useful."

Now why did I feel as though she were treating me like one of the village children, and why did that thought not bother me as perhaps it should have?

I couldn't resist her good natured challenge and quickly excused myself, stopping only to collect Nathaniel from where he sat playing chess with Fadi. Nathaniel had developed a strong attachment for the young human, and they often spent time together when the boy's chores were over for the day. They delighted in playing board games together, and I was glad that he had someone with whom he could not only spend time, but also learn self-restraint.

"What are we doing, Siofra? I just about had that little smart aleck beat this time!" Nathaniel asked as we hiked high up even higher into the mountains. It was dark out now, so I didn't have to worry about concealing myself in layers of heavy cloth, which was nice.

"The Leone's youngsters who have not shifted for the first time are about to go up into the mountains for their time away from their families. They shift for the first time at about puberty. The first time, they won't shift back to their human forms for at least a year's time."

"A year?" Nathaniel was aghast, and I couldn't blame him.

"Their bodies complete their growing during that time. When they shift back to human again, they will look like young humans in their late teens. They are planning a big celebration for that event the day after tomorrow, and we are to bring back some of the menu items. It's the polite thing to do, as their guests." I explained.

"What an amazing thing. A whole year in a different shape. Are they able to communicate with their humans while they are shifted?"

"No, and that's one of the reasons why they are taken away from here during that time. It will help to lessen any frustration they might feel at not being able to spend time in conversation with their families." I couldn't help but think of the sheer amount of frustration Leone cubs must surely experience during their first Year. "I believe they have a link similar to the one we have, where they are connected emotionally to other shifted Leone, but other than that, speech isn't possible."

"How do they know that it's going to happen to several of them at once?"

"Leone tend to mate at about the same time each year. They have heats, rather than a regular human-type menstrual cycle. Last year's cubs will be coming down the mountain tomorrow night to join in the festivities as well. They'll be the ones who take the new youngsters up to their new home when the celebration is over."

"Wow. Sounds like something you'd see on National Geographic, if they even knew something like that existed," he responded. I can't say I didn't feel that way, myself.

"Enough talking, Nat. We have to hunt, and talking isn't going to help us with that at all," I said, and the conversation shut down.

As we continued to climb, I enjoyed the cool night air and the glorious stars shining in the sky. The muted sounds of birds greeted our ears, and I had to admit that it was nice to get away from civilization and the big city for a time. I'd been a city vampire for several decades, so change was nice.

Even with our enhanced hearing and faster reflexes, the hunt was tough. The local gazelles seemed to have adapted to having Leone in the area, and were very good at hiding in nearly inaccessible places. Fortunately, since we were working together, Nathaniel and I were able to bring down three of the crafty animals. We were extra careful and only took bachelor males, as the species was not particularly plentiful, and the loss of a few bucks would not seriously threaten the species.

They had made the mistake of gathering at a pond, and so we were able to make quick work of them. They probably never knew what hit them.

We bled the beasts out by hanging them from a convenient tree, leaving a hemoglobin bounty out on the ground for passing carnivores and insects. Nathaniel carried two of the carcasses, while I took the other, and then started the long haul back down toward the village.

All was quiet and good until I realized I was hearing voices not far ahead, just above the village. I very carefully put my burden down on the ground and motioned for Nathaniel to do the same. I did not recognize the voices I was hearing, especially as they were speaking Russian, and did not at all like what it implied.

No one was going to threaten or injure the Leone. It just wasn't going to happen.

We crept forward until we were just above two human males who seemed to be carrying small cameras they had trained on the center of the village. My hunger tickled at me and it reminded me that it was time to eat. I batted it down and continued to listen to the conversation below me.

"Are you sure about what you saw, Ivan?" I heard one ask the other, who grunted an assent. "How do we know they will do anything while we are here?"

"I saw one of them change a few years ago, when I was on reconnaissance. My superiors never believed me and tossed me out, saying I was crazy. When I come back with evidence on film, they will have to believe me, and I will become a millionaire!" said the other, sounding very self-confident. "I am sure our scientists will want to study at least one of them. Perhaps we would be able to capture one of their women or children to take back with us."

I felt my brain fill with fire as I considered what I was hearing so close to me. That anyone would violate the Leone and treat them as freaks was beyond my ability to ignore. I glanced over at Nathaniel, and saw that his fangs were already out and that his attention was locked on those below us.

"Get just above them and I will move down below them. We will rush them at the same time. You take the tall one," I told him very quietly. Nathaniel nodded and moved to where I indicated he should. He moved silently and stealthily to his position and waited for my signal. We both usually hunted barefoot in the mountains, so that we could get better toeholds where necessary. I don't believe Nathaniel displaced a single pebble as he moved, as surefooted as he was.

I slipped around them and just under the rise on which they rested. I could feel Nathaniel's anticipation and knew he was picking up on mine as well. We would have no problem communicating when the time came.

"Maybe we could kill one to take back with us, Sergei. I don't know what dissecting the body would show, but maybe they could look at the DNA. I hear that you can tell a lot about something by looking at its DNA," Ivan said. "I wonder what you could see under a regular microsc..."

I chose that moment to strike.

He never finished his sentence, instead, his mouth opened and closed soundlessly, like a landed fish gasping for air it could actually use, his eyes were like the proverbial dinner plates as he stared his death in the face. His flesh had gone deathly pale, although I could heard his heart skip a beat and then begin thundering in his chest.

If this was his "fight or flight" reflex, it seemed to be stuck in neutral as his biological motor revved up to ridiculously high levels. The whisper of his blood racing through his veins was like a terrible death song that enchanted me, as his body sang its own lament at his pending passage into the Void.

My hands closed on his shirtfront and I clutched him to my chest before his brain registered what was about to happen to him. He really should have listened to his body's warning system before now, because it was now too late.

I didn't kill him immediately. I held him tight in my grasp, enjoying the feel of him struggling to escape. Out of the corner of my eye, I could see Nathaniel doing the same with his captive. I let the human see my fangs and smiled at him, though I know there was no humor in my eyes when I did so.

"There are more than just shape shifters in the world, human. Regretfully for you, you will not be able to share that information with anyone," I let him scream once, as only the Leone would hear him. "I guess we have a couple more carcasses for the celebration tomorrow!"

"What? What are you?" the one called Ivan begged me. "Please, let me go! I have family..."

"What am I? I am a vampire. The Germans call us *Nosferatu*. Some Slavic cultures call us *lamia*. Others, not really understanding what we are and do, have called us succubus and incubus. By any name, when you meet with one of my kind it will be time to sleep deeply, and there is very little chance you will wake up ever again," I replied. "These people are my friends, and I heard what you had planned, so that very little chance has just turned into no chance at all."

"No, please! I won't do it. I'll leave them alone!" he stammered. "Just let me go! I'll be quiet as a mouse!"

"Now why don't I believe you, Ivan? I have my doubts that you're telling me the truth," I purred at him, stroking the side of his throat suggestively with my elongated and talon-like fingernails. The broken edge of one of my nails scratched him a little, and I licked at the blood that welled up in the shallow wound. The spice of his fear had seasoned it deliciously and I could not restrain my groan of anticipation. Part of me wanted to drink him down quickly, while the rational part of my mind told me that it was important that he take awhile to die.

I glanced over at Nathaniel and his captive, and saw that unworthy had fainted dead away in his grasp. Spoil sport. I looked back at my own wriggling meat sack and smiled, showing him teeth that still sported some of his blood from when I had licked his wound clean.

"I'm hungry, anyhow, so you'll do just fine to help me ease my hunger pangs."

In a weirdly synchronized way, Nathaniel and I struck at the same time. Instead of drinking quickly, we stretched it out, so that the humans lingered as long as was possible before they died. The pain of Nathaniel's strike brought his captive back to consciousness, and he wailed into the uncaring night.

I wanted them both to suffer for what they had planned to do. I didn't worry that anyone else suspected anything about the existence of the Leone, as Ivan's words clearly indicated that no one had believed him when first he insisted on what he had seen. Both

Nathaniel and I needed to feed and I knew from experience that the Leone had no compunction about eating humans. It was the best way I could think of to eliminate he bodies and thereby, any evidence of their passage.

Several of the Leone, drawn by the death cries of the humans, made it to where we fed by the time the humans' hearts were beginning to falter. Some had shifted, while other retained their human forms. They stood and watched as we finished, and then dropped the bodies to the rocky ledge. The Leone waited politely for an answer to their loudly unspoken question.

"It seems that a few years ago, one of these two saw a Leone shift. They showed up here with cameras to try to record proof to take back with them," I indicated the cameras that lay in the dust. One had broken in the violence of the attack, snapping where the long zoom lens mounted to the camera's body, but the other seemed okay to my untrained eye.

Okay, so I know computers, not cameras. Sue me. I hadn't even used a camera since I had impulsively purchased an old Brownie, several decades earlier. It was probably still in a box somewhere in my collection, never having actually been used. I think I had entertained the idea of being a photojournalist, but decided that it would be too much work in the end.

"I heard them say something about either kidnapping or even killing one of you to take back for study, and I certainly was not going to allow that to happen," I told them, gesturing at them all. "It would be a terrible thing to happen to any of you."

"Thank you, my lady, for your kindness. Our sentries should have scented these two, but for whatever reason did not." Hamzah said formally. "I am surprised that they were able to get this close to our village without our hearing their approach."

"They were either being careful or were unbelievably lucky to be facing into the wind, but that's probably why their voices carried to us rather than you, so I hope you won't be too hard on your sentries." I honestly did not blame the Leone sentries, as I felt fairly certain the now dead interlopers had taken wind direction into consideration when making their plans. "We left three gazelle carcasses up on the ridge a little bit up the hill. They are our gifts for the celebration tomorrow. I guess you'll have a couple more to add to that pile."

The look Hamzah bestowed upon me let me know that while they appreciated our gifts, as well as Nathaniel's and my help in dealing with unwelcome visitors, I should leave community discipline to the Leone, themselves. He was right. We were only guests, and as such, unless specifically invited to offer them, our opinions were secondary.

The humans were vivisected and then eaten within an hour, in order to make them disappear as quickly as possible. Their bones were cracked open for their marrow, and anything inedible was thoroughly burned so as to make it indistinguishable from animal remains to the casual eye. The gazelles we had killed were gutted, the viscera consumed like some kind of treat, and the hollow carcasses hung in a cool subterranean storage chamber, where pests could not get to them before the ceremony.

Little Miriam and her cousin Ibrahim were about to head into the mountains. Miriam was the furthest along, and so she was not quite as able to focus as her cousin. She was far more likely to give voice to low hoarse calls than human speech, and a fine coat of downy fur had sprouted across the whole of her body, a precursor undercoat to the heavier fur that would soon emerge.

The first shift would take much longer to complete than any other, with the most dramatic changes occurring some few weeks before the full shift. Little Miriam's eyes had been the first thing to change. A few days later, her nose had broadened, seeming to take up most of the middle of her face, and her fingernails had come to more resemble claws than human nails. Her ears had begun to shift upward on her head as well. I could see that it wasn't an easy, painless transformation, as she spent a lot of time rubbing at the bits that were in the midst of changing from human to leonid.

She was far more catlike in her behavior. She slept away a good part of the day, only becoming active at night, when she would do such things as sniffing at various points and then rub her cheek against things such as doorposts, corners and rocks. For now, it was all about marking her territory.

It was fascinating to watch it happen. Little Miriam had gone from initially being frightened by the changes being wrought upon her body to embracing them and even losing herself in their throes. The day of the night of the celebration, she had lost the ability to walk upright, and moved about on all fours, even though she did not yet have full paws instead of hands and feet. I could smell the blood that oozed from the palms of her still partially primate hands, but it did not raise my hunger level. Leone don't smell human at all, so there was nothing to entice me.

The blending of human and feline anatomy left her rear end higher in the air than it would be once she was fully shifted, and it looked like an uncomfortable position in which to be stuck, even for a short time.

She would likely complete the change during the night of the celebration, while Ibrahim would probably not finish changing fully until he reached the retreat. I had seen the adults watching him and knew they were discussing something regarding him, but knew better than to interfere or be overly curious. Whatever it was, if they chose to share that information with me, it was wholly up to them to make that decision. I waited on their pleasure.

When Ibrahim got too close Little Miriam at one point, she turned and swatted at him with her unfinished claws, hissing in his face. Ibrahim yelped in surprise and fell on his ass in his scramble to escape the female's irritation. Fatima laughed indulgently, but still chased Ibrahim away from the understandably irritable cub. As Little Miriam was so close, it was best that Ibrahim be kept away from her as much as was necessary.

It was not that shifted Leone did not think human thoughts, but that the youngsters did not yet know how to process all the new information their changing bodies could now sense, so they tended to be more thoughtless and behaved in a more primal manner in their reactions to things. Thus, the adults did everything they could to minimize potential overreactions.

I was correct in my estimation of the nearness of the actual event, and Little Miriam completed her first shape shifting during the ceremony. In the midst of devouring a bloody chunk of gazelle, she had suddenly dropped her prize to the ground and began writhing in the dirt as the bones of her body started the last part of began their transformation from human dimensions to feline. Her screams were not that of a human, but of one of the great cats, and several of her clan mates, those who were able, shifted as well. I heard the terrible sounds as her bones were shifted around and reshaped within her own skin. Loud snapping and crackling sounds cut through the air as Miriam danced her agony in the dust. I'm sure that if I had still been able, the mere sight of what now happened would have made me feel nauseous.

I knew that Miriam's internal organs were being compressed as her ribcage changed to a more feline configuration, and that cannot have been a comfortable thing. I could hear her heart as though it were slamming against her ribs, the adrenaline surge that sparked the transformation nearly doubling her blood pressure. A mere human could never have survived the violence of this transformation.

At one point, I caught a glimpse of a bizarre melding of human and Leone features, seeing her partially human body with rear legs angled like those of one of the big cats, leaving her unable to stand properly, and her half-grown tail lashing about in a reflection of the agony her body was undergoing. Miriam's face was mostly feline now, although what remained of her human features was being shoved away into nothingness as the shifting continued. Her nearly flat human breasts were gone, replaced by a dual row of tiny pink nipples that paraded down her chest and across her now much narrower abdomen.

Suddenly, as though they had only now become aware that non-Leone were watching, those of her people who were already shifted surrounded her and became a wall of fur and flesh, as though to give the girl a living veil of modesty for what would be her transformation into the form she would keep for the next twelve lunar cycles. Those who were not able to shift still celebrated, dancing and ululating into the night with the joy of the occasion, as this meant yet another opportunity for an additional generation of the Leone and the survival of the species.

Little Miriam, Ibrahim and a small contingent of Leone left for their mountaintop retreat before sunrise, as they wanted to avoid both unwanted attention and the overbearing heat of the day. Being still mostly human-shaped and thus slower, Ibrahim had begun his trek earlier. His own changes were occurring, but he was still bipedal. Even when the time came that he could no longer move about on two feet, but had not yet fully developed paws, he would need to travel without assistance. He had been raised to know and knew better than to ask for it.

The Leone are a hard people, and unless one is very young, wounded or otherwise ill, they are responsible for themselves. It would have been humiliating for Ibrahim to have to request assistance during this, the pivotal moment of his young life. Survival of the fittest was a hallmark of Leone society, even with their species being in such dire straits.

Little Miriam had come to me to say goodbye, rubbing herself hard against me and nearly knocking me down. Remember that a ninety-eight pound Leone child is going to be a ninety-eight pound cub, so a well-aimed rub can put a two-legged human-shaped being on its ass if she is not careful. I was privately glad that Miriam had not chosen to jump on me and rest those great clawed paws of hers on my shoulders. She probably would have driven me to my knees, at the very least.

"I'll miss you, Miriam. I hope to see you again," I told her, rubbing the silken fur between her ears, for which I was rewarded with a pleased purr. "You are lovely, my dear!"

With a final flick of her long and very muscular tail against my chest, she bounded away into the darkness and off to her new life as a full member of her clan and her people. I quietly envied her that familial connection, as my own had only lasted until shortly before I had entered my teens.

Nathaniel and I smiled as the very pleased and excited young Leone went on her way, then went back to our quarters. We did not want to intrude too much upon the Leones' celebration. I had some reading to catch up on, and Nathaniel? Well, Nathaniel had something else to do of which he was not as yet aware.

Someone had been in our quarters and had been kind enough to tidy them up. The throw rugs had been beaten into submission, as had our lounging pillows. Taking a careful sniff of the pillows, I guessed it had been one of the younger girls who was still awaiting puberty. This one was particularly fond of strawberries, and I could smell their sweetness here and there amongst those items she had been forced to touch.

Nathaniel was cleaning his teeth and I was preparing to start reading when he suddenly sat back against one of his overstuffed cushions and just began talking to me. He was not normally quite so abrupt, so I put my book down and gave him my full attention.

"Why was it so painful for her to shift for the first time? I see other, adult Leone just slide right into it without any sign of difficulty," he asked me. "It doesn't seem to hurt them like it hurt her. You'd have thought she was being ripped apart inside."

"In some ways, they are being ripped apart. Their bodies are changing for the very first time. The soft parts of their insides have been doing all their developing for the past ten to twelve years. Muscles and tendons have had at least a decade in one configuration. Now it's time for the more solid bits to develop. Their bones have been in the same form since the day they were born. Fatima told me that even though the young Leone are finally learning their other shapes, it seems as though their bodies fight this most natural next step in their lives. Thus, the pain," I explained. "It will hurt a little when they become human-shaped again in a year's time, but after that, it won't hurt them at all."

"So Ibrahim is either going to go through that on the way up there, or shortly after he arrives."

"Exactly. I'll hope that he's able to hold out until he gets there," I replied. There was something else that could happen as well, but I did not want to worry Nathaniel, so I kept that piece of knowledge to myself. "It can't be fun to have to half-drag oneself up a mountainside."

"I think becoming a vampire was much easier," he said, his eyes full of earnest relief. "I can't imagine going through something like that."

It made me pleased that my offspring was now so very comfortable in his own undead skin. I rose from my chair and crossed the room to where he sat, leaning down a little to kiss the top of his head. He squirmed and batted me away with one hand.

"What's that all about?" He demanded suspiciously, rubbing his hair as though I had left something behind with my kiss.

"I'm just proud of you, Nathaniel. Very proud," I replied, cuffing him gently. "Now go and wash yourself again. You left a little mujahedeen in your hair. While a human might not be able to smell it on you, I know that I can, as well as the Leone. They're just too polite to say anything about it to you."

Swearing with embarrassment, Nathaniel lurched off his cushions and went out the door, taking what was left of a bucket of rinse water and a little soap with him, obviously determined to scrub the incriminating human tissue from his scalp. I laughed and went back to sit and return to the book I had been reading at the start of our conversation. It was a mystery novel by one of my favorite female authors, and I had been delighted to receive it in one of Janos' most recent CARE packages to the Leone. The inscription he had placed within it was both scatological and even downright rude, but knowing my friend, I considered it high praise, indeed.

A few days after the celebration that took this year's cubs up into the mountains, Hamzah and his people moved to a new location. They had held a council meeting and decided that they couldn't take the chance that Ivan had told anyone about their existence. Thus, survival demanded they err on the side of caution. Before they left, they more formally introduced us to another Leone community nearly a hundred miles distant from what would soon be their former village. We had met these other Leone in passing on a few occasions during trading discussions between "our" group and their representatives, who had come to discuss potential marriages. Fatima and Hamzah told them some of what we had done for the clan and stressed that we could also be at least as helpful for a new clan.

Fatima was the last to leave, but before she did, she came to Nathaniel and me to bid us farewell. What they had not been able to take with them was now in the process of burning to the ground. When I had explained about DNA and forensic science, they had very quickly understood the dangers of leaving anything behind unnecessarily.

"Take care of yourself, Fatima," I told her when we said our goodbyes. "I've arranged a scholarship for Fadi in London. It's an excellent chance for him to get a good education and make some good contacts while he's over there."

"Thank you, Siofra. You have been a wonderful member of our community, and if you ever need anything, please do not hesitate to contact us. If it is at all possible, we will come to help you," Fatima told me, enfolding me in a motherly hug. It surprised me to find out how much I enjoyed that body to body contact. "You are like my own daughter."

When I automatically laughed at that, she put a hand against my lips to shush me.

"You are both accomplished predators, strong women and you both have fine fangs. What more could a mother hope for, yes?" she asked me in English, smiling at me in a way that would have made me blush had I been able. At that moment, I found myself wishing I could do just that. "You are as much a daughter to me as my own. You make your mother proud."

She kissed me on the cheek and dropped her cloak to the ground, unabashedly revealing her nakedness to Nathaniel and me. Scars ran up and down her torso, but instead of making her ugly, it only enhanced her beauty, lending her a savage aspect, even in human form. Fatima was bestowing a great compliment on both Nathaniel and me by doing so, as she was revealing her true self to non-Leone, something that can only happen with those non-Leone who are especially loved and cherished. Those scars showed that she could fight and fight well, as she had not only honorably received those scars, but had survived to display them.

Then, in what seemed like half an instant, she blurred into her lioness form and ran to catch up with her husband and children. Her farewell roar's echo bounced off the mountains like thunder and I smiled a bit sadly.

"Goodbye, Fatima." I said softly after her, a single blood tear coursing down one cheek from the inside corner of my left eye. "Goodbye, Mother."

Upheaval. It had been a part of my life since I had still been human, so you'd think I would be used to it by now, but I had made some connections with these people and I would miss them. I started a bit when Nathaniel reached out a hand and squeezed my shoulder, trying to comfort me, also wordlessly handing me a tissue to wipe the blood from my face.

He was sweet that way.

With that, we turned to face the other direction and began our journey to our new home with a different and strange clan of Leone. If our luck held, it wouldn't take too terribly long for our new hosts to accept us. Otherwise, we'd have to fend for ourselves in a place where my deathly-pale skin would instantly mark me as an outsider.

Eight

O ur first meeting with our new hosts was tense and I could feel their resentment at our presence. Only their relationship with Fatima and Hamzah's clan made them allow our encroachment into their lives in the first place. Their children, curious as most youngsters can be, ignored their parents' hostile attitude toward us and pestered us good naturedly at every opportunity. Not being a fool, and seeing this as the ice-breaker it could be, I would answer the children's questions, whatever they were, as did Nathaniel.

I am sure that for a time, the adults grilled their children about everything that had been asked and answered during their visits. I would have done the same thing if such an opportunity had presented itself and I were in their place.

We learned to fit into our new hosts' community almost seamlessly, and Nathaniel picked up Arabic faster than I would have thought possible. Despite the fact that he wasn't one of their own people, the local young women loved trailing after him. I think it was more because of fascination, rather than teasing that made them do so. Leone had the curiosity of cats, and it showed with these young women.

Well, they understood once I took their Clan mother aside and explained the vampire birds and bees to her, including the fact that Leone did not register as prey to us, nor did he have a sexual or romantic attraction to any of them. Understanding what I told her, she passed the word along to the rest of the community and you could almost feel a clan-wide sigh of relief in response. It probably helped that Nathaniel was a nice young man who listened to what he was told, and didn't try to force his own ideas on the people of the village. Best of all, once the males understood that Nathaniel would not be taking advantage of their women, they visibly relaxed.

He took advantage of that unusual opportunity to learn the local language. When he pronounced something incorrectly, the young women would repeat the correct pronunciation of the missed word until he repeated it correctly. Once he did, they would giggle like schoolgirls and praise him for his cleverness. He would demur politely, but thank them for their many kindnesses, which endeared him to them even further.

He would have made an excellent cultural anthropologist.

The first five years after our move to our new hosts' village went by very quickly. Fatima visited a few times to share news and just keep in touch. Little Miriam had done very well, but Ibrahim had had some kind of issue with his shifting where he did not shift fully, so he had spent his year on the mountain in half-human/half-Leone form. Fatima had not given specifics, but I could see it still disturbed her greatly. I thought to ask about his current status, but decided that was a private matter and that if she decided it was my business, she'd let me know.

In other news...

Through the generosity and connections of Janos, Fadi immigrated to England and now attended Eton, where he was making new friends, polishing his English skills, learning French and loving his rare opportunity at a formal education. Fatima told me she would be sure to have his letters forwarded on to me as the opportunity presented itself. The ones I had received via her messengers thus far made him sound like just about any other Western youngster, and I was pleased to hear that he was so very happy with his very unusual opportunity to make so much more of himself than a manual laborer.

In her own private missives to me, Fatima shared that Hamzah was getting older, and so he was now being forced to defend his position within the clan on an almost daily basis from younger challengers. Thus far, he had been fortunate to keep his position, but he knew it was only a matter of time before he would be essentially dethroned and would have to either submit to his successor or go it alone.

She did not delve deeper into the consequences of Hamzah's eventual loss of position, but I knew that Fatima might or might not go with him when that time came, as females generally either died in their clan position or abdicated in favor of a younger female. I didn't know the mechanics of Fatima and Hamzah's relationship to know what would happen, but there did seem to be a genuine attachment between them. I decided not to pry, since it wasn't my business and she might share it at some point when she thought it appropriate.

As I said earlier, our current hosts were good people, if much less demonstrative than Fatima and Hamzah's. Perhaps part of it was because while Fatima and Hamzah knew Janos, this new clan had learned about the situation secondhand. Miriam would come to visit periodically, so I am sure those visits helped to ease our relationship with this new clan.

I think our hosts hoped that Miriam might one day join their clan, or that one of their males might join hers. Either way, a little genetic diversity would not hurt the Leone's chances of survival. Miriam was an exceptionally handsome female, with both her human and Leone forms bestowing a commanding presence upon her. Their males would practically follow in her footsteps when she visited, and competed with their fellows with presents and compliments.

Some of the local females felt threatened by Miriam, but with one or two exceptions, kept their opinions to themselves. The few who had been foolish enough to try to challenge her were left bloodied and beaten in the dust, which only bolstered her reputation and desirability with the clan. It was very clear that she would eventually be the matriarch of whatever clan she finally settled upon, or as near the matriarch as possible.

Our quarters were somewhat away from the main cluster of housing, and we eventually learned that our residence was usually used for Leone who for one reason or another were being excluded from the greater village community. It had no bedrooms, but was a single large room with cooking facilities we did not need lined up along one wall. The floor was hard-packed dirt with a woven mat lying atop it. The living area was festooned with large pillows piled atop a much larger single woven rug in a corner opposite the kitchen area. We could rest amongst the pillows and relax when we so desired.

Vampires do sleep, although we only need an hour or three of sleep at a time, and we adjusted our hours to sleep during the worst of the day's heat. That way, we could be out and about during the night hours, though that wasn't always the case. Well-intentioned humans tended to stay indoors or at least close to home at night, so we were fairly safe in our food choices when we elected to feed in this way.

I've commented in the past about how the human diet flavors the blood I eventually drink. Well, while Europeans had anything from rich to bland blood, the Middle Eastern people upon whom I now fed had blood that was almost spicy, due to the exotic herbs and spices their normal diet contained. It was a very pleasant change from the fatty blood that Americans seemed to have, almost without exception. Things such as this are what keep a blood diet from being anything but monotonous.

On the subject of the flavor of blood, trust me when I tell you that fast food does nothing to improve upon the taste of blood, and when you exist on such a limited diet, variety helps quite a lot. The blood of drug abusers tastes wrong, as well, although it is still usable by vampires.

Eight youngsters went into the mountains during those five years. Three females and five males made the climb. Six came back down again a year later. There was happiness at the return of the previous year's cubs, but a muted sadness that not all were successful.

We never asked what happened with the two cubs that did not, both male. I assumed it may have been something relating to dominance-play gone horribly wrong, but it was not my place to ask for specifics. I do know that male Leone are far more likely to engage in dominance displays that can and do often devolve into combat situations between two or more cubs attempting to establish their place on the clan scrotum pole.

In our third year amongst the Leone, there had been no cubs to celebrate a coming of age ceremony, and that had been a sad and terrible time for the clan. The Leone as a species was in trouble, and I hoped they could find a way to survive. When only about one in every four children born to the Leone is a shapeshifter, something had to be done, though I had no idea how that would happen, unless they became open to more relaxed intermingling with other Leone communities. There would have been only one cub, a female, to make the journey that year, but she had not survived an encounter with a scorpion. Alia had been a nice kid, wanting only the chance to get a western education and eventually come back to be a doctor for her people.

Alia's non-shifting older sister, Abir, was already in the United States learning about genetics. I had no idea how she would translate what she learned to the issues her own people currently experienced, but I was certain that was why she was there in the first place. Their family's only remaining child with a chance of being a shapeshifter was a dark-eyed and very serious little boy called Mukhtar, and would likely go up the mountain in another couple years if his genes were correct. If and when he did shift, unless he did some serious growing in the interim, Mukhtar would be small. Leone did not gain or lose mass when shifting. They were the same weight when appearing human as when they were feline.

Nathaniel and I made ourselves scarce for several days so that the Leone would be able to mourn their youngest daughter's passing in their own way.

WE MOSTLY FED ON THE bandits that roamed the hills and mountains around where we now lived, although when violence in an area was particularly bad, we would relocate for a short time to that area and we would feed well and often. Rare is the human in such a situation who notices more bodies than perhaps there should be, when bullets and explosives are carving large chunks out of your local population. A body is a body in that case, so we were able to feed with near impunity.

During those times, we fed mostly on those who were already dying, as it seemed a waste to allow that blood to become unusable. For now, I drew a line against feeding on children, and in fact would sometimes carry injured children near enough to other humans where they might be rescued and receive medical attention.

If you want to put a cold thought to my seeming altruism, think of it as a farmer saving calves who would otherwise die very young. If you brought them to safety and gave them a chance to survive, they just might eventually grow to full size and feed you some other day. I don't believe that Nathaniel was fooled by my apparent mercy. He knew enough about me to know who and what I am. He just never said anything about it when he saw me do it.

I have never claimed to be a saint. I am a vampire and so I do what I must to continue my existence.

I kept in fairly regular touch with Janos, though it had probably been four months since last I heard from him. Before you start thinking of this as a long time, keep in mind that to a vampire as old as myself, four months is barely the blink of an eye. To an older vampire like Janos, it was even more insignificant, so I didn't want to pester him. Consequently, I tried not to call unless it was absolutely necessary. I didn't want to seem like a needy child, especially as I had not been a child in over four hundred years. It was during one of our most recent conversations that I commented on his foresight in the location he had found for Nathaniel to learn while away from prying eyes.

"We had a fun little number called The Black Plague going on in Europe when I was still a toddler like your Nathaniel, Siofra. I remember well how much easier it is to learn what you are and what your limitations might be when no one's going to be looking askance at another dead body. I did something similar to what you are now doing each time I decided it was time for another child."

"I wish I had known about that earlier, Janos. It might have saved me a few headaches," I told him a bit tartly. "I wouldn't be calling you now for advice."

"Siofra, you of all people should know that vampires tend to be a bit reticent when it comes to personal discussions, and you certainly have never given me any reason to believe that you were even considering extending your family circle. It wasn't my place to say anything about it, although I had always hoped you would do so."

"Maybe that's not the best way for vampires to be, Janos. We're cutting off our own noses when we keep things like that to ourselves," I responded. "You'd think I would have put all of that together, myself, after all these years, but that didn't happen."

"I understand your feelings, Siofra, but what you and I have is not the norm, as far as openness is concerned. It will take those vampires such as yourself to make those kinds of changes, but that will take time and the stubbornness I know you possess in spades. The current vampire council will not be amenable to what you propose, so it may be another couple hundred years until you and your generation can make that happen."

"One thing at a time, my friend, but it's something to think about," I told him. "I have as little to do with the council as possible. They still consider me to be a dangerous aberration."

"I am aware of their feelings on the subject, but I disagree with their reasoning. We, vampires as a species cannot afford to be as coffin-bound as we are at this time. Our elders need to be open to the prospect of change and evolution. Just because we do not change physically does not mean that our society cannot or should not do so."

"You've always been a voice of reason in a sea of chaos, Janos. Why you never took a seat on the council has always puzzled me," I responded.

"I hate politics, my dear. I haven't the time for it."

"You've always been a realist, Janos. I respect you for that," I laughed. "I appreciate all the help you can offer me now, though. If I can avoid on the job training, I think that's a good thing."

"Truly, but for now if you have questions, feel free to give me a call and I will answer them as best as I can," he told me. "I think you would have been wasted if Janos had turned you the proper way and he had the raising of you. I'm glad you were able to raise yourself, child."

"You are sweet, Janos, and I thank you for your kind words. If I had been stuck under Andreas' power, I probably would have ended myself."

After a little light banter, we said our goodbyes and made arrangements for the next "official" call between us.

When the province wasn't being overrun with crazy humans who brought violence and other forms of chaos with them, Nathaniel and I would hunt in the villages at least ten to twenty miles away from where we were staying. It made sense to keep as far away from our hosts as possible.

It was also the polite thing to do. Good guests don't bring the authorities down on their hosts. I'm sure that some etiquette maven has covered the subject at one time or another. Keeping the long arm of the law out of the equation can sometimes get you invited back as well.

Even when it wasn't completely out of hand, violence was a daily occurrence for miles around, so a few more bodies here and there down in the other villages were not going to inspire much additional discussion. With death and destruction everywhere, it was the most appropriate place I could think of where I could let him learn about what he was, with little chance of discovery.

As he was now able to generally keep himself well-fed and as a result more focused, Nathaniel was able to concentrate on learning the tricks of his new race. He was an excellent pupil and learned how to hunt more easily than I had anticipated. I marveled at his ability to scent lone humans and take them out of the picture, quickly, quietly and efficiently. He seemed to be able to pick out particular scents very well, and probably would have given the best-trained hunting dog a real run for his kibble. It made teaching him much easier than it might have been possible.

The few times that someone had happened upon us during one of those initial "training sessions", those humans had become the next part of the lesson: Dealing with Inconvenient Witnesses. I had worried that Nathaniel might balk at the idea of taking an innocent, but there had been no option to let them leave after having witnessed our feeding. I had taken the first such unfortunate, but after that, I had sent him after most of the others. His greater speed usually allowed him to overtake the fleeing humans and kill them before they had the chance to make an outcry.

Janos' time frame was fairly accurate. Perhaps in another twenty to thirty years, we could go back with some measure of safety, but for now, short of something completely unavoidable which forced our return, we would stay away from the United States of America. The world can truly be a small place and one can run into someone they know in the oddest places, so choosing such a remote location was the best way to prevent that from occurring. The relatively low level of technology would also help keep the both of us safe.

There was little chance that anyone would be snapping pictures where we were, and contrary to conventional wisdom, vampires do show up on film, whether it be the old fashioned kind or the virtual film of a digital camera. I'm not really sure where the idea of vampires having no reflection came from, but I know that it would be something that would make my kind's continued survival virtually impossible. How is a vampire who has no reflection supposed to survive in a world with so very many reflective surfaces? Can you answer that question, as I certainly cannot.

Ignoring all of that, once we arrived at our destination, I still had my work cut out for me. It's not as though he would somehow magically be in control of himself with a change of venue. It was simply easier to keep him from running rampant through a community while losing his mind to the bloodlust that every fledgling experiences.

As a fledgling, Nathaniel would not have been safe for any human to be around without another vampire constantly in his company, and that simply was not workable. Also, what would happen when those around him began to age, and he did not? These are the kinds of things a vampire has to consider all the time. In my four hundred plus years, that thought had been the nagging harpy on my shoulder which had kept me moving from place to place every score of years or so.

At little over five years after his turning, Nathaniel was as near an expert hunter as I could possibly hope. He could separate out his prey from a public place or even a group without much difficulty, and could get them into a place where it would be safe for him to feed. For now, we were focusing on a group of anti-government extremists who had been terrorizing one of the small villages near where we had made our home. I had decided that since we had a little more control of what came to our table, we could be a bit more discerning about what ultimately was served.

Nathaniel liked attacking his prey from above, when the opportunity offered itself. I was more of a distraction and surprise kind of hunter. Except when absolutely necessary, I didn't exert myself any more than I must to feed myself.

Nathaniel, on the other hand, would leap from ground to branch to wall as soundlessly as possible. He could have been quite the acrobat before his turning, as he seemed to do it with a practiced ease that was thrilling to behold. Once, when I asked him about his acrobatic talent, he responded that he had always been a bit of a daredevil while he was a child and had never really lost that love of taking chances when he became an adult. It brought to mind the tree climbing of my youth, when I could look down at my world below me, suddenly taller than any other creature, and feel a sense of superiority that I could not when I was a tiny earth-bound human girl-child.

As vampires, Nathaniel and I were different than the other creatures that walked the earth with us, and our strength and abilities gave us an even greater edge than we had while we were still human, climbing trees and rocks to lift us above ourselves.

When Nathaniel felt he was in just the right place, he would leap down upon his prey, knocking them senseless before taking them with him to a safe place where he could feed in relative peace. At first, there had been a few instances where his prey had made enough noise that it drew unwanted attention, but those experiences taught him to be more careful and to render the human unconscious before taking them away.

Sometimes, though, Nathaniel chose to play with his food, and I would chide him for his small cruelties when they became truly excessive. Most times, I could not figure out why he chose to play cat and mouse with his food. For whatever reason, I couldn't bring myself to ask. Other times, however, he would take as his prey a human who had done truly terrible things to his or her own kind, and when that happened, I kept my mouth shut and often would enjoy the show.

In time, we had pretty much been accepted as extended family among this group of Leone. We kept watch over their village when times were tough, and had made quick work of a few bands of brigands who had attempted to invade and numbers were not on the side of the Leone.

We talked long into the night with them at times, helped them hunt and even babysat their little ones for them in a pinch. The Leone do not smell like food, so there was no danger to them from us. We could have been smothered in dozens of Leone children, and beyond perhaps being irritated at the chaos; we would have no desire to even take the smallest taste of one of them.

Our favorite was a precocious boy called Ahmet, so far the only child of Saleh and his mate, a platinum-furred female called Noor. He was funny and a delight to be around. At only eight years of age, he would not be old enough to shift until he hit puberty, which was about five years off, but he would still pretend that he was a big Leone like his older cousin Shiya, who had been named for her maternal grandmother, now deceased. Ahmet was old enough to get choice portions of the community's kills, and after securing his portion, usually chose to eat it at our back door and then would lick his bloody fingers clean.

Yes, you read that right. The Leone often ate their meat bloody raw and generally preferred it that way. They could and would eat cooked meat, but it was never their first choice. It probably lost some of the nutrients that could be found in unadulterated flesh. I'd seen them sometimes marinate raw meat, but they generally didn't use a marinade that would "cook" it, such as vinegar or lemon. The marinades they used were strictly to add flavor to their fare. As I understood it, they were rather fond of spicy foods, so most marinades would have peppers of various strengths added to them to flavor things.

When Ahmet visited, he would relentlessly nag us with questions about what we were and how we were different than the Leone and humans. He was like a sponge and wanted to know everything he possibly could about the odd creatures that lived in his now-deceased grandparents' cottage on the mountain. It helped, I am sure, that those same odd creatures were willing to give him at least an abbreviated version of their lives. He seemed a bit shocked at what he learned of Western culture, but with his parents' permission, we told him everything we could.

"How can these parents allow their daughters out alone without a chaperone?" Ahmet asked one day as we regaled him with stories of western children and the lives they led. "It is dangerous to let girls and women out on their own!"

"Ahmet, I can promise you that things are less dangerous there than they are here. Westerners don't generally kidnap and/or rape random young women out on the street. Things are a bit more socially civilized in the West," Nathaniel reassured him. "Also, the culture there isn't based on religion."

"But everything I hear says that the Americans are religious fanatics," he protested.

"Well, we do have our crazies, but those are the exception, rather than the rule. We've mostly learned to be tolerant of others beliefs and cultures, as long as no one is hurting someone else," I responded. "You'll have to tell me, sometime, where you've learned all this wild stuff about the West."

"We hear this all the time from travelers who visit and preach, but do not stay."

I sighed as understanding hit.

"Ahmet, keep in mind that what you are being told by these people is not always going to be the truth. I would suggest that when you are old enough and have your elders' permission, go to visit the Americans and see for yourself what is and is not the truth. Until then, keep an open mind and remember what I've told you here."

We argued back and forth for a little bit before his mother, concerned that he was spending too much time pestering us, called him home and apologized for his frequent intrusions.

"Noor, it's fine. He is not a problem as we both enjoy spending time with him. It helps the days go by a little more quickly than they otherwise might," I assured her.

Nodding as though in agreement, but apologizing, she backed out of our tiny home and went back to her own, where I was certain Ahmet would be lectured again about bothering us. Of course, he would not listen, and in a few days, she would be back to apologize once more.

Things were fairly idyllic as far as vampires are concerned, for the eight years we ultimately spent amongst both groups of Leone, I experienced a sense of peace and security I had not enjoyed for at least half a century. Sadly, such wonderful times rarely last, and this time was no exception. However, when things became horrific, due to the sheer level of violence, it marked the start of another kind of education for Nathaniel that I could not ignore.

Nine

Probably no one but his closest friends and family knew this particular human's name, but I doubt he had many close friends. People such as he rarely did, with the kind of paranoia they generally would exhibit. They were normally incapable of feeling that level of trust with another human being.

From what we had been able to gleam from talking with those victims who survived and from listening in on conversations between the humans, he was about six feet tall, skinny as a rail, with a thick dark beard, pallid skin and wild dark eyes. He covered himself from head to toe in loose-fitting black clothing and often when he spoke, spittle sprayed out from his mouth to cover his unfortunate audience.

His followers were those who embraced violence and were convinced of the righteousness of their actions, even if those actions resulted in the deaths of those to whom they preached who refused to accept their words and edicts. Ninety-nine percent of those followers were male and those who did follow and believe him did so unquestioningly, from what I had been able to discover.

Stories had been told of his harem which consisted of at least a dozen women, most stolen from villages he had raided. No one knew where they were hidden away, but local rumor had it that he had sired at least three dozen children from them. The women ranged in age from as young as twelve to at least twenty nine, and it seemed nearly every village had lost at least one daughter to his marauders. His chief wife, a Jordanian woman called Sarahi, was said to rule her husband's harem with an iron fist, tolerating nothing that might show thought or individuality amongst those wives. It was said that she was in her forties, but that for whatever reason, her husband held her far above his other wives with his regard.

According those with whom we spoke, he took a few of the most promising and beautiful women when he came to raid, killing most if not all of the males of each village. Only those men who had the relative good fortune to be away when he came calling, though obviously through no design of his own.

He was one of those "true believers" who seem to think that their brand of god, be it religious or political, blessed whatever atrocities were performed upon the innocent. That he did this in the name of Faith sickened me. While I was not much of a person of strong political or religious affiliation at this time, I still knew and loathed it when I saw it.

Those who challenged his beliefs, even obliquely, were made into examples for other people and villages. The people who were fortunate enough to survive one of his visits followed him out of sheer terror. They rightly feared that he might slaughter their friends and family if they did not do as they were told.

Women were expected to encase themselves from the tops of their heads to the tips of their toes in voluminous burqas while out in the open, though it was decreed that ideally, women should be shuttered away where they would not interact with the rest of the world. In his myopic view, men ruled the world and women were little more than bed warmers and walking incubators. In fact, several schools in the area that taught girls had been burned to the ground, and their teachers had been murdered to establish this point. He felt that education was wasted upon women who would never actually use an education, if they lived as he decreed.

He had his religious police periodically visit local villages to conduct so-called "virginity tests" upon the local unmarried women to be sure they were leading "pure" lives. Never mind that something as relatively gentle as a fall, or even horseback riding could tear a hymen, making it appear as though a young woman was no longer virginal. Those poor women and girls who ostensibly "failed" were murdered on the spot.

The families of those so murdered could do little more than stand back and watch, lest they be murdered as well. It was proclaimed by the invaders that this was something the Divine ordered, giving it some semblance of legitimacy in the eyes of those who perpetrated this atrocity. Perhaps they believed this was true. The human leader was very charismatic and able to talk people into believing and then behaving as he bade.

Not for the first time in my long existence, I wondered how a loving god could possibly demand the horrors this man and those acting in his name visited upon those who disagreed with him? Try as I might, I could find no validation to justify his actions or to find the peace that would allow me to ignore what he had done and would continue to do. It wasn't as though he was forced to kill in order to survive, so I had already decided that he had to die.

People in several villages from miles around called him "Death", as whenever he entered a village, he left behind death and destruction. His all-male gang of thugs embraced his cruel nature and displayed their own cruelties in the way they raped women, cut the fetuses out of obviously pregnant (and still living) women, leaving those women to die and slaughtering their innocent children. We had come across the results of one of Death's raids only a few days before.

It had been a very long time since the last time I had seen something so very awful. We could smell it long before we arrived, but we were unable to ignore it. If it had been silent, we might have been able to move on; however, the sounds of wailing carried on the breeze and let us know that humans still lived there.

We waited until it was dark enough that our comings and goings could be ignored, and then we moved through the village using their walls and rooftops as our road. The spectacle that met my eyes was horrific to behold.

Pale faced, slack-jawed women stood, crouched or lay on the ground, too shocked to even speak. Blood was everywhere, and the small limbs of their loved ones were strewn about the ground, flies and ants gorging on the gruesomely butchered remains that had already created such a stench that had we not been able to do without breathing, we might have fled, ourselves.

A few women cried, some rocked and moaned, while others appeared to have gone completely beyond the power of speech or even sound. I am certain that in some small part of their minds, there was now a new terror that perhaps they now carried the babies of those who had destroyed their families, and that would be a terrible thing to have to endure. It seemed that no girl child below the age of ten had been left alive by the marauders. Perhaps they had been deemed inconvenient.

"Why has Death come among us?" cried one woman who clutched a bloody blanket to her chest. At first, I thought she held the blanket to mop up her own blood, but then I saw a small pale arm dangling limply from the folds of the thing and knew the truth. "What could this little one have done to so anger Allah that he had to die?"

I had to hold Nathaniel back from going to the women when first we realized what had occurred. He was so angry that he had lost control of himself and his fangs had descended. This was not the best way to make a good impression on women who had recently been terrorized. The combination of hunger and fury that he felt was strong enough that I could catch the edges of it in my own mind. There was a familiar flavor to what I was feeling from him, so I had a pretty good idea of what he was thinking

We had had many conversations over the years about humans putting responsibility for the bad things that happened to them on some supreme being. If, in fact, such an entity existed he or she probably did not appreciate getting blamed for the tragedies that peppered the lives of humanity. Nathaniel had not been a religious person before I had brought him over, being more of a secular humanist.

Is it possible to be a secular vampirist? I think that might be an excellent topic of discussion sometime, don't you?

I knew that Nathaniel had only the best intentions in wanting to give them solace, but we needed to remain as incognito as possible, so showing our faces was not an option. We would investigate, find out exactly what had happened, and do our work from there.

Knowing that to waste an opportunity would be incredibly stupid, we made our way around the town until we found humans near death, but not quite dead yet and fed from them. I had taught Nathaniel that to waste the blood would be stupid, and stupidity could not be tolerated.

The man I found had his eyes open and I saw them follow me as I approached. They were wide and frightened, and I did my best to console him, even as I knew he was probably terrified at the sight of a barefaced woman, a stranger, approaching him. At least the scarf I had wrapped around my hair kept me from being entirely scandalous in his eyes.

"Be at peace, sir. I will help you on your way to Paradise," I told him softly, and cradled him in my arms, kissing him lightly and chastely on the forehead. "I promise that I will seek vengeance for what has happened to you, your sons, wives and daughters. Those who did this will not long poison this world."

"Who...?" he managed. "Are you one of the houri come from Paradise to see me on my way?"

"I am no houri, but you may consider me a kind of friend who will help you to get there."

His heartbeat was weak, and his voice very soft, nearly a whisper, but he fought his approaching end to get out his next words to me.

"Death's minions came to our village and killed so very many of us before they left. I crawled away before they could take my head," he said. "I had no desire to become another of his trophies, even if it would have taken me to Paradise much more quickly."

"I wish that I had been here sooner, that I might have kept so much of this from happening," I replied. "Rest assured that I will hunt him down and send him to Hell, itself."

"You are a woman. How can you expect to destroy the plague that is Death and his followers?"

"I am more than a simple human woman, and I swear to you that I will do as I say. He will never see Paradise." I saw the faintest curve of a smile form at the edges of his lips. "Such as he should never be allowed to taste the delights of the afterlife."

"Whatever you are, if you can make that a certainty, I can die happy," he told me. "Thank you. May Allah bless you."

I could see his eyes beginning to glaze over as he finally allowed himself to let go and shock set in. It would not be long before he became delirious from blood loss. He might even think he was imagining my presence, as he did not appear to be offended by my barehanded touching of his body.

"I am not human, and must feed. You are dying already, so I will feed from you. However, I will keep my end of the bargain in this gift of your blood," I told him, and then bit him as gently as I could, drinking in his salty, spicy blood. He had been terrorized enough and I had no desire to add to it.

What? Do you want to make something of it? I dare you!

Oddly enough, the human did not fight me; he merely relaxed into my grip and sighed deeply as he descended into unconsciousness. The man had seemed to accept his fate. Perhaps the promise of the end of the one called Death had something to do with that.

I stopped drinking just before his heart ceased to beat, and then laid him on the ground once more, wadding up a nearby piece of cloth to rest his head upon. I crossed his arms over his chest and then stood, looking down at his cooling body.

"Be at peace and may Allah be with you," I told him sincerely. "You and your family will be avenged. This I promise."

Then I went in search of Nathaniel. We had split up, as he wanted to hunt in his own way, versus my own, more direct fashion. As long as he found prey and fed successfully, I was fine with whatever he wanted to do.

I found him in an alleyway, where he had cornered someone who appeared to be one of Death's henchmen. I climbed to a convenient rooftop to watch the show and not disturb him, though I knew he was aware of my presence. While our emotional connection had nearly faded away entirely, our sense of smell and our hearing are usually good enough to keep us aware of our surroundings.

It wasn't looking good for the human, and I could see why he had not made good his escape from the village after the butchery. Nathaniel was having more than a little fun with the human, letting him think he could finally escape, but then closing the avenue just as the human thought he was home free. There is no way the human could have thought he even stood a chance of escaping, as Nathaniel, who was covered in blood that was not his own, darted forward to block the human each time he thought he had an avenue of escape.

My offspring had been busier than I had thought while I was seeing to my own needs. I didn't know how many he had killed during my absence, but it was clearly more than two other humans, just from the sheer amount of blood that caked his face and clothing. I knew it would be more difficult for him, once we rejoined the greater part of civilization, but we could not live the vagabond life forever. It just doesn't work very well in this day and age.

The human had a deep wound in his gut, and I could see his large intestine poking through the thick skin of his abdomen. Dirt, sand and lint had already made their way into the wound, dirtying it and opening the entire area to certain infection. Without professional medical care, he wouldn't survive his wound, but that was not going to be a possibility for this one anyway.

The human had not lost much blood, but the damage to his intestines was too great. He eventually would have died of peritonitis from the damage done to his guts if my child had not found him first. It would have been a waste of a good meal, and Nathaniel was a thrifty sort.

"Well, you piece of shit, I guess you're not going to get away," Nathaniel told the human in his own language. "Someone got in a good swipe at you before you killed them! Good for them!"

"Death will find you! Allah will keep you from entering Paradise, you infidel!" cried the thug hoarsely. He held a hand to the open wound, as though doing so would make any difference at this point. "Paradise and seventy-sex houri are awaiting me!"

"Oh no, I have something for you," Nathaniel said, and pulled a dripping human tongue from the small bag at his waist and showed it to the human. "I'm going to make you eat this before you die."

The human looked as though he was about to be sick. I wondered what had inspired Nathaniel to do such a thing. I'd never seen him do something like that before.

"It does not matter the tortures to which you subject me," he declared. "I will tell you nothing!"

"Torture you? Question you? I believe you mistake my intent," Nathaniel said softly in the human's own language, and then smiled, showing the blustering human his fangs. "I plan to eat you. Allah's not happy with you, my boy, no, not at all. So I've come here to deliver appropriate chastisement."

The human gagged and then tried to run away, but for some reason, he couldn't get any forward momentum to accomplish the action. I stood back and watched as Nathaniel leaped forward and grabbed one of the human's arms. He twirled him as someone might twirl their partner on a dance floor, the gentleness and grace of the movement at odds with the violence that would happen shortly.

At the end of the spin, Nathaniel held him close to his chest, the human's back flat against Nathaniel's front. The vampire leaned his face down and laid his cheek against the human's, smiling happily. He ran his tongue along the human's cheek, and crooned his anticipation of the feast to come.

The feeling of Nathaniel's cool, clammy flesh against his own warm skin seemed to throw the human over the edge and rid him of the last of his bravado. I caught the sharp tang of urine as the human lost control of himself.

The human monster was now babbling incoherently as Nathaniel pulled him even closer, almost gently pushing the man's head to one side in order to expose the tender throat. Nathaniel ran a finger along the skin that was directly over the carotid artery, wiping away the man's nervous sweat in the process. It was certainly theatric, which helped to increase the human's tension further. The sound of the human's pounding heart thrummed in my ears, even from several yards away.

"Blood..." Nathaniel said to no one in particular, and then struck, making a smallish hole in the human's throat and sucking there like a famished infant. He could have very easily made a much larger hole, but apparently felt that he wanted to drag things out as much as possible.

His eyes glowed as he gulped down the human's blood, but instead of being out of control as he had been during his first feeding,

Nathaniel was in complete control of himself. As he settled into the feeding, his eyes took on the abstracted appearance of a very young child nursing, thinking far away thoughts, lost in the surfeit of pleasure that feeding can give a vampire.

Nathaniel would eat his fill tonight, the lucky boy. He had certainly made an excellent start of it with his earlier kills.

The human initially tried to fight, but then fainted from terror before too long. Nathaniel did everything but hold the human upside down to get as much blood as he could out of the body. It was a trick I'd shown him long ago to use when a human was near death, but you wanted to drink as much of the blood as possible before the human died and the blood that remained became unusable. His skin was tight because of all the blood he had ingested, and he cannot have been very comfortable that way, but I knew that it was not in him to just leave it alone.

When the human had all but died, Nathaniel pulled the unknown human's tongue from his pouch and shoved it into the terrorist's sagging mouth. The local inhabitants would get the message when they saw it, and that was the message we wanted to convey. It did not matter that they would see a gaping hole in his neck. Let the villagers think of it what they would.

I could feel Nathaniel's pent-up fury as it continued to build, though he said nothing to me about it. I wondered how long it would take him to do so, and what form that explosion would finally take.

It developed that I did not have long to wait, in that regard.

"I want to tear his arms and legs off, one by one!" he shouted in our small hideaway up in the mountains, the only place he could safely vent his rage. There was not one human ear to hear him within a twenty mile radius. "It's bad enough that they are killing off the local humans, but it's not that far between there and here. From what you've said about the Leone, there aren't many of them left. I don't want to lose any of them when we can help to keep it from happening!"

"I know, Nathaniel. We've done what we can here," I responded. "We need to deal with what is going on as it affects the humans. If nothing else, we must protect them as they are part of our food supply."

Once upon a time, such a statement from me might have brought sounds of protest from my offspring, but now he simply took it in stride. This was one of the reasons that raising him away from large population centers had been a good thing.

Okay, Siofra," he said. "As long as we have the chance to make all of this end. It's not that far a step for them to come here and slaughter the Leone and their sweet cubs. Imagine what they would do to the Leone if they got hold of them. I guarantee they wouldn't kill them immediately if they knew what they were and what they were capable of doing. At the least, they would torture them, all of them. Even the children."

Just thinking about the Leone cubs in that way made me feel ill, and knowing that Ahmet was only a year or two from his first shifting made it all the more difficult. Over the years, Noor had finally understood that her son was fascinated by us, but also realized that we were not trying to take him from her, either. Both Nathaniel and I tutored him the best we could and gave him as much information as we could on western societies.

At the age of eleven, Ahmet had announced to all who would listen that he planned to take part of the clan with him to the Americas, where he would establish another branch of the Leone. Chuckles had sounded until one or two of the young girls had risen to indicate their intent to go with him, as well as a few of the young males. Then, adult eyes had widened and the elders began to consider Ahmet in a different light.

Knowing that he and his potential clan had a chance of surviving if they established in the United States, Nathaniel and I were a bit happier, but Ahmet's own decision would not protect the rest of the clan who chose to stay behind.

We had told the Leone about what we had seen of this latest terrorist and our suspicions as to the Leone's probable future if things were left as they were. Now our hosts were discussing what they should do, in the event Death and his cohorts paid them a personal visit. We had not been invited to participate, and I could not blame them for exclusion, as we were not "family".

"Thank you for this information, Siofra. We must confer and decide if this danger threatens us here as well," I was told and then they left us alone. Leone villages were fairly mobile affairs, as they had essentially been nomads for most of their existence, but unless one absolutely had to move again, it was always good to avoid such a situation.

I did what I could to help pave the way for Ahmet and those who wanted to emigrate with him. Janos, always seemed willing to lend a hand, and gave them the run of several thousand acres of property he owned through a proxy. It was large enough to give them privacy, but still relatively close enough to civilization to allow them to attend school and learn more about their new land. Janos told me that he had not been doing much with the property anyway, so it would be good for it to have resident caretakers.

His story could have been bullshit. Janos wasn't above that when it suited him, but when he did bullshit, it was for all the right reasons. A lot of vampires might have listened to what we said and then ultimately decided that it did not concern them, leaving the Leone to die. Janos had never, in all the time I had known him, been that kind of vampire.

Nathaniel and I had decided that we could not remain in the village, pretending that this did not concern us and just allow these terrible things happen to people about whom we cared deeply. We had to do something. The Leone were too rare a species for us to allow them to be exterminated, and the humans in the area should not be terrorized or at the worst, murdered, for not following the wishes of barbarians who seemed to feel they had all the answers.

This was not something we could ignore and allow the human authorities to resolve, as they could not be relied upon to handle it correctly. Even a cattle rancher goes after the predators who threaten her herd.

We said our goodbyes to our hosts, and were engulfed in embraces and well wishes. I think they would have pressed food upon us if they had not known such things would be useless. As it was, the Clan mother forced us to take some sweets with us for the human children. The package appeared to contain dried, sugared fruits and nuts. I'm sure they would be delicious if I were still human, and I actually felt a slight pang of jealousy that I would never know what baklava tasted like.

"When things are rough, sometimes sweets will help to ease a child's pain," I was told. "I would assume that human children are like Leone cubs in this way. Be sure they are put into the correct hands."

"Of course, Clan mother. Thank you for your thoughtfulness," I replied and meant it.

"It is everyone's duty to look out for the young," she said firmly as she enfolded me in a final hug. I believe she thought of me as being young because of my eternally youthful appearance, but I was circumspect enough to avoid bringing the truth of things to her attention. "Take care, my dear. You are always welcome amongst us, should you pass our way again."

"And you, Clan mother."

Ten

It was taking quite some time to locate Death. This wasn't one of those things that are of little moment and are resolved before you know it. This was someone who had been around for awhile, and who had learned how to hide very well. Maybe the Leone would have been of assistance in helping us to find him, but I refused to place them in that kind of danger.

While vampires have enhanced abilities, we are not magicians and can't pull the answers out of the air. This was something that was going to take a lot of thought and careful investigation before it finally came to a conclusion, and hopefully the one we sought.

With each village we visited, we took the time to clean out the extremists before we left. It might take a day or two for us to do it, but we wanted eliminate them as anonymously as possible, cutting them out of the community, root and branch. Also, we did not want anyone following along and setting up some kind of unfortunate ambush. Remember: even vampires can be hurt or even ended if we're not careful.

Death was a slippery son of a bitch, we learned that in a big hurry. We very soon were calling him "the Weasel", as he always managed to slip out of our grasp, just when we thought we'd caught a break.

Just because someone is a warlord, it does not mean that he's going to be at all easy to find. Rumors and complete fabrications only helped to muddy the waters that much more. Most of the misdirection was probably deliberate obfuscation on the part of those locals who were either afraid of him and what he might do to them or their loved ones if they revealed too much or those who actually followed his twisted version of the majority theology and wanted him alive and free to continue his reign of terror. Threatening to kill someone if they do not tell the truth doesn't mean anything when the person being interrogated believes that they will go to heaven if they die a martyr.

Sometimes, "true believers" really suck. No pun intended, this time, I promise.

We didn't take the time to interrogate all the humans we hunted. It all depended on how high up they appeared to be in the main organization. The rank and file members were usually dispensed with quickly. The ruling cadre, however, were granted a certain amount of very special attention.

More often than not, our encounters with the Weasel's capos ran along these lines:

Me (or Nathaniel): "Where is Death? Tell us now and I might let you die cleanly. Tell me where he is now, before I lose my patience."

Extremist: "You do not belong here! You are infidels! You will all die!"

Me: "Let's not talk about what's going to happen to us, let's talk about you. How long do you think I'm going to keep putting up with your blustering bullshit? It's only going to make me that much angrier and unpleasant with you. Where is he?"

Extremist: "You will die! You will all die!"

Me: "I've about had enough of this, junior. Give me answers and I'll kill you quickly. Try my patience further and I'll make sure you take a long time to die."

Extremist: "I will kill you myself! Allah will grant me the strength to kill you!"

Me: "Junior, you're too late. I've been dead now for a long time. Your threats mean nothing to me. Tell me where I can find Death and this will stop."

Extremist: "Are you deranged? You aren't dead. You are as alive as I am, although not for long, I promise you!"

That was the point when I'd smile at the stinking little prick and allow him to see my fangs. My teeth were always so beautifully sharp and colored a flawless ivory. It wasn't as though he would live to tell anyone about them, anyway.

Extremist: "<incoherent screaming and maybe even pissing himself a bit>"

Any further conversation tended to get a bit garbled at that point and usually I couldn't get much more out of the human before I finally gave up, lost my temper and killed him. Living as long as I have hasn't necessarily made me a more patient person, sad to say.

A few became a bit more talkative once I'd started their blood flowing, but so far, the information they provided has been less than helpful. The one of us who wasn't having fun with the human would jot down any pertinent information that slipped out before too much blood loss made the mouthpiece unable to continue.

Funny how they believed they'd go free once the feeding had started. The only freedom they would have was when they finally passed beyond the Veil. Until that time, they were mine to do with as I pleased.

Using these tactics, we would chase one rumor of the Weasel's current location only to find that either he had never been there at all, or that we had missed him by mere days or weeks. His minions had obviously been well-trained in misdirection and obfuscation. It frustrated the both of us and probably made us even more cruel than we might have been when we fed from his underlings. There were times when I would let the screaming go on much longer than was necessary before I allowed my prey to die. I could always enjoy a nice drink by merely sipping it. I didn't need to gulp it all down at once.

I'd learned that with one of my very first feedings some four hundred years earlier, and I had never forgotten how pleasant that could be, sometimes. Feeding isn't always about getting it all over with as quickly as possible. Just as humans will linger over a fine meal, even a vampire can savor her meal.

It was Nathaniel's idea to behead our prey and leave their disembodied heads speared atop sticks and poles, while their bloodless bodies could be found in piled nearby. This was not something we were keeping secret, as we wanted the locals who were being terrorized to know that someone was out there trying to make things right. Our hope was that eventually they would become brave enough to come forward and out the Weasel. What must they have thought about the nearly bloodless bodies that were left behind? Surely they could not even be coming close to guessing the truth.

"This son of a bitch is crafty and I'm starting to become a bit cranky about the whole thing. I can't understand why it's been so hard to find him," I said one night as Nathaniel and I left our latest dead end. The marks of tire treads were still fairly crisp on the unpaved road, so it could not have been that long since the Weasel left this place. The depth of the tread marks pointed to the fact that the Weasel's vehicles were heavily laden, but we had no idea with what. "He has to be getting reports that those of his people that he leaves behind are dying violently. You'd think he'd be looking for us at this point and make all of this a lot easier."

"Should we make ourselves known? Give the human somewhere to look for us?" Nathaniel wondered. It was a logical thought, but it wouldn't work well at all. He was young and had not been the target of a hunt, as I once had been.

"That's probably not the best idea. If we let him know where we are, he might send in more forces than even we could safely handle, and I'm not ready to be ended just yet," I told him. "It's obvious, even with questioning, that his people don't know where he is at any given time or that some believe that if they died without telling us that they will go immediately to heaven, do not pass Go, et cetera.

I suspect that's also being done deliberately to keep him safe from people like us. We certainly can't be the only ones who want to find him."

And we weren't.

We had overheard discussions amongst the villagers in many areas that American and British forces were searching for him as well, but I really wanted to be the one to find the bastard and end him. I wanted to be certain it had been done and that there was no way someone could pretend he was still around.

I did not want any government to be able to use him for their own political devices, as I knew they would if they had the opportunity. No open-ended detention or opportunities for political machinations and grandstanding by those wanting to make a name for themselves. This was about ending senseless violence, not creating opportunities for power and profit.

I knew that American Special Forces were being used to track the man called Death, but also knew they had had no luck in their search. The Brits, well, I'm not exactly sure what they were doing, only that it wasn't very effective in finding out anything meaningful. I suspected that Nathaniel and I had more recent information, such as it was, if only because we were willing to take things as far as they needed to go to get that information. Plus, we had options and abilities open to us that our competition did not possess.

"I'm thinking we need to start checking the caves in the next province over. So far, it seems that we've been deliberately directed away from natural concealment and toward civilization. It's only logical to now do the exact opposite and see if we can get anything from there," I said one day. "He probably does know that he's being looked for by more than international forces, and so that may drive him to ground. Let's get our shit together and get moving. For now, it's probably best that we travel by night. I don't want to have to climb up or over anything while fully shrouded in a burqa."

"No, they don't really help to show off your best features," Nathaniel grinned. He couldn't help himself, I guess. I couldn't, either.

I actually hit him hard enough to knock him on his ass. It felt good. Well, for me, anyway.

We were roughing it, since we traveled just about every day in our search. Our valuables were tucked away in a safe place until we could retrieve them. Laptops and the like weren't necessary at the moment. Fortunately, it hadn't taken much arguing on my part to make Nathaniel understand that.

Initially, I had thought about getting either a vehicle or animals for transportation, but it was easier to travel quickly on foot, while an animal could go lame on some of the terrain we had to traverse. Plus, I did not want to have to worry about the care and feeding of a horse or camel, especially one that might react very badly to the idea of a vampire on its back for any length of time. Most would go to any lengths to dislodge a vampire, actually. I had only known a few exceptions to that rule, and most of those animals had been raised by and for vampires. It was simply safer that way for one and all, as trying to maintain controls of a wildly plunging animal could be difficult, even for one with enhanced abilities.

Let me take a moment to say something about traveling at night.

You people in more civilized and populated areas generally have it easy and probably don't even realize how lucky you are. There was a very good reason why most people in non-industrial countries woke and slept with the rise and fall of the sun. A simple candle or oil lantern really doesn't provide enough light to do much after the sun goes down. Motion pictures, television and dramatic license to the contrary, moving around at night, even with the Moon hanging high in the sky often does not offer enough light to allow one to see where one is going.

You probably don't realize how dark things can be at night until there are no longer even peripheral lights around. Streetlights, ambient light from homes, traffic lights and the like provide an amazing amount of light to see what is around, believe it or not. For a human, without an external light source, it was virtually impossible to see even half a foot in front of them.

Vampires, fortunately, do not simply rely on sight to locate prey. I even used to be acquainted with a blind vampire who was a very successful hunter. Some other predators are the same as we in that way, and that is why so many predators choose to hunt at night, when they have the advantage against those who rely on their sight so very much.

Because of our unique situation, we can both smell *and* hear our prey, and most of us seem to learn this very early on. While humans creeping through the arid landscape might move at a painfully slow pace, we vampires are able to move at a reasonable speed and hunt at the same time. It gives us quite the advantage, especially when a human tries to hide from the inevitable. Only rarely are we taken by surprise, and then usually because our attention is focused elsewhere.

Perhaps an awareness of those mortal limitations caused the Weasel's compatriots to keep light to a minimum when they were on the move or camped for the night. The last thing they wanted to do was to draw attention to themselves. I will admit that it was much easier to hunt when someone pulled out a penlight or we encountered the glow of a campfire that had not been properly banked, but overall, unless we were inside or near a village, the anonymity of the blanketing darkness kept both us and our prey hidden from sight.

It became a kind of game between us to not only find encampments, but also to determine by sound and scent alone, the number and make-up of those encampments. At first, I was the winner of most of these impromptu contests, but as time went on,

Nathaniel's senses improved and he started giving me a run for my money.

Rather than being upset by this turn of events, I was very pleased at Nathaniel's success. These were lessons he would need to learn in order to survive as a vampire. Even though we had a specific target right now, overall, this was a wonderful opportunity in which he could hone new skills.

I lost count of the number of caves we searched. Some had been deserted for months, years or perhaps centuries, but for those that boasted human life, beyond a few refugees hidden in their depths, we encountered no extremists. We left the refugees in peace, as for now, we were eating fairly well and often as we culled the refuse from the human herd. In most cases, the refugees never knew of our passing.

Once or twice we discovered these bands of refugees as they were being attacked, and we would make quick work of the attackers. I thought we had been successful in avoiding the notice of the refugees as we did our deadly work, but later heard through the grapevine that there was talk of some kind of djinn who were decimating the extremists and protecting the weak.

Well, we certainly weren't djinn, but that was a better explanation than the humans knowing what we really were. Word had to have reached the Weasel about this new mystery, and it wouldn't be all that long before he was forced to step in and investigate whatever it was that seemed to take such joy in destroying his followers.

By now, I was beginning to wonder if the Weasel was hiding in plain sight, as it were, protected by an existing community. However, there was no way that he would continue to evade us, and that kept me from losing heart. No human could hide from a truly determined vampire for very long.

We vampires have all the time in the world, after all.

Eleven

"I think it's time we started searching the villages themselves, Siofra," Nathaniel said one morning as we prepared to rest for the day in the back of a very small cave. From what I could see and smell, there had not been a human anywhere inside in a long enough time that there was no residual aroma or other evidence of their presence, so I felt fairly secure in staying the day here. "I think someone is actually helping him to hide. Kind of hard to believe, considering what he's done to the people who live in this country. You'd think they would do everything they could to get rid of him."

"Both humans and vampires are prone to making stupid decisions, Nathaniel. They could be trying to curry favor with him and his followers. That's a common theme with people who collaborate with dictators and terrorists. They don't seem to see that it puts them right in the same monstrosity column with the people they aid and abet."

We had spent the past four months searching for Death with no substantial leads, and a growing sense of impatience. It pissed me off to think that someone would willingly shelter someone capable of such horrific violence, but it did not particularly surprise me. Humans, I had found over the centuries, can justify just about anything, as long as a fat payout is part of the bargain. Hard currency seemed an effective crowbar to work past potential reluctance, and once the payout is accepted, the recipient has put him or herself right into the clutches of the payer.

Whether the one handing out the rewards is of terrestrial or supernatural origin, you've made a deal with the devil, and there indeed will be hell to pay. And speaking of paying...

"We need to be following the money, Nathaniel," I decided. "I'll get in touch with someone I know and maybe we can ferret out that information. He's got deeper connections than most anyone else I know."

I pulled my precious satellite phone from my pack and dialed a certain number. It was only a few seconds before the call was answered.

"To what do I owe the honor of this call, child," Janos purred. "It's been a few months since last I heard from you."

I read Janos in on what we were doing and what I needed to know from him.

"*Must* you involve yourselves in the affairs of humans? They are capable of caring for themselves, you know," he chided me. "They can resolve their own issues on their own, for the most part."

"I might agree with you, Janos, but this motherfucker's range is getting wider and he's on the verge of endangering the Leone. There are few enough of them left without losing the entire species to human idiocy."

"You have a point, I suppose. I tend to forget that we are not the only sparse species out there in the world," he conceded. I bit my tongue to keep from reminding him that he'd set us up with the Leone when we had needed a place to stay when we'd left the States. Does testosterone survive the change from human male to vampire male? I wondered if anyone had ever researched that little detail. No, probably not. "Why did you not call me at the start? I could have saved you a lot of footwork and blind tunnels."

"You're right, Janos. I feel like an idiot for not thinking about a paper trail first. On the other hand, we've eaten very well and have thinned out his network fairly well in the course of our search."

"Your trouble, dearest Siofra, is that you like to do things on your own, since you have gotten used to your life being that way. I have told you time and time again that it doesn't have to be that way, but you choose to ignore me when I tell you that."

"I don't want to be a part of a –"

"No, Siofra, I'm not talking about your joining a kiss. I know that's not the way you are comfortable. What I am saying, however, is that you do not have to keep to your own devices when you need help with something. I'm always happy to help."

I mumbled an apology, ashamed that I'd jumped to a conclusion when I should have known better. In some ways, Janos knew me better than I knew myself. I think that in some ways, I was an unofficial member of his own kiss, although neither of us had ever suggested that idea aloud.

"Anyhow, Janos, I need you to get back to me with whatever information you have as soon as possible. Last I heard, the Americans and British were both on the verge of sending in their own forces to find and capture him. I don't want that. I want him dead."

"So I gather, Siofra. I'll let you know as soon as I know anything. Please give my best to your Nathaniel," he told me, and then hung up. I wasn't offended, as I knew Janos would even now be setting the ball rolling on finding out everything he possibly could. In all the time I had known him, he'd never been one to dilly-dally and I liked that.

I put the phone away before I filled Nathaniel in on everything.

"We can keep looking for now, but it may be a waste of time. What do you think? Should we hole up and wait on him or...?" I let my voice trail off and just looked at him.

He appeared to consider it for a bit before he responded. That was something I really appreciated about him. He had the kind of maturity where he would think about something before saying anything.

"Well, as much as I want to find this bastard and wipe the earth with him, it's probably better that we wait. No sense in expending energy senselessly, I suppose," he shrugged. "I'm not hungry right now, anyway, so feeding's not something currently on my radar."

So that night, having decided to take a break, we went into the uninhabited areas and raced the wildlife that would try to outrace us if they could. It was fun, relaxing and brought us back to our basic predator selves. We weren't going to kill any of the creatures we hunted that night, but they didn't know that, so they gave us a merry chase before we caught them and then after a short time to count coup, turned them loose once more.

When we tired of our games, a low cave gave us a good place to rest for until we heard from Janos. It lacked any scent of humans, so it seemed a reasonably safe place for us to remain for now. I put the satellite phone on a very low ring and set it in a place where it could pick up signal. Even with the sound turned very low, I would still be able to hear it ring when Janos called with whatever information he could glean from his many sources.

The call came about midday the next day, and I leapt to the phone before the first ring had died away.

"Yes? What have you found out?" I demanded without even a polite greeting.

"And a big hello to you, too, Siofra," Janos replied. He sounded a little irritated at me, and I couldn't blame him for it. I'm sure I wasn't the easiest vampire in the world for whom to do research. When I'd still been directly running my business in Los Angeles, I went through employees like some human kids go through boxes of sugar cereal. No, I wouldn't eat them. I'd just make them decide to quit and go to work for someone a little calmer than I. "I would hate to think you've been sitting around, waiting for my call. I still don't understand why you feel you need to interfere in this mess."

"It doesn't make much sense to keep wandering around the country like idiots when you might be able to find more concrete information for us," I retorted. He made a sound of acquiescence.

The irritability was gone, replaced with something that appeared to be closer to resignation. Janos knew I wouldn't leave this alone. "It was the only thing we hadn't yet done to try to find him."

"Indeed. I suppose that makes sense. Anyhow, using the information you provided as a way to narrow things down, I have found that a fairly large influx of money has been pouring into a local hamlet about forty miles from where you indicated you are at this time. Things seem to be fairly hush-hush about the whole thing, but someone was all too happy to do me a favor and give me the information I sought."

"Where is this place?" I asked, and wrote down everything he told me in great detail, having him repeat even the most minute details. He was right. It wasn't too terribly far away, and while the Weasel might not be there right now, he or his henchmen would likely come by in the near future for provisions. When that happened, we could either follow them back, or we could use more entertaining methods of extracting the information we needed. "Thank you, Janos. I should have called you before about all of this. It might have ended much sooner."

"Actually, Siofra, it is probably better that it happened this way. You are in a fairly large country, and in your search, you have narrowed the playing field quite effectively," he told me. "Now go and find this "Death" person, kill him and get on with your and Nathaniel's lives. A vampire's life is meant for so much more than what you are doing right now."

"Thank you for everything, Janos. I'll give you a call once we've resolved this and let you know how we're doing. I'm hoping we can get him alone and take him out that way. I think we've already taken a large chunk out of his manpower, so he can't be ignoring what's going on."

"Well, keep your eyes and ears open, child. He may decide that he's not going to wait for you to find him and create a surprise for the both of you," Janos chided me like a concerned grandfather. "I don't want to find myself mourning you."

I thanked him and hung up, taking a moment to savor his words and the warm feelings they created in me. The idea of someone actually mourning my ending was something I had not really considered in a few hundred years, and it brought up feelings I thought I'd tucked away forever.

"I'd miss you, too, Janos," I thought in silent reply. "I'd miss you, too."

Twelve

It was another two weeks before we eventually tracked the Weasel down to the semi-remote village in which he had holed up. He had to know that he was surrounded, and that whatever final battle he was forced to have probably would not end at all well for him. I felt exuberance that an end was finally in sight and that we would soon be looking out for just ourselves once more.

The information Janos had supplied was excellent, although there were a few hiccups along the way. There were about three villages that fit the description he had given me, and we had to be absolutely sure of ourselves before we acted irrevocably. That required careful surveillance and the determination that there was absolutely no chance we were mistaken.

The first village took us the longest to eliminate as a candidate, as it was peopled with several males who fancied themselves to be the next big thing in martyrdom. While annoying, it slowly became obvious that these men were no threat to their neighbors much less the rest of the world, so, with the exception of one or two excisions, we left the village and its people in peace.

Doing the equivalent of listening at peepholes and going through the contents of the humans' laundry lines was a massive pain. One can only fondle so many pairs of socks and undershirts before even a vampire starts to get a headache. I have a hard enough time dealing with my own laundry, much less someone else's.

That's probably something you've never thought of...a vampire having to do their laundry. It's not like we just go and get new clothes every time whatever we've currently been wearing gets dirty. Most of us, beyond our predisposition for feeding off human society, are otherwise law-abiding citizens. Really.

Now you stop laughing, you might hurt yourself. Anyhow...

I wanted all of this to have been over with months ago, but as you can see, wanting wasn't getting. It all pretty much sucked and I wanted the opportunity to just be a modern vampire and maybe enjoy some of the more mundane benefits of the civilized world. I don't think I'd been able to wash the sand completely out of my hair for at least as long as we'd been hunting the Weasel.

The first thing that grabbed our attention was the huddled body that lay on the outskirts of the village. A quick look showed the death-blackened face of a young girl of only perhaps fifteen or sixteen years who appeared to have been beaten to death. Clumps of jet black hair had been yanked out of her scalp, leaving clotted blood behind. A note pinned to the black cloak that was now her shroud proclaimed that she was a harlot who had smiled openly at a male to whom she was not related, and so she had suffered the consequences. Huge black flies clustered on both exposed flesh and her clothing, doing all the things carrion-eaters do with decomposing flesh.

Circle of life and all that. I couldn't begrudge them their grisly task. They kept the world from being more of a cesspit than it already was in many places. It wasn't pretty, but it got the job done.

As we stood there staring at the rotting remains of the girl, I was glad I didn't have to breathe, and wondered if Nathaniel was thinking the same thing. The body had been out in the open for at least a day and even without the presence of the flies, wasn't looking all that presentable anymore. I was a little surprised that the local carnivores hadn't yet carried away her remains, but perhaps the humans felt she made a better object lesson to their own people by keeping the corpse close by.

Condemned for smiling at another human. Yes, that seemed like the kind of thing that the Weasel and his men would decree. Of course, even beyond this example of random cruelty, there was other evidence that he had most likely made his permanent camp here. There would have been no other explanation for what we beheld when we arrived.

Heavily armed sentries walked the perimeter of the village, keeping a close eye out for anything amiss. What few women appeared outside the few small domiciles were heavily veiled and only emerged to collect water or small items from the other women of the village. It crossed my mind that perhaps the Weasel was concealing himself in a woman's burqa, but decided that he was too much of an extremist to allow himself to hide in that fashion. He was someone who refused to be furtive. While he was indeed hiding from those who wanted his head or hide, he wasn't pretending to be someone else while he was doing it.

His ego was entirely too large to allow him to consider concealing himself from his pursuers. His followers had concealed his whereabouts from prying eyes and ears, which was obviously something the Weasel had little problem tolerating.

The sheer number of soldiers and the variety of weapons they carried as they guarded the town convinced me of his presence. These were men who were sworn to protect the Weasel, and I knew from experience that most, if not all, would give their lives to help him survive to terrorize even more people.

"We need to find out which building he's in, Nathaniel," I told him during our second night outside the patrolled perimeter. "We don't know what he sounds like, but I suspect that he's probably pretty vocal about his beliefs and what he wants to do. We'll need to listen very hard to see if we can narrow down his location even further."

"What about the guards? Shouldn't we be getting rid of them?"

"No. If we do that, he'll find out quickly that he's in trouble, and that would be entirely too dangerous for the both of us. It's best if we can bypass them and just focus on the house he's staying in right now," I said. "With luck, maybe we can empty the house and not alert his followers until it's too late."

Luck. Right. I don't believe that either of us really believed in luck, but it was one of those talismans that was hard to ignore entirely. You never really give up the hope of a completely satisfactory resolution to something like this. I'd gone through this same feeling the times I'd helped to end the periodic rogues who would threaten the secret of our existence through their thoughtless and selfish actions.

Then I had a fantastic idea, its brilliance almost blinding me.

"I know how we can get his undivided attention. I would normally avoid doing things this way, but from everything I've heard about her, it makes her the most appropriate bait for our target. Certainly no great loss to the world at large, should something go wrong."

"What? Who?"

"We know that his senior wife rules his harem with an iron fist and that even his men fear her. I'm thinking that she should be the rabbit to lure in our weasel. We can use her to draw him out and make him do what we want," I explained eagerly.

"It might work. Does he care for her that much?" Nathaniel asked reasonably. "These ass hats seem to regard their vehicles with more value than their women. What makes this any different?"

"If she is his senior wife and still wields that kind of power when he also has younger and presumably more beautiful wives, I can just about guarantee that there is a strong emotional attachment between them. He won't let us get away with stealing her from him."

"Stealing? Don't you mean 'kidnapping'?"

"No, you were right and I said what I meant. He doesn't look at women as people, they are possessions and this one wife of his is one of his most valuable ones. Women may be prized possessions to the Weasel and his people, but they remain possessions, nonetheless. We're going to be stealing his stuff."

"But how are we supposed to find her? Isn't she going to be wrapped from head to toe in cloth, just like the other women? This is going to be like looking for that needle in a haystack." He protested. "I don't think we can get away with grabbing random women off the street without someone noticing fairly quickly. How do we identify her from the rest of them? Isn't this going to be a nightmare?"

"Not necessarily. Just look at the body language you see between the men and the women who come outside. In most cases, the men are obviously in charge of the situation and the women meekly follow the orders they are given. However, there is one woman who, when she comes outside, the men never loom over her or attempt to force her to do anything. This one has the power to do whatever she wants to do in whatever time the doing requires."

Nathaniel looked thoughtful for a few minutes before he spoke. A beatific smile blossomed on his face as what I was saying sunk in and he had time to consider it. His eyes twinkled with delighted anticipation and he motioned for me to continue.

"Obviously, you've figured it out. I believe that our most successful option is to kidnap his favorite wife then make our demands. I suspect that he will be much more amenable to listening to what we have to say." My own smile must have mirrored his, and I felt my appetite blossom as I considered the possibilities of hot rich human blood filling me as I eventually drained the life from her well-fed body.

The small fly-ridden corpse I'd seen earlier in the day strengthened my resolve. While I would be unable to bring her back from the dead, I could and would still seek some justice for her. Killing the Weasel wouldn't make crimes like this go away entirely, but it would remove at least some of those who did such things.

"I'd like to bury that body when we have a chance, Siofra. I know she's already dead and that it doesn't matter anymore to her, but it just seems wrong to leave her there," Nathaniel said quietly. "I don't normally get all upset where the humans are concerned, but for some reason, this bothers me a lot."

So he'd been thinking about her, too. I shouldn't have been too surprised.

"That's fine, Nathaniel. I think I understand how you feel. While we can't do it right now, if there is still anything left when we are done, we can give her a proper burial."

I knew that the odds weren't in his favor for the body still being there in a day or two, but if thinking he could do that made him happy, I wasn't going to gainsay him about it. No matter how much the humans would try to make the body linger, the wildlife would have their say in the matter, and it was generally useless to argue with them.

Besides, they could make far more use of it than the dirt. The body was only a husk now, with nothing of that young woman remaining. She'd gone on to whatever afterlife she would and that was that, but Nathaniel was still young, and hadn't gotten to the point where he could see that.

As it turned out, we spent in the neighborhood of three days narrowing down locations and planning out how we would separate Sarahi, or as we tended to call her, the Dragonlady, from her keepers. While she pretty much had carte blanche in her movements, the Weasel's people kept a fairly close eye on her. There was probably no way we could get hold of her without at least seriously damaging her guards. Determining her routine was boring to observe, but necessary, under the circumstances.

She appeared to do most of her outside time during the early part of the day, before the heat became so oppressive that it was easier and far more comfortable to stay indoors. I suspected that she was the one who took messages back and forth for her husband, keeping him under cover when there was no real "need" for him to travel. There were two or three residences she visited every day, and a few more that were visited every other day or so. Since we couldn't rely on the more random locations, we decided that it would need to happen first thing in the morning, before she was able to make her initial contact of the day.

She was always accompanied by a single guard armed with an elderly but apparently still serviceable Kalashnikov. It was always the same guard, an older, dark-skinned male who showed great deference to the woman, but was never afraid to brandish his weapon to intimidate anyone who might approach too closely. He certainly never let anyone near the briefcase the woman carried, cradled to her chest like something dearly precious. I suspected that he was some brother or cousin to the Weasel, as it was the norm in this part of the world for a woman to be escorted by a male relation of some sort.

The security measures enacted upon the briefcase made me more than a little curious to see what might be inside. I wondered if she had a key on her person, or if I would have to tear the thing off of her to see what it held. Yes, sometimes vampires can be more than a bit like cats. We are infinitely curious and often will go to seemingly impossible lengths to investigate things better left alone.

There is an old wives' tale about distracting a vampire by spilling out poppy seeds, with the idea that the vampire will be forced to stop and count (not my pun, someone else's) the seeds and won't stop even with dawn creeping up. The people who came up with this idea are part of the crowd who seem to think that the sun destroys vampires. That was kind of obvious though, wasn't it?

A distant cavern would be our hideaway. We'd found it one night after feeding from and slaughtering a small group of patrollers. One of their number had tried to conceal himself within it and had become lost in the pitch blackness of the quarter mile long tunnel that concealed numerous dead ends and obstacles. It had made hunting him down all that much more delicious.

The cavern had everything we would need, including a means to keep our captive in one place and at our mercy. We had stocked it with other items we required, including some rough rations for Sarahi. I don't know, and honestly, really didn't care, if she'd appreciate stale bread, a few dates and water ladled from a bucket, but it's what we could gather without acquiring unwanted attention. It was difficult enough transporting the water without spilling it. There wouldn't be much, but it wasn't as though she had to share it with anyone. Nathaniel and I certainly couldn't use the stuff.

As for our own needs, we fed well the night before on the outskirts of a nearby village. It would have been better and more efficient to feed at the Weasel's location, but the last thing we wanted was for either he or his people to get any more nervous and perhaps become more cautious than they were already. It was one of those times when we didn't have the option of only feeding on the dregs of society. Both men and women died in order to feed us on the eve of our attack. Children were left alone, as they don't hold enough blood to sustain us, so they would have been a poor choice as a food source.

Both Nathaniel and I wanted to be sure we were completely sated and wouldn't be in anything like a weakened state if we were going to brave automatic weapons' fire. It's not like we hadn't dealt with bullet wounds in the past, as we had, more than once, but even though you know it's likely not going to end you, it's still not a fun thing to endure and then have to spend time and energy recovering.

The Dragonlady and her escort would head out around six each morning, right after morning prayers. She would stop at the communal well that served the village to wash her face and hands, and then go to her first stop. I didn't understand why she didn't do this before she even left home, but it appeared to be a part of whatever ritual was involved in her daily messenger route.

It dawned on me that perhaps it was a signal of some sort, and if it was, then what we were going to do would be noticed and responded to very quickly. I didn't have time to really think about it, so I pushed it from my mind and focused on my target.

A rooftop perch offered decent cover that morning. A pigeon in a filthy nest constructed in a small overhang nearby cocked its head and looked us over, but didn't fly away at our presence. Maybe it knew we were no threat to it. I'd seen that kind of indifference to my presence from other wildlife since my first days as a vampire. Obviously deciding that we were harmless, the bird fluffed its feathers and put its head back under its wing to sleep.

The fingers of the dawning sun had not yet appeared to caress the ground and the village, so the remaining shadows helped to conceal our forms against the clay exterior of the building. Another half hour went by, with Nathaniel and me crouched on the rooftop, as still as we could possibly be. Vampires can stay in the same position for hours at a time, since we aren't prone to sore muscles or other kinds of muscular cramping. That ability served us well, as when you don't move, you can blend into the shadows that much better.

As time passed, signs of life slowly began to return to the village, the animals being the first to greet the day in their own way. Goats began to bleat in their pen as increasing human activity caught their attention and their stomachs began to rumble with hunger. Even the pigeon decided to begin its day and after giving us another long look, glided down to nibble at the treats it found on the well-traveled pathway to the well.

Sarahi arrived on time, as she always did, kicking at the pigeon irritably to get it out of her way. The bird fluttered to the top of the wall and watched her pass. I wondered if pigeons had any feelings about the treatment they get from humanity and what the bird might have been thinking as the woman went by. Pigeons always seem so slow and peaceful, but what if there was something more going on in their tiny brains? I guess we'll never know, will we?

We waited until she had finished her morning ablutions and then we moved. We were barefoot, in order to get the best traction possible, our talons extended and digging into the dirt as we ran. Our talons give us the ability to push off much more strongly than a simple human toe would, so we can gain greater speed much more quickly than if we didn't use them. Of course, unless you really want to shred your shoes, you should always remember to take them off before allowing your talons to extend.

I'd learned that the hard way, a very long time ago while I was still a fledgling vampire in Ireland. I'd given Nathaniel the gift of my experience that way, so he'd not had to discover it the same way I had found out. While the old stories talk of vampire fangs, retractable finger and toe talons aren't generally part of the discussion. Mine have been invaluable over the years, both for hunting and for defending myself when I had no other options.

Nathaniel grabbed the guard and disarmed him in a single movement, snapping his neck and letting him drop to the ground. The guard never uttered a sound, other than the dull thud of his body striking the dirt. The stink of the contents of the dead guard's emptying bowels exploded into the air as his body settled into death. Nathaniel caught the Kalashnikov before it hit the ground and then swung its strap across his shoulder to nestle the weapon at his side. We had decided to bring it with us, as we might have a use for it later, but I also wanted to avoid the sound of the thing clattering against the ground or worse, against the stones that ringed the well.

Having left the guard in Nathaniel's capable hands, I grabbed Sarahi and clamped a hand over her mouth as we sped away. Of course, she didn't accept her new state calmly. The Dragonlady fought me at every step, trying to break free or at least voice a cry of alarm. I knew it would be a pain in the ass to try to run with her fully conscious, so I thumped her gently alongside the head.

Let me say here that there is a huge difference between a human's "gently" and a vampire's, and I was forever forgetting that difference. One day, it would be something I couldn't take back.

For a split second, I became concerned that I had hit her too hard. Fortunately, my fear was short-lived, as I was reassured when I felt her take a deep, shuddering breath. As a dead body, she was little use to me. Still breathing, she was more than passing useful, even if she remained unconscious.

I knew that whatever trail we left before the sand swallowed our tracks would confuse our pursuers. The marks of our talons on the dirt would indicate that whoever had killed the guard and absconded with Sarahi was at least accompanied by something that wasn't human, but it certainly wouldn't be immediately assumed that the kidnappers themselves were non-human. It's just not something someone would normally think.

The sound of hoof beats equals horses, not zebras.

In any case, it wouldn't be long before someone discovered the guard's body and raised the alarm. At that point, things would become very busy and unpleasant in the village. Homes would be searched and violent interrogations would follow, but no one would have an answer for Death. Instead, the people of the village would be terrified and would be doing everything they could to help him and thus avoid anything nasty happening to them or their families.

I don't think they would be very successful in dissuading the Weasel from what appeared to be his favorite pastime. I think he enjoyed the terror he caused in the people he encountered, as their fear kept them obedient and passive.

In this case, if bad things happened, they happened. As I already well knew, and as Janos had reminded me more than once, I was not the caretaker of the human world. Shit happened and that was that. It wasn't my place to step in all the time. Anyhow, I'd rather have the Weasel nervous and unhappy than comfortable. The fact of his favorite wife's unexplained disappearance would have him very nervous, especially as that special briefcase was also nowhere to be found. It had been chained to the lady's dainty wrist to keep it safe. Well, safe enough from mortals without handcuff keys, anyway. We had our own methods of getting what we wanted.

We chained the Dragonlady to a boulder that had apparently been used for that purpose in the past: it had a single iron wrist shackle attached by a chain to a sturdy ring. The ring had then been attached to a boulder with heavy metal strapping. Although it was all quite old, it appeared to be in good condition, certainly, anyway, for the use I intended. Perhaps it had escaped too much deterioration because it had been housed in a cavern that contained little to no natural moisture, which would have sped oxidization and more than likely made them unusable.

The slightly rusted shackle itself was at least two inches wide and closed around her dainty wrist with little room to spare, so I had little concern that she might find a way to slip out of it. I wondered if anything like this had ever happened to her before, as from what I had been able to deduce during our surveillance, she was someone who was rarely on the bottom of the societal totem pole.

I wasn't too worried about her yelling for help, as the cave wasn't anywhere near any inhabited areas, and the odds of it being found anytime in the near future was unlikely. I'd chosen the location deliberately, as there was no earthly reason why I should make it easy on him. I wanted the Weasel off kilter and nervous as hell. This would do that.

Nathaniel had ripped the handcuff from her wrist as soon as we reached our destination, a small cave about ten miles from the village. Of course, removing the handcuff forcibly had seriously damaged the human's wrist and hand, but we weren't really planning to turn her loose again, once we had what we wanted. The ancient shackle now covered the wrist that had not been damaged, as we both decided it would be better that she not really have full use of either hand while she was in our custody.

We didn't need anything like a martyr to the cause. The plan was to feed on her if we had the chance and then make both her and her sick bastard husband's bodies disappear, never to be seen again. You can't make someone a martyr if you can't find their body. It's hard to have a very public burial when there's nothing to bury, right?

Our captive played possum for a couple hours before she allowed her eyes to open. She didn't know what we were, so she did not know that we were very much aware of when she awakened. I must say that I was impressed that she didn't rouse much earlier because of the broken bones she had in her wrist and left hand. The deeply gouged flesh that was a result of the removal of the handcuff couldn't have been particularly comfortable, either. I could see why the Weasel liked this woman so much. She was one very tough cookie. Well, I was here to make her crumble, and I knew I would enjoy it very much.

How would her attitude flavor her blood? There was every chance I would find out, and I might decide to share with Nathaniel. But then again, maybe I wouldn't.

"I know you're awake, Sarahi, so you might as well stop faking it," I told her brightly in decent Arabic. "Your wrist has got to be hurting pretty badly right now. It's broken."

She let loose with a string of obscenities I found marginally creative but knew I could do much better, even in a language that I wasn't particularly good at speaking. I laughed.

"I don't believe that's physically possible, even for someone of my particular talents, young lady." Nathaniel heard me and laughed from his place at the mouth of the cave. That boy had a wicked sense of humor of which I was fond. I think it was one of the reasons we got on so well, even beyond our connection as maker and one-time fledgling. "You seem to lack creativity in your insults. How disappointing."

Well, I guess that wasn't the right thing to say, as she seemed to take my words as a personal affront and let loose with a brand new list of suggestions and accusations. I wondered if her brand of religion even allowed women to talk that way. I refrained from asking her that, though. It was much more fun to learn the new words she was sharing. They might be useful at some time in the future.

"You're mine, Sarahi. An escape from me just isn't going to happen, no matter how much you might hope for it or think that it's even the barest possibility. I'm a far better and faster tracker than you could ever hope to have in your filthy husband's band of thugs," I taunted her. "Once I take care of him, I won't need you anymore and then you're mine to do with as I please."

I knew that she got the gist of what I was telling her, even though I hadn't been specific. She now knew that her life wasn't worth a pile of dirty couscous. Of course, that made her begin to pull at her bonds and try to work her way loose, but it amused me to see her so very frantic. I imagined that she had enjoyed watching her husband's female victims do the same. Well, turnabout is fair play.

She yanked and pulled at the chain for some time before she finally gave up. She sat back on her heels and glared at me. Over time, her expression became speculative and I guess that's when Sarahi thought she could play the girl talk card. For now, she had no reason to think it wouldn't work.

"How can you do this to another woman? All women are sisters and should take care of one another," she told me, her eyes guileless. Her dissembling and patently false words infuriated me. I could hear her heart pounding in her chest as she tried by sheer force of will to get me to believe her. "I am a victim, too, you know."

She didn't know what I was. Yet. But she would, soon enough.

"You, a victim? All women are sisters? Like that poor little girl who was murdered by your husband and his followers? For all I know, you stood by and encouraged it!" I shouted at her from across the cave floor. My voice echoed against the walls, and she flinched in response.

The look on her face turned ugly for a moment as her anger betrayed her, but she wrestled back some control and put her "kum-ba-ya" face on again. She'd obviously played this card before and found it successful. How many had died as a result of her expert play-acting?

"Women in my culture are limited as to what we can do, unlike you Western women. We do not have the freedoms" it seemed she made the word an epithet, "that you have had."

"Freedoms? You make the assumption that I don't know what it's like to live a tightly circumscribed existence. When I was a little girl, I was sold off to pay my father's debts," I told her. "Women have far more rights here in your country than the one from which I came."

I saw as disbelief registered on Sarahi's face before she regained control of herself enough to continue her tale of woe which was supposed to bring me to her way of thinking and gain my allegiance.

"How could that be? You come from a country that has great wealth and gives its people carte blanche to do whatever they like. There is no way you could understand what it is like to live or die at the pleasure of a man."

I couldn't help the bark of laughter that forced its way past my lips. It was only natural that she assumed I was just a very young woman, since that's what I looked like to her human eyes. There was nothing, really, to reveal to the casual observer that I was more than I appeared to be. Needing a moment to gather my thoughts, I waved a hand vaguely at her and went toward the front of the cave to talk with Nathaniel.

Nathaniel was leaning against the rocky entryway, arms crossed against his chest and a sardonic smile on his face. I knew he'd been listening to the exchange in the cave, and could only imagine what he thought of what he'd heard thus far. If his expression was anything to go by, he wasn't believing a word of what she'd said, either.

"Quite the pile of shit, isn't it? Please tell me you're not believing anything she's telling you, Siofra."

"Oh, come on, Nathaniel. You and I both know that I'm not that gullible. I've been around for several more lifetimes than she, and have heard more sob stories than you ever could imagine from humans desperate to save their own lives," I responded. "If she thinks her story is having any kind of success with me, she's very wrong. Even if I had even the slightest idea that what she was telling me was true, the sound of her heart slamming against her ribcage tells me that she's lying."

"Maybe she's just scared, Siofra," he suggested reasonably.

"She may be a little afraid, but the Dragonlady is just a little too sure of herself. I think she's pulled shit like this so many times that it's become a script of sorts. Her story has gotten so good that she's got it memorized. It's like watching one of those bawdy, overacted telenovelas."

"Well, at least you know when someone's throwing bullshit in front of the door and have learned to duck. What are we going to do now?"

"We need to know what's going on in the village and how close they are to us here. I really don't want a pitched battle between a horde of angry fanatics and us trapped in the back of a cave. I have no desire to go out like Butch and Sundance did." I thought about the very end of the movie, where they leapt out of their hideout and into the brightness of the day...

Fade to white.

"Make a run down to the village and keep an eye on what they're doing. Come back here either once they start moving or if there is something I really need to know," I decided. "I know you can handle this on your own, but there's always an element of danger to surveillance."

Nathaniel gave a quick nod and smiled at me.

"Okay, boss. Either way, I'll check back in a few hours to see how things are going here. This Sarahi may be simply human, but even crippled on the one hand and shackled on the other, I think she's dangerous. Don't underestimate her." Now why did he sound as though he were lecturing *me*? I had to smile back at Nathaniel, showing a bit of fang as I did so. Insolent whelp!

"Don't underestimate *me*, Nathaniel. I know a wolf in sheep's clothing when I see one. She's going to get her tail cut off, trust me on that. It remains to be seen whether that will happen sooner, rather than later," I told him. "I can feel her fear and smell her anger, even from out here. I think she's far more than what she appears to be, and she's been at this game for a long time."

"What's that supposed to mean?"

"It means that I think that I might have to look further into her part in all of this. She's a cunning bitch and its becoming obvious that I can't trust her, even just a little bit," I explained. "She's trying to get on my good side. Is it too bad that I don't have one?"

Nathaniel laughed, kissed me on the cheek and was away and out of sight before I could react. I chuckled softly, shook my head and went back into the cave to renew my interrogation of our captive. This was showing signs that things were going to get particularly ugly, and I wasn't yet sure if I wanted her to think she had any kind of upper hand in our "discussions".

Thirteen

I walked as quietly as possible to the rear of the cave, considering that the cave's floor was hard-packed dirt. No sense in letting her know I was already on my way back. I was forced to duck at times to avoid low-hanging projections and at other times to walk sideways in order to slide past narrow areas, as the corridor wasn't of a uniform size. The cave was natural, rather than man-made, after all, and nature tends to be more of a freehand artist than one who colors within the lines.

The soft glow at the end of the tunnel grew a little brighter as I got closer to the main cavern, and let me know that the single thick candle I'd left to light the otherwise pitch-black room was still lit. The candle flickered fitfully, its dancing flame creating odd shadows on the walls and adding to the atmosphere of fear and uncertainly I had wanted to create for Sarahi. Sometimes, a bit of dramatic flair can add just what one needs to keep a captive off their game, but I had a feeling that this human was an old hand at dissembling to the point where she could give her captor an unpleasant surprise.

While the slender flame of the candle allowed her at least some visibility of her surroundings, albeit heavily shadowed, the slight light it provided gave me all the detail I needed. Excellent vision is one of the perks of being a vampire. Well, providing that you were turned while you still had your eyesight. While you can re-grow an eyeball or a limb if you lose it after you have been turned, if it's not there before you become a vampire, you're not going to get it back. However, if you lose your head, it's not going to re-grow a body beneath it. There are limits to vampiric abilities.

I could hear Sarahi mumbling softly to herself, and at first I thought she was praying, but after listening for a few minutes, realized that she was making plans. I doubt that she realized she was verbalizing them, and decided I didn't want to bring that fact to her attention. I didn't know if it was something normal for her to do, or if this situation was making it happen. Either way, it was something I could use to my advantage. Before I allowed myself to be seen again, I deliberately kicked a pebble on the ground so that it ricocheted off one of the walls and made enough noise to startle the crap out of her.

"Well, hello there, Sarahi. Busy trying to get loose while I was gone? Unless you're really into doing even more damage to yourself, that's just not going to happen. That chain looks like it's been a part of that rock for at least the past hundred years. Which begs the question as to why someone felt it was necessary to put it there in the first place," I told her conversationally, squatting nearby, but out of arm's reach. "Who else has used this cave as a prison? I haven't seen any bones, but then, maybe the scavengers have already been by to make off with the evidence."

Sarahi looked a bit shaken as she was reminded that there was no guarantee that she would ever again see the light of day. Good. I wanted her scared and off-kilter a bit. I knew she was planning something, but as yet, had no idea of what that plan might be. Even though she talked to herself, it had been more muttered sounds of frustration than anything else.

"My husband will be looking for me, and when he does, he will kill you slowly. He won't let you get away with this," she insisted.

"You can plead all you want to, Sarahi. You're not going anywhere."

"If you let me go, I won't tell him who or where you are and you can escape," she cajoled. Maybe she thought I hadn't heard her threat just a moment ago. I gathered that this had worked for her before, but then, she probably had never before dealt with vampires.

Of course, most people who dealt with vampires rarely dealt with anything else again. "Just release me now and you can go about your life!"

Her pleas fell flat with me. I'd heard similar litanies many times over the centuries, though most often with prey I had brought back to wherever I was currently residing for a future meal. It had probably been at least a century since I'd been able to do something like that, but it was a bit humorous to hear this kind of escape attempt again.

"Oh no, you are here for a reason and I'm not letting you loose. Not yet, at least. I need your husband to come to rescue you, and if you're not here, that wouldn't work very well for me, now would it?" I smiled at her insincerely. "I know how much you'd hate to miss seeing his face before..."

I let my voice trail off but continued to smile at her. She began yanking desperately at the chain that held her, but neither the chain nor the shackle so much as creaked in protest. I knew that if I allowed myself to breathe, I would probably be able to smell her blood as it rose to the scratches and gouges she was making on her own flesh. While I had eaten very well last night, I didn't want to find myself being tempted, so I only breathed when I was going to speak, and then only through my mouth, rather than my nose, since that was the only way to avoid catching the scent of her blood. It probably made me look like a slack-jawed idiot, but so be it.

"Let me free!" she shouted at me. "Let me loose right now! I am First Wife to Death, himself!"

Like that was supposed to impress me. Well, maybe it might impress and even frighten the average human, but again, I was anything but average and I certainly wasn't human. I laughed.

"No, I think you're going to stay right where you are, woman. Screaming and threats aren't going to get you anywhere with me."

"He will kill you slowly," she hissed at me, her eyes mere slits. She'd have made a good vampire on presence alone, if I had wanted to bring a homicidal psycho over to terrorize the world, but that was never going to happen. "He will not rest until he has found me and put an end to you!"

I laughed again, which seemed to upset her. I guess that wasn't the proper response when she made such declamations. Now, instead of trying to yank her arm free of the bracer-like manacle, she tried to lunge at me, the fingers of her crippled free hand curled into a claw. I noted that the nails that had previously been painstakingly manicured were now torn and ruined. Sarahi had done it to herself as she ineffectually tried to dig at the bolts on the shackle. I imagine that it must have hurt, since there were numerous broken bones in her unshackled hand. Perhaps adrenaline was keeping her from realizing how bad things really were with it. She might have even been missing at least one of her nails, but I couldn't be certain unless I came closer, and I really didn't feel like doing that right now.

"I've been hearing threats like that for longer than you can imagine, Sarahi. To this point, no one's been successful when they've told me they or someone they knew was going to kill me, and it's not as though they didn't give it the good old college try." Sarahi's brow lifted at what was probably unfamiliar slang, so I tried again. "They took their best shot."

"You've just been lucky so far, but that cannot last forever," she insisted. "Your time *will* come!"

"Forever's a long time, Sarahi. A very long time." I shook my head at her sadly.

"Everybody dies," she asserted. Her haughty expression grated on me. "You are no different. It is the difference between dying young or growing old. Wouldn't you rather die an old woman with your grandchildren and great grandchildren around you?"

I snorted.

"I'll never have grandchildren or great grandchildren and I'm much older than I look, so save your breath," I told her, smiling. "There's no way you could ever tempt me with something like that."

With that, I got up and walked back out of the cavern. Even though I don't breathe, I needed some air. Sarahi's very presence fouled the cavern. She was lucky I left the candle burning, and I almost went back to blow it out, but I restrained myself. It didn't matter how much she pissed me off, I couldn't be petty. At least, not for now.

She'd kept on with variations on a theme, and I'd have had a headache from it, if vampires were able to get them. Sarahi was best taken in small doses, I was fast discovering.

I'd save that for later, when I could savor and enjoy it ever so much more.

It was about midday, and because of the heat, the local wildlife was nowhere in sight. Taking a deep lungful of air through my nose, I enjoyed the clean dry scent of the air. It was a far more pleasant aroma than the stale air in the cavern. No, I didn't need to breathe, and so the atmosphere in the cavern shouldn't really matter, but even a vampire enjoys nice-smelling things over things that aren't quite so fresh.

Leaving the Dragonlady alone in the cave would scare her even more, especially as it was already so unnaturally quiet. I decided that giving her a few hours of solitude was just what was needed to soften her up a bit. There was little to no chance that she would be able to free herself if left alone, so I wasn't too terribly worried about it. I'd examined the strapping, chain and shackle for structural weakness and had found none, so I was feeling pretty confident.

I went for a short run to clear my head, keeping to the nearby rocky shadows in the event that any humans were nearby. I startled one of the local deer-type animals and watched it bolt out into the desert heat while in the throes of its fight or flight instinct. From the moderate pile of dried and drying feces it left behind, I could see it had been standing there for quite a while, or at least had used the area many times before. An industrious but ball-less dung beetle caught my attention as it wandered over and began to examine its stinking treasure, perhaps in the hope of finding something it could use.

Mother Nature's clean-up squad was here. It seemed that there was almost always something that would and could deal with natural waste that had been left behind. I found this kind of thing fascinating, actually. As the local vermin had cleaned up what Nathaniel had left behind while he was dying and then after he died, so did the dung beetle in its own small way. I squatted for a time and watched as the little guy chose his favorite bits of crap and then slowly worked them into a larger dung ball. It was the work of a few hours, but I had the time and no real inspiration to go back into the cave. The Weasel was my target, and Sarahi was my bait.

Bait generally has no need to be entertained while it's being concealed, and I was tired of being entertained by her histrionics. It was too much like watching a badly scripted movie.

Finally, the dung beetle, apparently happy with what it had accomplished, wandered away again, pushing its new ball of dung in front of it, using his agile rear legs to steer the thing. What a way to go through life, backward, and with a giant ball of shit announcing your presence. You'd have to be an eternal optimist to be able to do something like that, I think.

The little guy was nearly ten feet away from me when Nathaniel came back again. He had an urgent look on his face, and I stood up so he could see me better. Gesturing to me, he went to the cave entrance, and I followed. As I got closer, I could hear Sarahi screaming for help deep inside. The sound of her voice was very hollow, as she was, after all, probably a quarter mile down into the earth. A human wouldn't have been able to hear her, though, so that was a blessing in disguise.

"It looks as though the Weasel has probably killed off a third of the villagers. Most of it apparently happened shortly after he discovered she was gone. He's really off his nut. More so than he was before any of this happened. I found a place to hide and watch, but finally left when they started searching the rooftops for evidence of her kidnappers," he told me.

"Is anyone headed this way yet?"

"He sent out three groups that I saw. None was headed in this direction, but I would imagine that they will eventually end up out this way. His men are scared shitless of him already, and this has really got them on edge. I'm sure it's possible that some may go AWOL because of this, but then, the true believers are all over it. We just have to be very careful now."

"I'm always careful, Nathaniel. I thought you knew that by now," I remonstrated, shaking my head. "Sarahi's been alone in the cave for a few hours now. She kept up with the same song and dance and I decided I'd had enough. If you go in there alone, she's probably going to try to appeal to your sense of honor and male protectiveness, you know."

"Oh, it wouldn't surprise me a bit if she did, Siofra. In overhearing some of the conversations in the village, the men aren't too terribly fond of her. The general opinion seems to be that she's got an awful lot of power for a woman and that the Weasel pretty much hangs on her every word. It's entirely possible that he's reacting this way because he doesn't know what he'd do without her."

"Well, he could actually love her, you know, Nathaniel."

"Actually, it seems more of a maternal fascination, if you know what I mean. It doesn't feel like love to me. More like a sense of missing a parent or mentor," he replied. "It's like he's bereft and completely at sea without her around."

That was an interesting thought. I hadn't considered that Sarahi might indeed be the brains behind this whole thing. If the Weasel was truly so fixated and dependent upon her that he couldn't operate without her, then we needed to look at the Dragonlady much more closely.

If we were to kill her outright and leave her body where he could find it, what would he do? Would he go completely bat shit crazy, or would he just become catatonic? Was it worth that kind of experiment? It seemed we may have kidnapped the actual evil mastermind of the horrors that had been visited upon so many humans these past several months. Could a real end actually be in sight?

"Something to think about, Nathaniel. We have to decide how we want to handle this, though. From what you've told me, the Weasel's pretty unhinged right now. I'd rather he stayed that way, rather than going out on a campaign of revenge. Some humans are like that. Confused and at sea is good. Murderous is not. Was there anything else you might have seen that would be of help here?"

Nathaniel stood and thought for several minutes. I could see him considering and then dismissing things in his mind. He'd always been fairly observant, so I trusted his memory of things. He wasn't prone to embellishment in these kinds of situations.

"He seems to have a lieutenant to whom he's looking for suggestions. His own are mostly along the lines of "find her, you lazy bastards" and the like. The lieutenant is the only one I'd really be concerned about. I can already see that "when I'm the boss" look in his eye when he thinks no one else is looking," he told me. I'd seen that look before a few times myself, although in different circumstances. This could be a problem.

"So you're pretty much saying that we're going to have to take out this lieutenant as well, then?" I asked. "We don't need to have someone else stepping in after the Weasel's gone to whatever hell he's destined for."

"Well, he's sticking fairly close to the Weasel, or at least he was when I left. There's no knowing if he's gone off on his own since I took off to come back here."

"There is that, yes. We really can't drag this out any further. It's time that the Dragonlady left the earthly plane, I think," I decided. "This is going to be an interesting kill, to say the least. You know that she's going to try to talk you into letting her go?"

"I'd be disappointed if she didn't at least try, Siofra," he replied, chuckling dryly. "It's not as though she could say much of anything to change my mind about her final disposition."

Laughing, we both headed down the long corridor toward the screaming woman who would shortly be a very silent corpse.

Fourteen

Sarahi stopped screaming for help once we reached the cavern and she saw Nathaniel amble in. I stayed just past the entryway, so she couldn't see me, but I could still see her. I was curious to see what tack her attempt at escape would take now that she was dealing with a man, rather than a woman.

From my vantage point, saw her eyes go to Nathaniel, narrowing as she considered her options. Her look was calculating, and her eyes cut over to the entrance to the corridor where I hid, a sneer crossing her face as Sarahi began to think she might have a chance of survival. I had no idea where she might have thought I'd gone to, but it was clear she wanted to take advantage of having Nathaniel to herself. She'd probably had a lot of success dealing with unwise human males who underestimated the level of cold calculation she employed to get her own way.

Nathaniel looked young, open-faced and friendly. Gullible, even. If she had been dealing with anyone else, he might have been right up her alley for a rescuer, but she didn't know that yet. It was actually kind of fun to watch it all unfold from the sidelines. I wondered if she ever even considered that I might be coming back again.

"Oh, please, sir! Please, let me free! I'm only a woman, and of no value to you," she cried. "Surely you would have better luck at a ransom if you kidnapped one of my husband's men. I know nothing valuable!"

He looked down at her, seeming to consider her plea. From my vantage point, it was anything *but* an award-winning performance on her part.

"While you might not know anything valuable, he certainly trusted you to carry his important papers, Sarahi. I found some very interesting documents in there when I opened it. Those are going to go out to the proper authorities who can make sure they don't happen."

She appeared shocked at Nathaniel's words, although I think it was more by the fact that he had been able to open the securely locked briefcase than because of what he intimated the contents revealed. While it would have been quite difficult for a normal human to open the thing, Nathaniel had been helped by the fact that he was stronger than a human and that the briefcase was of a fairly standard design with minimal security features beyond the easily thwarted lock.

If your hearing is good enough, you can hear tumblers clicking into place when you turn them, and yes, vampire hearing *is* good enough for that. I'd used the ability dozens of times in the last century, when I was after something someone no longer needed.

"You really want to go back to him, eh? I got the impression that to him, one woman is the same as any other. In fact, last I saw, he was being held by some other woman in a pretty green veil. They seemed pretty comfortable in one another's arms," he lied. We were rewarded with a look of shock which changed to an anger that made her eyes seem to burn with hatred. "I think he may already have moved on."

Nathaniel could really be a bastard when he tried. I was so proud of him. There must have been at least a grain of truth to his words, since he had been pretty specific with the color of the veil. The reaction he got from Sarahi was laden with venom and unabashed hatred. I wondered if each woman was identified by a specific color of veil so they could be told apart from a distance. I supposed you'd need some sort of an identifier if you covered your women in a voluminous burqa from the tops of their heads down to the floor. It gives a whole new meaning to the word "shapeless".

"Na'eemah! That conniving bitch!" she almost screamed. This Na'eemah must be her competition for the Weasel's favor. That was something that was good to know. Hopefully she wasn't anywhere near as scary as this one was, as I really didn't feel like slaughtering anymore humans than I really must. It's not as though I was really all that hungry right now. "I should have had her killed when I had the chance!"

Sarahi seemed to only then realize what she had uttered aloud, because I saw her face become flustered. She had made an irreversible mistake and we had heard it. How would she try to get out of this one now? I wondered if this Na'eemah was anything like Sarahi, or if she was simply a threat to the Dragonlady's dominant position in the Weasel's harem. It could always be this Na'eemah's way of protecting herself from an abusive husband. I'd seen that kind of thing happen before.

"Na'eemah is a snake in the grass! She's not to be trusted. She only wishes our husband ill," she tried to convince us, but it was clear she couldn't even convince herself of the truth of those words. Maybe she thought she could make us forget what she had said. I'd have felt sorry for her if I didn't already hate her so much. I remembered what may have been her most recent victim and shook my head. "Please, let me free so that I can save my husband from this temptress!"

"Really, now. She's that bad?"

"Even worse," Sarahi insisted. She seemed to have forgotten me in her zeal to get Nathaniel to free her. "Hurry, before it is too late!"

Nathaniel was already walking over to her, a soft, sad smile on his face and the key we had made for her shackle in his hand. Sarahi's face grew cunning as she thought she now had a way out. I saw her grasp at a small rock on the ground with her mangled hand and conceal it in her palm. It was obvious what she planned to do, but she would be very surprised at the outcome of her scheme.

As the sides of the shackle parted to free her wrist, Sarahi swung at Nathaniel's head with the rock. It was apparent that she intended to brain him if it was at all possible, but I didn't know how she planned to deal with me once she had. Perhaps she thought me weak, despite all prior evidence to the contrary.

Sarahi screamed when Nathaniel's hand came up and intercepted her own hand as it approached his temple. I'm sure she'd never seen anyone move that fast before and it probably scared her more than a little bit. He twisted her fingers until she gasped in pain and was forced to drop the stone or risk fracturing what few of her finger bones had escaped earlier damage.

"Now, Sarahi, that wasn't a very nice thing to do when I was going to turn you loose," he chided her, shaking his head in mock sadness. "I don't think I can let something like that go."

"I was afraid. You can understand that, can't you?" she blurted out, her plan undone and now trying to save herself. "Forgive me!"

Nathaniel shook his head sadly and put a finger to Sarahi's lips to silence her, his own pursed in regret. I wouldn't have wanted to listen to any more of her lies, either. It's funny that people actually *do* stop talking when you do that.

"I don't think I can believe anything you're telling me, Sarahi. I think all you've done so far is tell me lies. I don't like liars at all."

"I'll never do it again! Please, let me free!"

"You've said that before and look where it got you. Why should I believe anything you tell me now?" he asked her gently. His tone was almost parental, which seemed to throw her off course. "Give me a reason why I should trust you, Sarahi?"

"If you set me free, my husband will shower you with wealth," she lied. "I will tell him that you rescued me from my kidnappers and he will be so grateful that he will give you more money than you could possibly ever hope to spend in this lifetime."

"I still don't believe you, you know."

She put her free hand out onto his cheek and stared deeply into Nathaniel's eyes.

"Please," she breathed, coming in close to his lips, but not quite touching them. "Please set me free."

She thought that the tease of sex was going to help things go her way?

As I watched the drama unfold before me, Nathaniel smiled at Sarahi and I saw her relax, apparently convinced that her gambit had succeeded and that her release was imminent. He smiled a bit wider, and she gasped, drawing back as far as Nathaniel's grip would allow, which wasn't much. Only now could she see his fangs, which gleamed in the flicker of the candle's light. Most definitely not what she had expected to see, but then, what modern civilized human believes in monsters?

"Tell you what, Sarahi," he said, letting go of her wrist and standing back, and holding his now empty hands down by his sides. He sounded so very reasonable, but I'd heard similar promises from him before when it came to humans, so I knew how trustworthy the following statement was from him. "If you can escape to the open air before I catch you, I'll let you go back to your husband. I'll count to fifty and then I'll be right behind you."

She showed a look of relief and then started for the entrance to the corridor, but I stepped up right into her face, grabbed her and spun her about, not wanting her to have her bearings that easily. From the expression on her face, she hadn't expected me to show up again.

When I was almost done spinning her silly, I nodded to Nathaniel and he moved while I continued to spin the human around until she was surely quite dizzy, and most certainly nauseous. What a wonderful way to send someone out in a bid to save herself.

With one quick stride over to the single light source in the cavern, he blew out the candle, plunging Sarahi's world into total darkness. I could hear the woman blundering about the space as Nathaniel slowly began his count to fifty in Arabic. He'd keep his word about counting all the way up, of course.

She finally found the opening and she started to run, but shortly thereafter, I heard her yell of pain as she impacted the first low spot in the corridor. Nathaniel had reached the number thirty, and so he remained behind as he'd promised, but I walked slowly behind Sarahi, not to keep track of her, as our senses could have picked her out of a dark warehouse filled with non-human wildlife, but because, dammit, it was fun!

"Oh, you smell so good, Sarahi! I can't wait to sip you, myself," I teased her softly, my voice gone husky with anticipation. I let her hear me inhale deeply through my nose, and in response, her heart seemed to jump a beat. "I love the spicy taste of your peoples' blood!"

"You are responsible for all of our soldiers who were lost! You will pay for your crimes!" she hissed at me as she continued to blunder forward. "We are on a holy mission!"

"You've been killing too many of the local humans, Sarahi. If you'd kept things small, I might have left you alone, but you just had to spread far and wide. Now you're going to pay the price, and so is your husband," I told her quietly.

"Your man said that if I can find my way out, I can go free, and I will be free!" she swore. "I have always survived and I will survive this, also!"

"You can hope you do, but then, this is a very long and dark path to the light," I taunted her. She didn't respond, but took a deep breath and kept moving forward. I had to admire her tenacity, but that was the only thing I could admire about her. "I'm a survivor, too, Sarahi, and I get what I want."

It was the truth, and I'm sure she could hear that in my voice. Fear is a wonderful source of adrenaline and it spiked her fight or flight reflex right up into the stratosphere. I'd had a lot of practice at doing things like this over the centuries, and it never ceased to amuse me. I couldn't imagine going back to being human, even if such a thing could have been possible. I had talents as a vampire that no poor mortal human could ever truly enjoy. Most of humanity had become far too domesticated since man first began plowing their fields to grow the barley that became the beer and ale they craved, and modern day hunters enjoyed only the barest essence of what I experienced when I sought my prey.

I heard the human's heart begin to pound even harder in her chest as she realized that she was listening to the sound of her own impending death. I smelled the aroma of fresh blood in the air, so she had damaged herself with that first impact. She knew now that running was out of the question, and she wouldn't really have anything to light her way until shortly before she emerged into the sunlight. The myriad twists and turns of the corridor kept the light out of most of the cave.

I laughed as she became confused and lost her way inside a side tunnel. Profanity spilled from her lips as she encountered the dead end and was forced to turn around.

"My, but what a mouth you have! You kiss your husband with that mouth?" He probably let her get away with just about anything, but I wasn't going to bring that up. "I'm shocked to hear such unladylike words coming out of you."

"Let me go!" she begged me. For once, she sounded sincere, but she'd worn out any sympathy I might once have held for her. Bitches like this one were better off dead. "Just let me go!"

Nathaniel had long since finished his count and was slowly walking toward us. I knew he would drag this out as long as possible before bringing her down. I knew how he thought, and he was treating her the same way he treated the human males who disgusted him. He'd lied to her and didn't really care that he had. As far as I was concerned, this woman had lied to a lot of people, so it was time the karmic two by four paid a visit.

"I'm coming for you, Sarahi," Nathaniel called. "I want the taste of your throat in my mouth. It will feel *so* good!"

Sarahi ran a few steps and then encountered one of the several narrow places in the corridor. I heard the sound of her skin tearing as she pushed her way through, terror acting as a temporary painkiller in her effort to get as far away from her tormentors as possible. My own fangs emerged of their own volition as the sound of her pounding heart teased the predator that I am.

I could have reached out and grabbed her arm, taking her for myself, but this was Nathaniel's game now. He had decided to mete out her execution in his own way, and I would not interfere. He had gone from being my child to being his own vampire. I was done training him and would respect his decisions.

By now, Sarahi was sobbing in terror, the salty smell of both her tears and her blood spicing the air. Terror is to a vampire as catnip is to your cat, and I couldn't help but be drawn in closer to her. I actually had to restrain myself at this point, as I found myself fantasizing about what her blood would taste like now that it ran hot and fast in her veins and arteries.

"I can't follow, Nathaniel, or I'll feed from her myself," I told him too softly for Sarahi to hear me. It was shocking to me that I was having a problem with self-control. I should have been much too old to suffer from something more common with fledglings. "It's up to you."

"Yes, you can, Siofra. We can both feed from her, if you like. There is no way I'd let her go after what she said back there. She needs to die badly, very badly," he urged me. He put a hand on my shoulder and squeezed it firmly, urging me onward. When we had still had our emotional connection, the shoulder squeeze had become our silent form of reassurance when things were chaotic, and we'd not yet lost the habit.

Reluctantly, I continued on with him as we followed our prey. I so wanted to leap on her and end it all right now, but I wanted her to feel as though she was actually going to make it. Something told me she'd done similar things to her victims in the past.

Finally, a couple hours later, after taking several wrong turns and having to regain her bearings, she encountered the pale light of the setting sun and with a cry of triumph, began running for the entrance to the cavern and supposed freedom. Nathaniel and I were both very close behind her, but she never thought to look behind herself until she reached the actual entrance.

As she saw her death, Sarahi's scream echoed in the entryway, despair and defeat coloring it the crimson hue of blood. Her throat must have gone raw with the sheer power of her wail.

"You're mine, Sarahi!" Nathaniel hissed, and grabbed at her broken wrist, pulling her in close to his mouth. The glow of the setting sun highlighted part of his face while plunging other parts of it into shadow, giving him an otherworldly, surreal aspect. He was a terrible thing to behold. "You just couldn't run fast enough, could you? Not that you really had any chance of getting free, human! You and your husband are just too dangerous to allow to live. You're killing off far too many humans, and we just can't let you do that anymore."

She fought him like an enraged wildcat, scratching at his face, tearing his skin to the point where bone showed through the tatters of his flesh. Nathaniel flinched a little, but he'd suffered worse over the years during particularly intense hunting. Sarahi must have been expecting to see blood flowing from the damage she caused, but instead, only the thick dark fluid that vampires all bleed oozed from the wounds she had made. Nathaniel seemed to want to delay ending her, and I simply watched.

"Why don't you die or faint or something?" she muttered as she managed to tear part of his throat with the shreds of one of her long sharp fingernails. Her hands were coated in the thick fluid that oozed from Nathaniel's torn flesh and she stared at it as though noticing it for the first time, which it may have been, now that I think about it.

"I'm already dead, Sarahi. You can't kill a man twice," he replied, feeling gingerly at his face with his free hand at the damage she had caused him. While his injuries weren't something that would end him, I knew it would still hurt like a bitch. "Feel how cold my body is right now? Think about how the last corpse you touched felt in your hands."

She suddenly jabbed at his eyes with her fingers, to which Nathaniel jerked back in order to protect his eyes and snared both of her hands tightly in his own. I smelled what amounted to vampire ambrosia as one of her rings cut into the side of one of her fingers under the pressure of Nathaniel's grip, spilling the delectable aroma of her blood into the corridor.

Anger flared in his eyes and I could almost swear that Nathaniel's fangs lengthened, although that couldn't happen. He was royally pissed off, and she'd really done it to herself now, not that she'd ever really had a chance of actually being released, but she'd ensured that her ending wasn't going to be anything resembling merciful in the least.

He hissed at her, much like a cat would, showing his fangs and the dark rich red of the inside of his throat, which stood in stark contrast to the pallor of his skin. I heard her heart begin to race even faster, if such a thing were even possible.

"You stupid bitch, you very stupid bitch," he breathed at her, crushing her fingers and thumbs until they were dangling bags of flesh and crushed bone. Blood dripped from punctures caused by the destroyed bones, and then leaked onto the dirt below. "I would have thought you'd have learned your lesson already, but you appear not to benefit from your mistakes."

She screamed in agony at Nathaniel's torture and nearly fainted, but he slapped her with the flat of his hand, jarring her back to alertness. I saw her go very pale then, whether through pain or fear, I couldn't say. He had her undivided attention now, and her eyes only left his to take in the sight of his perfect fangs. I could see that a part of Sarahi knew she would eventually feel them tear into her flesh, but she couldn't seem to help babbling anything she could to try to change Nathaniel's mind.

"I—I can make you rich! I can give you many children! I can give you the power I brought to my husband—" she blurted out desperately.

"You really don't get it, do you, Sarahi? It doesn't matter what you may offer me. I'm not interested in whatever promises you make. You're only getting one way out, and it's not going to be one you're going to like," he told her sternly.

She screamed a name, her voice cracking as her vocal cords refused to hit the range she attempted. It may have been her husband's name, but I had no idea, and with her voice's mutiny, it was garbled too much for me to understand. Sarahi tried to pull herself away from Nathaniel, but all she succeeded in doing was splashing her blood around some more.

"I think she finally gets it, Siofra," he said to me as he beheld Sarahi's antics. "Notice that the begging and scheming finally appears to be done. It's just a big pile of crazy now."

Nathaniel was right. Sarahi's words, interspersed with the occasional random scream, had become crazed, making no sense at all. It was entirely possible that he had completely broken her mind, but I doubted that. Sarahi was too strong a person to completely lose herself. At least part of her self-absorbed mind had to be locked on what was happening to her now. With all the plotting and scheming she had done over the years to achieve the position she had created for herself, she was being ended like a cow going to slaughter, and not being ceremoniously mourned like a deceased queen or princess might.

"Nathaniel, I have an idea. Hold her still a moment. I need to get something from her," I interjected as he appeared to be about to take his first sip of Sarahi. I'd seen the flash of something under her clothes as the light of the setting sun crossed her chest and I wanted to get a closer look.

Heeding my request, he held her easily and waited as I came forward and began my investigation.

A little shifting of burqa and bodice revealed a cloth-wrapped piece of jewelry hung around her neck that could have very easily funded a small insurrection. The only reason I'd seen the thing was that part of the wrapping had come loose, revealing the treasure therein.

Precious stones studded the golden thing like gobs of rock candy on a string. It was probably Sarahi's safety net in the event she needed to make a considerable bribe to get herself out of something. I was going to assume that the Weasel knew about it, as this wasn't something anyone would be able to easily hide away.

Perhaps that's the reason why the Weasel was so crazed right now. We both knew he valued her, as she was his first wife, but he knew what a windfall something like the medallion she wore could bring him. Sarahi hadn't offered it to Nathaniel or myself to free her, so maybe she was merely the caretaker of the thing, and it wasn't hers to offer as ransom. In any case, it was ours now, and I knew of several places I could turn it from the beauty it was now into something far more negotiable and compact.

Keeping clear of her bloody hands and arms, I undid the heavy chain and jeweled medallion that she had been concealing under the front of her gown. I immediately tucked it into the small leather bag I had secured to my hip and stepped back, nodding to Nathaniel.

"We can use this thing as bait, Nathaniel. I can guarantee he'll do anything and go anywhere to get it back." I told him. "Once we've dealt with the Dragonlady, get out that little camera phone of yours and we'll get a picture of it. I'm sure we'll have his attention very quickly."

"Glad you saw it before we left her. That thing looks like it's worth a hell of a lot of money, no matter what culture you're in," he grinned at me. "It's time that we end her and get on with the next step. I've wasted enough of her blood already."

Indeed, there was a sizeable amount of Sarahi's blood spattered on the walls of the corridor, the dirt floor and ourselves. It seemed an enormous shame to let it go to waste.

Nathaniel pulled the human close again, tipping her chin up and exposing her throbbing carotid artery. He licked at the skin there and then shook his head in negation. What was the matter?

"No, I think taking her throat would let her die too quickly. She's got to linger," he said aloud to my unvoiced question. "I think I'll start somewhere else. Somewhere much less vital."

With that, he raised her arm and found the large veins near her elbow, the ones the folks at the Blood Bank like to use when humans donate blood. They would provide a good flow without letting to go too soon. He licked the fold, then almost daintily broke the skin over the largest vein, allowing her blood to pour forth.

Instead of drinking deeply, he played with it, never allowing it to coagulate and seal, taking small sips while the majority of her blood flowed down onto the thirsty sand. So much for his earlier comment about wasting food. This was more cruel play and a bit of vampiric first aid than anything else.

The small amount of her blood that he did ingest did its work and I watched as the edges of his torn skin on his face moved together once more and became whole again. It was as though he had never been injured by Sarahi. No scar, not even a blemish, remained to show that she had done her best to break free of his captivity.

Being a vampire can be awfully cool, sometimes.

Once we could both hear her heartbeat beginning to falter further in its downward spiral into death, Nathaniel gestured to me to join him. She had stopped even attempting to fight by then. It was what I had always considered to be the best time to have a shared meal with another vampire.

Once I moved next to Nathaniel, he shifted position slightly, but never moved his mouth from where he fed in the bend of Sarahi's elbow, and then offered the human's other arm to me. Wordlessly, I moved to him and took the human's arm, wiping sand, clots and dirt from the skin before opening the vein to make my own feeding location. I locked my mouth to that salving river and hungrily swallowed the hot fluid that obligingly pumped out of her body and down into my throat. I was correct, and whatever the human had been eating had added a certain richness and energy to her blood. It made me think of a human having an energy drink to break a drowsy experience.

I assumed that she must have been eating a lot of nutrient-rich food for a long time, since a day or two's feasting isn't going to affect the flavor of blood as much as hers was this evening. She'd eaten very well for at least a month's time, and as I thought of the condition of the underfed humans from whom we'd taken our meals for the past several months, it offended me.

How dare she feast while others starved? Islam has a concept of being good to the less fortunate that she and the Weasel seemed to have missed somewhere. It didn't seem quite right that I appeared to know more about her faith than she did. I certainly hadn't seen her attempting to do any of her five daily prayers while we had had her in captivity.

Well, she wouldn't be the first member of a religion who was a member "in name only". All faiths seem to have people like that in their ranks.

I must admit that in the end, I did drink more than Nathaniel. It turned out beyond the deliciousness of her blood, that I was much hungrier than I had realized, and my instincts kicked in, not wanting to waste this opportunity to feed myself. We've gone through a lot of exertion before and after we'd taken Sarahi today, so my body had dehydrated a bit more than I had expected it would. As Nathaniel wasn't necessarily drinking a lot, he may have fed while he was gone earlier in the day. Hell, if I'd had the opportunity, I might have done the same thing.

She had some of the finest blood I'd had the pleasure to drink in a very long time. Sarahi had probably gotten the best food her husband could offer her, and here I was, drinking in the benefits of her generous diet. My mind wandered as I enjoyed my repast, thinking about the human's mostly mysterious background.

I was reminded that she'd given her husband at least one son, but I didn't know how old he was and whether or not he was going to find himself in my crosshairs at some point, but for now, I just wanted to revel in the taste of the Weasel's favorite bride. She had served her purpose, and now we could take a short break before all hell broke loos

We left Sarahi's empty naked husk in the dirt, laying half in and half out of the entrance of the cavern, the ants already working on scavenging what they could from it. It seemed somehow appropriate to leave her in the illusion of having just achieved her freedom before being torn from this life into whatever afterlife awaited her.

I hoped it really sucked for her, and not in that sexy vampire way, either.

We took pictures of the medallion using the burner phone Nathaniel had taken from one of his most recent meals. It had made sense to keep the phone, since it apparently had cell service through Zain, and it certainly couldn't be traced back to us. We weren't the ones who had purchased it in the first place. It had been a fortunate find, as our meals generally had nothing more than the robes they wore and the shoes on their feet. This one had probably been a lieutenant or something like it. Its charge was almost gone, so it would soon be useless to us, but we made use of it while we could.

Several phones had come to us that way. This one had been fairly unusual in that it had come to us with almost a full charge. Turning it off between uses didn't keep its power from being discharged, but it certainly slowed things down for a bit. We'd had a long-term standing joke about our food's thoughtlessness in never supplying a recharging cable for the cell phone we scavenged from them.

While the pictures this phone took weren't fantastic, there was enough detail available that it was obvious what it showed. We decided that it was best to take the pictures with the medallion lying on the remains of Sarahi's veil. No sense in giving them any more identifying information than was absolutely necessary. After that, we sent the picture, along with pictures of the papers we had discovered in the briefcase, off to Janos. He would make sure the information in the pilfered paperwork would go to the appropriate authorities and that the picture of the medallion would get it into the hands of the Weasel.

Our message to the Weasel included a not so gentle request for contact and gave the phone number attached to this phone. It was a safe thing to do, as it wasn't as though he could track our identities or location with the number. The implication of our message was that the medallion would go to the highest bidder if we didn't hear from him in the next twelve hours.

We heard from him a mere four hours after we sent the images. I imagine he must have been frantic, thinking he'd never hear anything from whoever had taken his portable treasure trove.

He never even asked about Sarahi, only about the medallion. He was intent on knowing its current condition and what we had in mind for it. He even offered us a large amount of money for it up front, but both Nathaniel and I knew that his offer was empty. The Weasel didn't strike me as a man with a lot of cash reserves. He would meet us, and then probably try to end us in order to take it.

Oh, and he signed his message "Boulos", so we finally had a name to put to the monster who had destroyed so many innocent lives. It seemed kind of innocuous, and not really something you'd attach to a murderous son of a bitch. No wonder he'd embraced being called "Death", instead. It surprised me a bit that he hadn't signed his nickname to his response, but he'd long ago shown that he had a chaotic personality.

"You know we can't trust him, right?" Nathaniel asked needlessly. "This thing is worth far more than he's even pretended to offer us."

"Yes, I know he's a sneaky son of a bitch. At the very least, he'll have guards around him when we meet, if not snipers on nearby buildings," I noted. "We need to take him out at our first opportunity, but we have to get close enough to make that happen and then get out again fast enough so that we don't end up as dried up corpses in the desert."

"He's going to try to put us at a disadvantage, wherever we meet. Do you have a place in mind where we might have an even chance, at least?"

"I'm thinking about meeting him outside one of the villages, so there will be fewer places for his men to hide."

"If there are fewer places for his men to hide, that means there will be fewer places for you to hide as well. Are you sure you want to put yourself in that position?" he asked reasonably.

"You have a point, but I don't want to get my brain splattered all over the place. Our kind can't come back from something like that. I'm open to suggestions, Nathaniel."

After some discussion, we got back to Boulos with a proposed meeting site. Of course, he didn't like our first choice. He wanted some control over the situation and wanted to have the upper hand. We countered with the fact that we were the ones with the medallion he wanted back, and then the serious negotiations began. Boulos had figured out that Nathaniel wasn't a complete fool when it came to negotiation.

Several text messages later, we finally agreed to meet Boulos the next morning, outside a nearby town where we had searched for him earlier. Well, Nathaniel agreed to meet with him, as the Weasel wouldn't have taken a woman seriously. I was glad that we'd come to a compromise, as our cell phone was on the verge of becoming an electronic brick, useful only for throwing through windows.

Before and during their meet, I would be doing surveillance inside and outside of the town. If and when I found anyone belonging to him, I'd end them then and there. Hopefully, I'd be able to take most of them out before he actually met with Nathaniel. I doubted we would escape things without a scratch, but if I could arrange for as few "scratches" for the two of us as possible, that's what I'd do.

As Boulos would obviously have already sent out patrols to safeguard the village where he would meet Nathaniel in the morning, we didn't have the chance to feed during the night. His heavily-armed men appeared to be traveling in groups of at least three, so it wasn't worth the risk. Because of that, I was glad that I'd fed from Sarahi, instead of just leaving her to Nathaniel. If I had the opportunity, I'd feed from whomever I found during my surveillance.

It was about three in the morning when we left for the village. We weren't supposed to meet Boulos until about seven in the morning, but that didn't mean that we couldn't show up earlier to check out the lay of the land, now did it? Besides, I needed to see what he had in store for us long before he could spring it on Nathaniel. Yes, for now, he had the upper hand, as he had quite a few of his own men, but perhaps I could thin out his herd a bit before the sun rose. If I got a bite to eat during the process, I wouldn't complain.

We'd already discussed the plan up one side and down the other before we left our rude encampment, so no more was necessary as we ran to the village, which was about thirty miles away. Nathaniel would do what he could to help me out beforehand, but he wanted to avoid attracting any more attention than he must before they met. Besides, showing up with blood on your clothing is going to cause a lot of undesirable talk when you're trying to make someone feel overconfident. Yes, we both wore black, but blood can still show up on black clothing if you haven't laundered it yet. It's not like it's something thin and translucent, such as water.

Normally, we would have run pell-mell for the village, but that wasn't wise at this juncture, so we ran for as long as we felt was safe. There was no chance of our being spotted by anyone using infra-red technology, as we gave off no body heat, but there was no sense in pushing things. At least two of the patrols we'd evaded so far had contained at least one member who used it and would pass along what was revealed to his compatriots. They chattered and gossiped between one another like old grannies as they made their rounds, so it wasn't that difficult to locate and avoid them. If I had been Boulos, I probably would have at the very least beaten them for being so unprofessional, if not killed them outright for being fools.

I'd liked hunting at night a lot more before the damned things had been invented. Again, it wasn't as though I had any chance of being seen by those who wore the things, but if our passing startled unsuspecting wildlife or disturbed something that should not be moving in the first place, thus alerting any humans that *something* wasn't right, that wasn't going to be of help to us at all.

We evaded three more of Boulos' patrols before we reached the perimeter of the village and finally split up to check out the lay of the village, its buildings and outbuildings. Although we did locate some of Boulos' men in various stages of alertness or complete lack thereof, we left them alone for the time being. It would be a disaster if he called upon them for something and they failed to answer because they were simply a quickly cooling body. I'd made that mistake once, a couple hundred years ago, and had learned my lesson then, escaping my own ending by only the smallest of margins.

Nathaniel was supposed to meet Boulos by the old dry well on the outskirts of the village, so we took up a position almost directly across from there before the sun's blush touched the horizon. I, on the roof of an outbuilding, him waiting nearby. I had mapped out the locations of the most dangerous of the Weasel's henchmen, and would begin killing them off at about five in the morning. So far, only two or three had shown that they had anything like a walkie-talkie or other radio device, so that made it easier for me. Those without such a device would be the first to die. It only made sense, under the circumstances. Those seemed to be the ones closest to the meeting point, as they would probably be relying on such things as hand signals and shouted commands from their leader.

When it was about an hour and a half before the appointed time, I indicated to Nathaniel what my route would be, and then nodded at him to move off so that he could "enter" the village on his own a little later. By that time, the majority of Boulos' snipers would be entering rigor mortis.

I was only a few dozen yards from my first target, who dozed on a nearby rooftop. Stealthily climbing the roof, careful not to jog any of the tiles too strongly and make them fall, I was soon standing behind and over him. He twitched in his sleep, his fingers curling and uncurling from around the old rifle he held as he dreamed.

Squatting down only a few inches away from his back, knife in hand, I reached forward and sliced quickly across his Adam's apple. His eyes shot open in shock, and he slumped forward, blood pouring across his rifle and his lap, only the slightest of gurgles coming from his mouth as he died.

The scent of his blood was maddening, but I knew that feeding from him was out of the question. He was already dead, and as I've said in the past, vampires cannot drink blood from a dead body. My nostrils flared and my lips and mouth twitched involuntarily as my cravings tried to get the best of me. Part of me wanted to lick up the blood that pooled on the ground, but the sane part of my mind knew that would be the worst possible thing I could do.

As quickly as I could, I moved on to my next victim, and after that one was dead, the yet another.

With the third one, I couldn't restrain myself any further. Having killed twice already and my victims' blood in the process, I had to allow myself to feed. I had no choice in the matter. I wasn't sure what was wrong with me, as I normally had far more control over myself. This might prove to be even more dangerous than I had anticipated.

Fangs extended, I dropped down behind my third victim, hands out and ready to grab him. I don't know what got his attention, but he suddenly whipped around and stupidly raised his rifle, pointing it at me awkwardly. He was a young kid, barely an adult, but even kids as young as he was can be monsters. I jumped forward and clamped a hand over his mouth before he could utter a cry. Fortunately, the rifle hung from his shoulder by a worn leather strap, so I was saved the task of keeping if from hitting the ground and causing a racket.

The boy's eyes grew wide and terrified as I leaned forward, showing him my fangs.

"You dumb little bastard. What the hell are you doing working for this monster? Well, if you're old enough to kill for him, you're old enough to die for him, too," I told him in his own language, and then ripped a hole in the side of his neck, latching on for all I was worth and sucking there as though I had not eaten in an eternity. In a normal situation, I would have simply allowed his blood to pour into my mouth on its own, but some overpowering urge made me do things differently.

I didn't have time to think about it, as I had one more sentry to end, so I let his dying body drop to the walkway and I moved on to my final victim for now, an older male with a pair of rifles strapped bandolier-style across his chest and an enormous serrated knife hanging from his belt that was big enough to be used to decapitate an opponent easily. He would not be an easy kill by any means.

Jumping from one balcony to another, I made my way over to where my target perched. He appeared to be wide-awake, as opposed to my previous targets, so the element of surprise would be even more difficult to achieve. It seemed that my only option would be to jump from my current location to the balcony on which he stood, but I wasn't comfortable with that idea. Any number of things could go wrong, and considering that things had gone pretty well so far, the odds weren't really in my favor anymore. I refused to allow myself to get cocky and just hare off without even thinking about my next move.

He made a habit of pacing from one end of the balcony to the other, and several minutes of watching him showed that he wasn't varying from his established routine. I would wait until he was at the opposite end of his path and then move to where he was not.

I waited several more minutes to further reassure myself that he wouldn't change course, and then I leapt to the far end of the balcony. I hid myself amongst some barrels and wooden boxes that were stacked near to where I landed and waited for him to return. I reasoned that it shouldn't be long now.

I was wrong. It was quite a long while, and it reached the point where I left my concealment to find out what was going on.

Peeking around the corner, I saw him standing at the corner of the balcony, his robes carefully pulled aside, and urinating out into the dirt below. I shuddered involuntarily at his filthy habits and as he shifted his clothing back into place, I moved to my hiding place and waited for his return. He wasn't very obliging, so it took at least another several minutes before he came close to where I hid myself.

Once he had his back turned from me, I stood in order to attack and kill him, but he must have seen something, because he whipped around, drawing his knife and feinting at me with it.

I stifled a scream of pain as his knife sliced into my side, ripping out the contents of my abdomen and spilling them to the ground. I saw him smile, but was surprised that he made no outcry. Was he that overconfident that he thought he did not need assistance? I'd seen such humans before, but they were few and far between. He stood back and watched, waiting for me to crumple to the ground, which I did, holding onto my side and trying to push things that should never be seen on the outside of a body back in.

I mean, would you want to have dirt on your innards, even if you didn't have to use them anymore?

He gave a low chuckle and moved forward, as though to finish me off. I let him get quite close before I responded, pretending to be a dying human woman. I felt a wave of disgust rise in me as my opponent came close, the reek of sweat and some other foul aroma I could not identify emanating from his robes.

He said something softly in a language I didn't understand, and I suddenly realized that the Weasel must also be using mercenaries who might only be there for the money he paid them, or worse, the opportunity to rape and pillage at will. I had an idea what drove this human, and I wasn't about to let it happen.

"Go screw yourself!" I said in Arabic, and he started a bit, but kept coming, his knife still in one hand and reaching for me with the other. The shock on his face changed to a smile of anticipation as he came closer. I must have looked quite frail, as I'm only about five foot two and have a very slender build. Some have described me in the past as being "waif-like", whatever that means.

At some point, he must have noticed that I wasn't actually bleeding like a normal human and that brought him to a halt. He raised his knife to plunge it down toward my head, but I twisted sideways at the last minute, leaving him to slash only empty air at my passing. The movement caused the edges of my wound to rub together, and I grunted in very real pain at the agony that shot through me. Vampires are dead, but we can still feel things.

I would have to feed to heal the damage he had caused me, but I wasn't sure how long it would take me to be in that position. I was confused at his continued insistence on facing me alone, but had neither the time nor inclination to think it through very much. I was simply grateful that he had not sounded an alarm.

Rising in a single fluid move, I pulled out my boot knives and drove them into each side of his throat, turning him into a bizarre-looking knife block. He dropped to his knees, shock once again registering on his face as he finally realized how overconfident he had been in dealing with me. Weakly, he tried to remove my knives, but his strength was already failing him, and he could only wave ineffectually at them.

"I've had those knives for over three hundred years. I've kept them very sharp and pointed. I hope you've enjoyed them at least as much as I have," I told him, and smiled, showing my fangs. His eyes widened in horror and he fell backward onto the walkway, his legs folded uncomfortably beneath him.

This time, knowing he was done for, he tried to call out, but was only able to make a soft gurgling noise as his blood drowned his vocal cords. At the same time, I fell on him, desperate to drink any of his blood that I could start to repair the damage he had caused. I wouldn't be able to drink much of it, as he was dying right before my eyes.

I yanked one of my blades out of his throat and drank from the deep wound it left behind. I only got in about two deep swallows before I was forced to pull away. His heart was dying too quickly from the combination of a lack of oxygen and blood loss. When his heart did stop, his remaining blood would be poison to me, but at least the two swallows I'd managed had started the repair process. Removing my second blade, I wiped it and the first blade carefully on his tunic before sliding them back into the sheaths housed in each of my soft boots. Finally, I secured them with a thin but sturdy loop of leather then fitted over the hilt of each to keep them from sliding out uninvited.

There was no sense losing those knives now. I'd had them entirely too long to take any chances with them. I had even missed their presence while during our flight to the Middle East in the first place. I hadn't felt completely comfortable until Hamzah had handed me the package containing them at the airport.

Looking at my gut wound now, I saw that while it still wasn't pretty, my innards weren't going to be falling all over the ground now. I'd been through much worse in the past, to the point that I'd actually had to kill more than once to recover, but this had been bad enough on its own.

Turning my attention back to the dying human, I watched as his mouth opened and closed soundlessly like a goldfish out of water, as he was unable to take even a single breath. His eyes were wide and staring, and I knew that whatever it was he stared it, it was not on this earthly plane. Eventually, I heard his heart finally shudder to a halt, and then proceeded to search the body for whatever I could use.

I took the rifles and all the ammunition I could find, reasoning that if I could avoid outing myself to the rest of the Weasel's crew as being something not human, that would be for the best. I'd not fired rifles very often, but had done it enough that I knew what to expect when I did. I'd decided when I first scouted the area to leave the weapons of my first kills behind, as this human's arsenal was of a far better quality than theirs. There is a huge difference between a decrepit old shotgun with a broken stock and a pair of .22s, compared to a 3.08 and a 30.06 believe me.

Before I left for what would be my main hiding place during the coming meeting, I also took the wide dark muslin cloth belt the human had worn around his waist and tied it around my own to protect the area. For now, I felt it was important to keep everything as clean as possible. I didn't want to have to open myself back up again later to clean out things that had accidently been sealed inside of me when next I fed. I'd had an issue with the point of a blade shortly after I'd been turned that had shown me how important it was to be as sanitary as possible.

My watched showed that it was nearly seven, but I hadn't seen any of the Weasel's people yet in the area, which gave me some concern. What was going on that no one was here to prepare for something the human obviously had thought was important enough to agree to terms set by complete strangers?

Women and children came and went, doing their morning chores, while some of the men gathered outside a small cafe and drank steaming cups of thick demitasse while they smoked reeking cigars and cigarettes. One small boy came perilously close to where I was hiding, and did the equivalent of holding my breath until he turned and ran the other direction, making for a taller boy who was apparently his brother. I didn't pay attention to the conversation once I heard one of them mentioning if their mother knew about something the other had done.

It was at least another couple hours before the Weasel finally deigned to put in an appearance in the village. Nathaniel was out of sight, as he wasn't going to play the part of someone who had been cooling his heels, waiting for the brigand. It had been decided that he would wait for at least fifteen minutes before he put in his own appearance, looking as calm, cool and collected as he possibly could.

He walked to the cafe where the Weasel had come to have his own cup of demitasse and then sank into an empty chair next to him, where he picked up a random demitasse spoon from the detritus of Boulos' earlier cup and idly tapped it across the top of the table, not saying a word to the brigand. It made for quite the bored performance.

I was impressed.

Okay, the spoon dance told me that Boulos was armed, but with only one gun that Nathaniel could see. I could see the two henchmen who hovered on the periphery, waiting for their boss' next order. With luck, they'd never hear another from him. I listened closely to try to follow whatever conversation they had.

"So you're the fool who took the woman and my money," Boulos began, sitting back in his chair and wrapping his arms around the back of his head. "What possessed you to do something so very stupid?"

"I know an opportunity when I see one," Nathaniel replied. "The woman tried to escape and it ended...badly. I'm assuming you have more, however."

If I didn't know Nathaniel as well as I did, I might believe he was the unfeeling ass he was pretending to be right now. Just the right amount of disdain and uncaring attitude about the guns just about, but not quite being pointed at him by Boulos' men.

"I want that medallion. You will give it to me," the Weasel said suddenly, leaning forward again and putting his elbows on the table. "My men will not let you escape from here."

"You said you'd pay to get it back, and that's what I want. Money. Lots of money, and it had better be cash. Don't think I'll take a check from you."

The Weasel actually laughed.

"I'm not giving you anything, American," he snarled. "As I said, you'll be giving that medallion to me now!"

Boulos waved his hand and the two guards came to attention, pointing their guns at Nathaniel's chest. Idiots. Pointing them at his head would have been far more threatening, and Nathaniel knew it, but he continued to play the cool interloper and tapped the spoon a few more times on the tabletop.

"No, you're going to fork over half a million US dollars, or you'll never see it again. I can have a buyer for that in a matter of hours, and I'll get far more cash for it then. I'm just trying to avoid the middleman if I can," he replied urbanely.

Boulos actually got up and walked up behind Nathaniel, drawing his belt knife. He reached over and grabbed Nathaniel's hair and jerked his head backward.

"You really want to die?"

"Do you really want to lose the medallion entirely? I never said I'd bring it with me, now did I? You're just making an unfounded assumption that it's here as well," Nathaniel laughed. The spoon continued its curious tap dance as the standoff continued.

As long as the spoon's dance continued, I would stay out of their way. If it stopped, I would have no other choice but to step in.

Boulos dropped his handful of Nathaniel's hair as though it had burned him. He stomped back to his seat and slammed down onto it, glowering and muttering curses under his breath. This wasn't turning out as he had planned, and he might actually have to part with real money to get back what he wanted.

Yes, this was one seriously pissed off terrorist.

"Mahmet, Achmed, go find something else to do for now. This *American*," he made the word an epithet as he waved them off, "and I have things to speak of in private."

Looking a bit confused, but not wanting to arouse further ire in their employer, the two humans left the vicinity. I took the opportunity to follow them. With luck, I'd be able to take them out of the equation before anyone knew what was going on.

"Must you continue that infernal tapping," Boulos demanded of Nathaniel. "It is annoying and it makes it difficult for me to think."

"I'm a musical kind of guy, Boulos," Nathaniel replied. "I do it all the time. You might try it yourself sometime. Very relaxing!"

"Would you not rather have a cup of demitasse, so we may discuss this as civilized men," Boulos inquired, holding tightly to his temper. His face went beet red when Nathaniel demurred.

"Sadly, my stomach is touchy and so I cannot have such things anymore," he replied truthfully, smiling ruefully at the Weasel. "It has been years since I was able to have even a single cup of coffee. I do thank you for your offer."

Over-actor! Well, if he'd been taking a lie detector test, he certainly would have passed it. He hadn't lied about his aversion to the delightful-smelling cups of caffeinated stuff.

I liked the smell of hot coffee, myself. The stronger it was, the better. Sometimes, I felt it as though it had somehow wandered down around my toes and lingered there, tantalizing me.

I'd never been able to taste coffee before I died, and I wondered if it tasted anywhere near as good as it smelled. Nathaniel had once told me that it could be bitter, but there was no way I would ever know that now. I could only sit on the sidelines and sniff it, like a crazy person.

The argument outside the cafe continued, with the Weasel trying one threat after another, and Nathaniel pretty much throwing it back in his face. We both knew the humans didn't have even half of what

Nathaniel had asked for the medallion, and Boulos probably knew we knew.

"Trust me, Siofra," Nathaniel had said before we parted in the dark of the early morning. "He's going to be pissed off and threaten all sorts of nasty shit at me. Hell, he may even try to kill me. If he does, I'll just have to out myself earlier than we had planned."

I knew he was right, but I didn't have to like it now, did I?

Finally, the Weasel shot up out of his chair and stood next to the table, his arms crossed as he scowled down at Nathaniel. I'm sure it was intended to not only be an intimidating pose, but downright threatening. He should have learned by now that Nathaniel didn't intimidate easily.

Nathaniel rose from his chair gracefully and stood almost nose to nose with Boulos, showing with calm eyes and an unruffled expression that Boulos' grandstanding wasn't having the desired effect on him. He gestured for the Weasel to go ahead of him, and for a few minutes, it turned into a black comedy of manners as Boulos tried and failed to get Nathaniel to walk ahead of him.

Finally giving up, the Weasel began walking toward the desert, with Nathaniel just about standing by his side, but slightly behind. It was time for me to leave them to whatever they were going to do. I, meanwhile, would be taking care of Boulos' henchmen in a very final way.

With luck, I'd be able to finish healing up while I did.

Fifteen

It turned out that I was luckier than I thought I might be and I fed well from the guards. My gut healed over as though it had never been damaged. I happily discarded the cloth belt and left it in the sand next to one of the two newest bodies. I'd let the people in the town wonder what had happened to the Weasel's henchmen, because, as far as I knew, I'd killed all of the guards who'd remained in town between the moment I arrived and now.

I wondered what had happened to Boulos' patrols, as they had not returned to town with the rising of the sun. Had they gone back to the other village or maybe even decided that it was best to leave while the leaving was good? There was little chance that I would find one to ask that very question, so I put it out of my mind and went to find Nathaniel and Boulos.

Nathaniel had taken him to a location not too far from our actual encampment, but since he wasn't going to be leaving his current location, it didn't bother me. I could hear Nathaniel's reasonable counterpoints to Boulos' angry denunciations, and couldn't help smiling. I knew that in some ways, attempting to have an argument is like arguing with a cat. You're not going to get anywhere, and the cat is going to enjoy frustrating you.

I approached silently from the rear, and though Nathaniel knew I was coming, Boulos had no idea that he was about to meet a surprise and likely a very unwelcome guest. If he was argumentative now, this should put him through the roof. I rocked to a halt as Boulos finally lost his temper and pointed his pistol at Nathaniel's head.

"Listen, you stupid American! Give me the medallion or I'll put a bullet in your fat head!" the Weasel exploded. Nathaniel had finally taken the brigand to his limits, emotionally.

"I told you, it's not here," Nathaniel told him quietly.

"Then why did you have me walk all the way out here with you? What foolishness is this?" He held the muzzle of the gun frighteningly close to Nathaniel's cheekbone. If he shot downward, Nathaniel had a chance. If he shot upward...well, if he shot upward, he'd lose his head a half second later when I tore it from his shoulders. "I'm tired of this bullshit!"

I had to keep from laughing as Boulos pronounced the last word as "bull sheet".

People if you're going to use swear words borrowed from other languages, at least make sure you pronounce then correctly, okay? It's the polite thing to do.

"I don't know what to tell you, Boulos. Waving that gun around isn't going to solve anything," Nathaniel responded. He kept his hands very carefully at his sides, knowing that any unexpected move on his part could result in his ending. "Relax and we can talk—"

"Screw all this roundabout talking! Tell me where it is now!" Boulos bellowed, pressing the muzzle of the gun hard enough against Nathaniel's face as to push the skin in and make the outline of his cheekbone stand out dramatically. "I must have the money that medallion will bring me if I am to salvage the plans you have stolen from me!"

This wouldn't be good at all if Boulos followed through on his threat. A whole pile of not good. I'd have to tread very carefully now if this wasn't going to blow up on us. It probably would have been a very bad idea to tell him that the United Nations now held them and were probably studying them at this very moment. The pile of papers had held a treasure trove of information that would not only help with dealing with the Weasel's thugs, but with others of similar ambition who were named as pawns in the plot that had been hatched.

As soon as we had seen the content of the papers, it had been obvious what they meant to more than just a small corner of the world. These plans were deliberately designed to make countries act against one another in a case of finger pointing, while this asshole and his whole contingent sat back and laughed at the destruction their actions caused. Rather than just send them to one government, Nathaniel and I, as well as Janos, had decided that it needed a much wider reveal, which is why we'd had them sent to the United Nations. This was something that would have affected more than just humanity. It would have expanded to affect vampires and even the Leone, eventually. In bringing this into the light, we were hoping to save us all.

I moved as quietly as I possibly could toward the horrifying tableau in front of me. If I startled the human and he inadvertently squeezed the trigger while he still held his gun on Nathaniel, it would be all over, as far as I was concerned. Nathaniel was the longest-lasting near-family I could remember having, if you didn't count Janos. I really didn't remember much about my original human family. No one was going to take something like that away from me once more when it didn't have to happen. It was just too difficult to tolerate again.

Nathaniel was doing everything but looking over at me in his attempt to keep things on as even a keel as possible. There was actual fear in his eyes, which was something I hadn't seen there in a very long time now. Perhaps it was even as long ago as when we had first started our trip to the Middle East nearly a decade earlier. He was very much aware of his predicament and knew that the mercurial Boulos had a hair trigger. For now, only the knowledge that he might never get his precious medallion back was keeping him from doing the unthinkable.

"Boulos, if you kill me, you'll never know where the medallion is hidden," Nathaniel reminded him, trying to bring the human back to something resembling sanity. "Can't we just sit down and discuss this reasonably?"

"All you've done is talk, American!" Boulos screamed at him, flecks of foam spraying out of his mouth. I saw teeth yellowed from continued smoking and coffee drinking, which wasn't a pretty sight to behold. "I am done with all your talk!"

"But—"

Boulos' brought the gun up so it aimed skyward and pulled the trigger, sending a bullet past Nathaniel's left ear as it shot toward the stratosphere.

"You need to take this seriously," Boulos hissed at him. "They won't wait on payment and I won't waste another bullet on your games."

"*They won't wait on payment*"? Who were "they", and should I care about it? The human was obviously frantic about it, however.

I don't know how Boulos would expect anyone to be able to hear his words after firing a gun next to their ears, but he seemed to think that wouldn't be a problem. Perhaps he just didn't care. In Nathaniel's case, his eardrums would be fine, although the sound and vibrations generated by the explosion of gunpowder would have hurt him deeply.

Knowing I could no longer be stealthy, I decided I had to intervene. Boulos was bringing the gun back down toward Nathaniel's head, and I didn't know how long it would be before he finally pulled the trigger and ended the whole discussion. The human was already past reason, and realistically, he couldn't be trusted not to shoot Nathaniel, even if he *did* reveal the location of the medallion.

Nathaniel threw his hands up alongside his ears and crumpled to his knees, moaning from the effects of being in close quarters to a gunshot. The Weasel angrily reached down and ground his fingertips into Nathaniel's shoulder, demanding that he get back up, to which the vampire shook his head in negation.

Boulos swung the gun around again and pointed it at Nathaniel's head once more.

"Do you want to die?"

"Too late," Nathaniel ground out, and stood back up before Boulos knew what was going on. "It's already several years too late."

The Weasel staggered backward toward me as Nathaniel seemed to loom over him, baring his fangs at the suddenly terrified Weasel. It was all finally too much for the terrorist, who fell onto his back, his gun arm extended.

He pointed the gun in Nathaniel's general direction and just started firing, the bullets hitting random points on Nathaniel's body. Although most of his shots hit non-vital areas, Boulos managed to squeeze off one more shot, which was aimed slightly higher than the others. The result wasn't pretty.

The bullet's trajectory took it across the right side of Nathaniel's face, and took his cheekbone and a good number of his teeth with it as it passed through flesh and bone before continuing its journey out behind his ear and into the desert beyond. Fragments of Nathaniel's flesh and bone scattered across the sand like so much gruesome confetti. He gagged and dropped to the ground, his hand involuntarily going to his face and finding only exposed muscle and jagged points where the right side of his upper jaw and part of his face had been obliterated. It wasn't long, however, before he turned toward Boulos, his remaining fangs extended, a hungry and desperate look in his eyes, dark drool running out of his mouth and the side of this face as he beheld his attacker.

Boulos, too busy doing a "deer in the headlights" impression to notice me behind him, screamed in shock as I grabbed his arm, wrenching it around and twisting the gun out of his fingers. I flung the weapon in some random direction; it didn't matter where, as long as it was nowhere he could reach it. I might have dislocated his shoulder and broken a few of his fingers when I did it, but I really didn't give a crap.

Nathaniel pulled himself to his feet and slowly began to approach the human, his eyes taking on the same kind of glow they had the night of his first feeding. Boulos tried to scramble away, but I held fast to his arm. There was no way I was going to let him escape. We had known a long time before that he would be ended, but now it was going to be even more horrific than even we had imagined.

Thick dark fluid oozed down the side of Nathaniel's face and down his neck, and then was soaked up by the collar of his shirt. When he reached Boulos and gently took the arm that I had been holding, I released my hold on the human. I knew from the expression on Nathaniel's face that he wouldn't be paying attention to anything external for now. He was entirely fixated on the human before him, like a guitarist playing a solo. There was nothing here but Nathaniel and Boulos the Weasel.

Nathaniel helped the human to stand, holding his undamaged hand firmly, but offering him no violence as he did so. It was almost hypnotizing to watch the tableau unfold before me.

Almost nose to nose with the human, Nathaniel said something to him, something that must have been warm and intimate, but his speech was too soft and garbled for me to understand. There had been too much damage done to the side of Nathaniel's face, and apparently his tongue as well, but Boulos never so much as flinched.

It could have been a dance, rendered in slow motion. Nathaniel, fingers entwined through the human's own, pulled the Weasel even further toward him, bringing the human in toward his chest. He reached out his other hand and pushed back the hood that had concealed Boulos' balding head and scraggly-bearded face, cupping the human's chin in his palm as one would do when imparting a lesson to a child.

Boulos stood very still, staring up at the ruined visage that loomed above him. Nathaniel looked down at him, encircling his free arm around the human and bringing the human in close until they stood together, their bodies pressed close. If it had been any other situation, it might even have had romantic overtones.

Nathaniel turned Boulos' head to the side, exposing his throat, which was covered in parts of his untrimmed beard. I saw a look of realization cross Nathaniel's face, which changed to one of consideration. A moment later, he gently pulled Boulos' robe further to the side, revealing a reasonably hairless junction between his shoulder and throat. The human, silent during all of this, stood stock-still.

I think I would have killed Boulos myself, if I didn't know that Nathaniel would have to feed from him to heal. As it was, it took all the restraint I could muster to keep from turning the human into a loose sack of shattered bones and ruptured viscera.

Nathaniel lowered his mouth to the Weasel's shoulder and neck in a move that was vaguely reminiscent of a lover moving to nibble on his beloved's neck. Silence reigned supreme until the dance went from a nibble to a ragged bite, when Boulos shrieked and tried to pull free of Nathaniel's death grip. It looked almost comical, seeing Boulos' arms and legs wriggling wildly as he fought his impending death.

At first, Nathaniel's feeding was sloppy, since so much of the human's blood was lost from the open side of the vampire's face. I watched from the sidelines as the damage was healed as Nathaniel fed, beginning with the cheek and then moving inward to the damaged bones and teeth.

The wriggling was becoming weaker as more blood was drained from the human's body, but he hadn't yet given up. You saw that sometimes, when humans refused to accept the inevitable. It was so cute and had the added bonus of keeping the heart racing, which in turn, helped the blood flow longer for a feeding vampire.

"You've lost everything, asshole. You've lost your power base, your selfish, egotistical first wife, and now that medallion. I saw what you and your people had planned. Did you think you were just going to start a war, watch it escalate and then sit back and wait until you were the only ones left?" I said quietly, not caring if he actually heard me. Maybe it would follow him into whatever afterlife he might receive, if such a thing existed. "You're not only going to pay for what you've done to Nathaniel, you're going to pay for all those lives you and that bitch of a wife of yours have terrorized and ended since you started your little foray into religious fundamentalism."

Boulos died about fifteen minutes after Nathaniel began feeding, a footnote in the history of this area, and one who would not be missed by any of those who he had terrorized during his short but very bloody reign. I stood over his body, looking down at the pale, bloodless face and empty, staring eyes, glad that the piece of crap was ended. The sense of satisfaction I felt was tremendous. Nathaniel stood beside me, looking off into the distance, a thoughtful look on his face.

"I know I've been hurt before, but nothing like this. No human could have survived something like this without having a fully supplied medic on hand. It's another reason I'm glad I'm no longer part of the human race," Nathaniel told me, pressing hard on his cheekbone. "It's so nice to be able to speak again, too. I never really realized how important a tongue and mouth are to saying things without sounding like you're talking around a mouthful of food."

"I'm just glad that the last bullet wasn't aimed just a little higher. That might have destroyed your brain, and then you'd simply be gone," I replied. "I don't know why you kept egging him on about things. Everything that happened was at least partially your fault, you know."

"I know, Siofra. I just wanted to get him away from the village and as many of his men as possible. I'm surprised we haven't encountered any of his patrols from last night," he noted. "I thought that we'd be faster than he was, but he managed to surprise me with that gun of his, and then everything went to hell in a hand basket. You know, even if you had been faster, I don't think I could have avoided being shot, once he had that thing pointed at me. I'm just grateful that it wasn't aimed higher, like you said."

"He put at least nine bullets into your body, Nathaniel," I reminded him, gesturing at the multiple holes that had destroyed his clothing. "If you'd been human, we wouldn't be having this conversation right now. Next time, don't worry about how far you're taking him away. Just end him and get it all over with. It's not worth being ended, yourself."

Nathaniel snorted humorlessly and nodded.

"So, do we just leave his body here, or do we move it elsewhere?"

"I don't really want anyone making a martyr of him, so he needs to disappear. That's not going to be that easy. I know there are a few dried out and abandoned wells in the vicinity, but most are near population centers, and I don't want the stink of his rotting body to get any more attention than necessary before he decomposes enough that he can't be easily recognized," I said. I blew air out between my lips and made a raspberry noise. "Well, we might as well pick him up and move him to a more concealed location until we figure out what we're going to do."

Motioning me out of the way, Nathaniel bent and picked up the corpse, throwing it over one shoulder in a fireman's carry. He must have had something in mind, as he never said a word as he began moving northward at a fast pace. I followed along, curious to see where he was taking us.

Sixteen

After several years living in rural areas, we'd finally decided to move to the city and had taken up residence in a long-term stay hotel. It wasn't the Ritz, but we had real beds, hot showers and laundry facilities that didn't require hauling your own water. A few pretty gems pulled off of the medallion had given us a tidy windfall, and the remainder made an excellent savings account.

By now, Nathaniel was much better at controlling himself around humans, so I felt reasonably comfortable with him in a large population center. Over the past few months, we'd managed to thin out quite a few of the more unsavory individuals who haunted the tourist district, making things safer for everyone else. Anyway, it was about time that Nathaniel had some practice feeding in the city.

The phone rang, startling me out of sleep. Next to me, Nathaniel mumbled, opening his eyes and glancing blearily at the phone that was on the table next to where he slept. Grabbing it, he threw it to me and rolled over, pulling the blanket over his head to get more sleep. It had been a long night of hunting and we'd only got back in a few hours earlier, so I couldn't blame him.

I looked at the caller ID screen and seeing that it was Janos calling, I clicked the Answer button. We'd just spoken the night before, so there was no reason we should even be talking again for at least another week. Something was up, but what?

"Hey, Janos, what's up? It's still early here."

"Siofra! Shut up and listen to me!" he shouted into the phone. I could hear what sounded like violent banging going on in the background. "This is important!"

Was that fear I heard in his voice? Janos was *never* afraid, not once in the time I'd known him.

"What? What's going on, Janos?"

Nathaniel sat up in bed, the idea of more sleep forgotten. I knew he was listening as closely as he could to what he could hear of Janos' call. His hearing would be good enough to hear most of it, including the commotion in the background.

"Remember when I warned you about certain individuals who didn't like what you represented to the more conservative part of our community? Well, they've finally decided they're not going to wait on things." there was a huge crash in the background, and I could hear voices in the room with him now.

"Janos! Who is there? What's—?"

"Be careful, child! Don't let them—"

There was more crashing and banging on the other end of the phone, as though there was a pitched battle going on. From what I had heard so far, that assessment was probably exactly right.

"Siofra, protect yourself! They're coming for you next, I'm su—!"

There was the dull wet sound of something impacting flesh, an oath, a scream, the sound of gurgling, and then a sharp thud from the other end of the line as the phone landed hard on something. If I had a heart that could beat, it would have been trying to bang out of my chest at that moment.

"Janos!" I screamed into the phone. "Janos, are you alright?"

There was a scraping sound, which I assumed came from someone picking the telephone receiver off the floor.

"This isn't Janos, little girl. Don't worry, your end should be coming right along now," said a high-pitched and very unpleasant voice from the other end. "There are rules you must follow in our community, little one, and this is what happens when you flout those rules."

"Who the hell are you?"

"That's not important, child. As you won't be here much longer, there is no reason for you to know," came his reply.

"I'm nearly four hundred years old, asshole. I think I can make decisions for myself by now. I don't need anyone's permission."

"Asshole? Really, young lady, you should show some respect for your elders," he clucked at me disdainfully. "Siofra, there are vampires far older than you who know how things should be. You set a bad example for our youngsters, and it was high time we did something about it. Mustn't let the children get inappropriate ideas, now should we?"

"There was no reason for you to end Janos. He was a powerful vampire with lots of connections out there. You probably just shot yourself in the foot, doing something that stupid," I shot back. "He's got friends who will probably come after you."

"His so-called 'friends' know better than to come after me, Siofra," he retorted. "They will not lift a finger in retaliation. They all know better."

"He didn't deserve this!"

"He allowed you to be as you were, and didn't bind you to his kiss. We can't have irresponsible vampires out there, letting you youngsters do whatever you want, whenever you want."

"Oh, I promise you, whoever you are, I will find out who you are and where you are, and you'll wish you'd made sure of me, yourself!" I told the voice at the other end of the phone. Blood tears ran down my cheeks as I cried silently. "I'll see you ended."

The only reply I got was derisive laughter.

That was when our door burst open and we found ourselves set upon by three unknown vampires who bore both modern and medieval weapons. One was armed with a Lochaber axe, another with a handgun of some sort, and the third seemed to be some sort of martial artist. Throwing the phone at the would-be assassins, I managed to hit one of the three in the head, giving him a significant and ugly dent to his temple and knocking him to the ground. I was gratified when I saw that I'd actually opened a wound and that he didn't seem to be at all interested in getting back up again.

I guess cellphones are more dangerous than I thought they were, and we were down to two assailants already. That upped our chanced immensely, but these were still trained assassins, and they were going to be doing their very best to put us down.

Nathaniel rolled backwards in his bed and into the space between the bed and the bathroom wall as one of them swung an archaic Lochaber axe deep into the center of his mattress. While the other vampire tried to pull the thing out of the fiber and wire coils that made up the mattress, Nathaniel rose, leapt forward and backhanded his assailant with a force so strong that he actually knocked the vampire across the room and out into the hallway. Unfortunately, that vampire bounced back onto his feet and darted back into the room, this time trying to distract me while his remaining partner started shooting.

Now I had two of them on me, with one making feints at me while the other kept trying to fill me full of bullets. I heard screams from the rooms near us as some of the bullets that missed me pierced the walls and apparently found targets elsewhere. It probably wouldn't be long before the authorities were notified and we would have even more unwanted company.

A few bullets actually hit me, doing varying amounts of damage. One in particular tore into my left elbow, effectively rendering that arm useless for much of anything until I fed again. It hurt so much that profanity flew from my mouth like startled bats from the mouth of a cave.

The shooter crowed with delight as he realized he'd actually managed to hurt me, and I called him a few choice names in reply.

"You might as well just give up," he goaded me. "You're not going to live through this, you know."

"Go fuck yourself," I suggested blandly.

"Now, now, Siofra. Language! It's this defiant attitude of yours that's gotten you the kind of attention that's brought us here. Hans is already ended, and now it's your turn."

Hans?

"Who is Hans?" I asked, genuinely puzzled. The other vampire raised an eyebrow as he looked at me.

"Hans the Waymaster. I suppose you knew him as Janos. No one knows his true name, but Hans was the name he used when he was doing things that weren't necessarily allowed by the Council," the gunman told me. "It took a while, but his true identity, such as it is, was finally ferreted out and he has been dealt with appropriately."

This vampire seemed to be fairly well informed on what was going on in the upper ranks. I wondered if that was normal for a Council assassin, or if there were special ranks of assassins who did the dirty work those in power occasionally required.

"I'm almost four hundred years old. I'm not a fledgling. This is how I've lived my life for most of that time. Why is that a problem to the Council?"

"It's not my place to question the Council, only to do as they bid. They have decreed that you must be ended, so that's the way things are. Your roommate is here, so he must be ended as well."

The talkative vampire's companion, perhaps thinking I was distracted, tried to come at my head with a kick, and I surprised him by ducking down, grabbing one of my boot knives from the floor and hamstrung him. My target screamed something in a language I didn't understand and fell to one knee, no longer able to support himself properly. Unless he fed, it wasn't going to heal, so things were improving for me now.

Cut someone's Achilles tendon, and it's going to have a nasty effect on their getting around very easily. It's one of those anatomical bits that's rather important to being able to move around.

"Dammit, you know better than to be so careless, Stefan! You're useless, and I should have left you behind. Your fault, refusing to carry a weapon," my remaining attacker exploded. "Get out of here before she ends you completely, or I decide to end you, myself."

Lovely vampire. Threats like that do nothing to engender loyalty in minions.

"S'not my fault. She came at me with the knife!"

"Just shut the hell up, get up and end her, Mr. I Know Kung Fu!"

The injured vampire in question pulled himself to his feet, but when he was finally upright, he wavered and wobbled in place because of the damage I'd caused him. The slice was deep, and I'd felt it hit bone, so he wasn't going to be doing any standing on one leg kicks like you see in the movies anytime soon.

Maybe I could use the obvious dissention in the ranks to my advantage. I had to do something if I was going to survive this, but what?

"I'm going to end you if you don't leave," I told the crippled vampire. "Leave now, and I won't come after you later, if you continue to leave me alone."

"Shut your mouth, Siofra! He's not yours!" the mouthy vampire shouted at me, almost sounding desperate. "He's got a job to do!"

Now that was an interesting development, wasn't it? Could there be enough dissention that I could make use of it?

"You haven't done anything to me yet, Stefan. Take this opportunity and leave now," I urged him quietly. "You have my promise that I'll let you leave with no further damage."

I could see interest in his eyes, accompanied by a wince as he was reminded of the damage I had already done to him. In his current condition, there was more chance that I would end him, rather than his being able to end me, and he knew it. Stefan could easily feed off one of the humans in the nearby rooms, heal himself and be away before the authorities arrived. That part was the only certainty in his favor right now.

"Is it worth dying for this loudmouth?" I asked him in what I thought was a reasonable voice. "Aren't there other things you'd rather be doing than dying?"

"If you leave now, Stefan, I'll tell *him* what you did and your life won't be worth shit," the other vampire replied in the same tone of voice I had used. "I'll hunt you down and end you, myself."

"I can't do anything unless I'm healed up, and I can't do that until I've fed," the injured vampire told the other. "I'll leave while I can, Martel, and take my chances with *him*, should it come to that. You try to end her. I don't think it's going to be as easy as you implied."

I stood back carefully as the one called Stefan limped past me carefully and went out the door, stepping as wide as he could around the battle Nathaniel was having with the third remaining vampire. At this point, the other vampire was ducking behind the ruined mattress and trying to avoid the sweeping threat of the Lochaber axe that Nathaniel swung in a surprisingly expert-seeming manner.

The one called Martel was shouting profanity and threats at Stefan's retreating figure, but the latter vampire never slowed. He knew a gift when he saw it, and I wasn't about to break the promise I had made to him.

I heard a thud, then a cry and looked over to see that Nathaniel had buried the blade of the wicked-looking axe down through the top of the other vampire's head, destroying the connection between both halves of the vampire's brain. That vampire was now making odd grunting noises, and was staggering around as his body didn't know how to deal with disconnected information. As Nathaniel stepped forward to yank the blade out of the top of the other vampire's skull, he took part of the crown with it, exposing the other vampire's brain to the air, and damaging it further.

All movement on the other vampire's part ceased as he fell to the ground and half of his brain fell out of the exposed part of what had been the protection of his skull. He was ended now, and no amount of blood would bring him back from his final death.

I shouldn't have taken my eyes from my own assailant, as I heard a shot, and jerked backward as this last bullet took me in the chest, knocking me backward and against the wall, even as it exploded out my back, leaving a softball-sized hole where my right shoulder blade had been. I slid down the wall, leaving a long smear of thick, dark fluid behind, feeling boneless. A tiny part of my consciousness wondered if my spine had been damaged.

The vampire Martel stepped forward, his gun aimed between my eyes, and I watched as his finger began to squeeze the trigger. I'd failed both myself and Janos. I hoped that Nathaniel would be able to escape before he was ended as well.

"He'll be so pleased that you're finally gone," Martel sneered at me. "I'll let him know after I've dealt with that traitor, Stefan. You really should not have interfered, little girl."

There was a *swooshing* sound...

I continued to stare blankly as Martel's disembodied head suddenly thunked down in front of me, his eyes showing displeased shock. Why didn't he stop fooling around, put his head back on and just hurry up and pull the trigger?

"Siofra?" I heard Nathaniel's voice as if from a distance, and looked stupidly around until I saw him coming to me. "Siofra, are you alright?"

"I—"

FIACH FOLA

Glossary

Ádhamh: (*Gaelic* AY-thuhv) red, earth

Boulos (*Arabic* BOO-lohs) Arabic version of "Paul"

Fiach Fola (*Gaelic* FEE'awk FO'luh) Blood Debt

Hamzah (*Arabic* Hahm-zuh)

Mathúin (*Gaelic* mah-HOON) Bear

O'Se (*Gaelic* Oh-Shay) Child of Se

Sarahi (Suh RAH Hee) Dragonlady, wife of The Weasel

Siofra (*Gaelic* She-fruh) Irish Gaelic meaning "elf"

Sumaire (*Gaelic* Shoe-mah-REE) Bloodsucker, void, vortex

Don't miss out!

Visit the website below and you can sign up to receive emails whenever Anna Rose publishes a new book. There's no charge and no obligation.

https://books2read.com/r/B-A-MFMF-LUTS

BOOKS 2 READ

Connecting independent readers to independent writers.

About the Author

Anna Rose is the author of the Tales of the Dragonguard (about dragons, of course!) and The Sumaire Web series of vampire novels.

She is currently working on KAL'S HEART, the third story in the Tales of the Dragonguard, that began with AYA'S DRAGON, and continues with SARA'S FIRE. which is now available in both e-book and softcover at Amazon, and in ebook format at iTunes, Barnes & Noble, and other fine merchants.

KAL'S HEART continues the story of the high-flying Dragonguard. Kal, the Aerie-born son of Dragonguard parents, is faced with a mystery that affects not only the whole of the Dragonguard, but his family as well. Together, he and his unusual dragon, Spirit, must use their unique abilities to find out who is causing trouble for the Dragonguard and to his family.

Her newest venture with her stories and novels is turning them into audiobooks for those folks who prefer listening to books, rather than reading them, for whatever reason.

Amongst her other writing, Anna writes vampires who like what they are and aren't looking for a rescue. Her vampires bite, drink and kill. No bottled or bagged blood for these vampires!

The first novel in the series, SIOFRA, was released in late January of 2012. The first novel was followed by FIACH FOLA and then DROCH FOLA. There is also a short story called FEASTA FOLA.

She lives in usually sunny Southern California.

Read more at www.sumaire.com.

www.ingramcontent.com/pod-product-compliance
Lightning Source LLC
Chambersburg PA
CBHW021319250626
47155CB00002B/546